HIDDEN IN PLAIN SIGHT

ALSO BY JEFFREY ARCHER

THE WILLIAM WARWICK NOVELS

Nothing Ventured

THE CLIFTON CHRONICLES

Only Time Will Tell • *The Sins of the Father* • *Best Kept Secret* •
Be Careful What You Wish For • *Mightier Than the Sword* •
Cometh the Hour • *This Was a Man*

NOVELS

Not a Penny More, Not a Penny Less • *Shall We Tell the President?* •
Kane and Abel • *The Prodigal Daughter* • *First Among Equals* • *A Matter of
Honor* • *As the Crow Flies* • *Honor Among Thieves* • *The Fourth Estate* •
The Eleventh Commandment • *Sons of Fortune* • *False Impression* •
The Gospel According to Judas (with the assistance of Professor Francis J. Moloney) •
A Prisoner of Birth • *Paths of Glory* • *Heads You Win*

SHORT STORIES

A Quiver Full of Arrows • *A Twist in the Tale* • *Twelve Red Herrings* • *The
Collected Short Stories* • *To Cut a Long Story Short* • *Cat O' Nine Tales* •
And Thereby Hangs a Tale • *Tell Tale* • *The Short, the Long and the Tall*

PLAYS

Beyond Reasonable Doubt • *Exclusive* • *The Accused* • *Confession* •
Who Killed the Mayor?

PRISON DIARIES

Volume One—Belmarsh: Hell
Volume Two—Wayland: Purgatory
Volume Three—North Sea Camp: Heaven

SCREENPLAYS

Mallory: Walking Off the Map • *False Impression*

First published in the United States by St. Martin's Press, an imprint of St. Martin's Publishing Group

HIDDEN IN PLAIN SIGHT. Copyright © 2020 by Jeffrey Archer. All rights reserved. Printed in the United States of America. For information, address St. Martin's Publishing Group, 120 Broadway, New York, NY 10271.

www.stmartins.com

Library of Congress Cataloging-in-Publication Data

Names: Archer, Jeffrey, 1940– author.
Title: Hidden in plain sight / Jeffrey Archer.
Description: First U.S. edition. | New York : St. Martin's Press, 2020. |
    Series: William Warwick novels
Identifiers: LCCN 2020024223 | ISBN 9781250200785 (hardcover) |
    ISBN 9781250200792 (ebook)
Subjects: GSAFD: Mystery fiction.
Classification: LCC PS3616.I425 H53 2020 | DDC 813/.6—dc23
LC record available at https://lccn.loc.gov/2020024223

Our books may be purchased in bulk for promotional, educational, or business use. Please contact your local bookseller or the Macmillan Corporate and Premium Sales Department at 1-800-221-7945, extension 5442, or by email at MacmillanSpecialMarkets@macmillan.com.

Originally published in Great Britain by Macmillan, an imprint of Pan Macmillan

First U.S. Edition: 2020

10 9 8 7 6 5 4 3 2 1

JEFFREY ARCHER

HIDDEN IN PLAIN SIGHT

St. Martin's Press ❧ New York

To John and Margaret Ashley

Acknowledgments

My thanks for their invaluable advice and research to:

Simon Bainbridge, Jonathan Caplan QC,
Vicki Mellor, Alison Prince, Catherine Richards,
Marcus Rutherford, Jonathan Ticehurst,
and Johnny Van Haeften.
Special thanks to Detective Sergeant Michelle
Roycroft (Ret.), Chief Superintendent John
Sutherland (Ret.), and Detective Superintendent
Robin Bhairam QPM (Ret.).

1

April 14, 1986

The four of them sat around the table staring at the hamper.

"Who's it addressed to?" asked the commander.

William read the handwritten label. "'Happy Birthday, Commander Hawksby.'"

"You'd better open it, DC Warwick," said the Hawk, leaning back in his chair.

William stood up, unfastened the two leather straps, and lifted the lid of the huge wicker basket that was packed with what his father would have called "goodies."

"Clearly someone appreciates us," said DCI Lamont, removing a bottle of Scotch from the top of the basket, delighted to find it was Black Label.

"And also knows our weaknesses," said the commander, as he took out a box of Montecristo cigars and placed them on the table in front of him. "Your turn, DC Roycroft," he added, as he rolled one of the Cuban cigars between his fingers.

Jackie took her time removing some of the packing straw before she discovered a jar of foie gras, a luxury way beyond her pay grade.

"And finally, DC Warwick," said the commander.

William rummaged around in the hamper until he came across a bottle of olive oil from Umbria that he knew Beth would appreciate. He was about to sit back down when he spotted a small envelope. It was addressed to Commander Hawksby QPM, and marked *Personal*. He handed it to the boss.

Hawksby ripped the envelope open and extracted a handwritten card. His expression revealed nothing, although the unsigned note could not have been clearer. *Better luck next time.*

When the card was passed around the table the smiles turned to frowns, and the recently acquired gifts were quickly returned to the hamper.

"Do you know what makes it worse?" said the commander. "It *is* my birthday."

"And that's not all," said William, who then told the team about his conversation with Miles Faulkner at the Fitzmolean soon after the unveiling of the Rubens painting, *Christ's Descent from the Cross.*

"But if the Rubens is a fake," said Lamont, "why don't we arrest Faulkner, send him back to the Old Bailey, and Mr. Justice Nourse will remove the word 'suspended' from his sentence, and lock him up for the next four years."

"Nothing would give me greater pleasure," said Hawksby. "But if the painting turns out to be the original, Faulkner will have made a fool of us a second time, and in the most public of arenas."

William was taken by surprise by the commander's next question.

"Have you warned your fiancée that the Rubens might be a fake?"

"No, sir. I thought I'd say nothing to Beth until you'd decided what course of action we should take."

"Good. Let's keep it that way. It will give us all a little more time to consider what our next move should be, because we have to start thinking like Faulkner if we're ever going to bring the damn man down. Now get that thing out of my sight," he demanded, pointing at the hamper. "And make sure it's entered into the gratuities register. But not before it's been checked for fingerprints—not that I expect the dabs expert to find any prints other than ours, and possibly those of an innocent sales assistant from Harrods."

William picked up the wicker basket and took it into the next room, where he asked Angela, the commander's secretary, if she would send it down to D705 for fingerprinting. He couldn't help noticing that she looked a little disappointed. "I was hoping to get the cranberry sauce," she admitted. When he returned to the boss's office a few moments later, he was puzzled to find the rest of the team banging the palms of their hands on the table.

"Have a seat, Detective *Sergeant* Warwick," said the commander.

"Choirboy is speechless, for a change," said Lamont.

"That won't last long," promised Jackie, and they all burst out laughing.

"Do you want to hear the good news or the bad news?" asked the commander once they'd all settled back down.

"The good news," said DCI Lamont, "because you're not going to enjoy my latest report on the diamond smugglers."

"Let me guess," said Hawksby. "They saw you coming and have all escaped."

"Worse than that, I'm afraid. They didn't even turn up, and neither did the shipment of diamonds. I spent an evening with twenty of my men armed to the teeth, staring out to sea. So do tell me the good news, sir."

"As you all know, DC Warwick has passed his sergeant's exam, despite kicking one of the anti-nuclear protesters in the—"

3

"I did nothing of the sort," protested William. "I simply asked him politely to calm down."

"Which the examiner accepted without question; such is your choirboy's reputation."

"So what's the bad news?" asked William.

"In your new role as a detective sergeant, you're being transferred to the drugs squad."

"Rather you than me," said Lamont with a sigh.

"However," continued the commander, "the commissioner, in his wisdom, felt a winning team shouldn't be broken up, so you two will be joining him as part of an elite drugs unit on the first of the month."

"I resign," said Lamont, leaping to his feet in mock protest.

"I don't think so, Bruce. You only have eighteen months left before you retire, and as the head of the new unit, you'll be promoted to detective superintendent."

This announcement provoked a second eruption of enthusiastic banging on the table.

"The unit is to work separately from any of the existing drugs squads. It will only have one purpose, which I will come to in a moment. But first, I wanted to let you know that the team will have a new DC added to its complement, who may even outshine our resident choirboy."

"This I want to see," said Jackie.

"Well, you won't have to wait long. He'll be joining us in a few minutes. He has an outstanding CV, having read law at Cambridge where he was awarded a blue in the Boat Race."

"Did he win?" asked William.

"Two years in a row," said the Hawk.

"Then perhaps he should have joined the river police," said William. "If I remember correctly, the Boat Race takes place between Putney and Mortlake, so he'd be back on the beat." This elicited more banging on the table.

"I think you'll find he's just as impressive on dry land," said the commander, after the applause had died down. "He's already served for three years with the Regional Crime Squad in Crawley. However, there's something else I ought to mention before—"

A sharp knock on the door interrupted the Hawk before he could finish the sentence. "Enter," he said.

The door opened and a tall, handsome young man entered the room. He looked as if he'd stepped straight off the set of a popular television police drama, rather than just arrived from the Regional Crime Squad.

"Good afternoon, sir," he said. "I'm DC Paul Adaja. I was told to report to you."

"Take a seat, Adaja," said the Hawk, "and I'll introduce you to the rest of the team."

William watched Lamont's face closely as Adaja shook hands with an unsmiling superintendent. The Met's policy was to try and recruit more officers from minority ethnic backgrounds, but to date it had been about as successful in that ambition as it had been at arresting diamond smugglers. William was curious to find out why someone like Paul had even considered joining the force, and was determined to make him quickly feel part of the team.

"These SIO meetings are held every Monday morning, DC Adaja," said the commander, "to bring us all up to date on how any major investigations are progressing."

"Or not progressing," said Lamont.

"Let's move on," said the Hawk, ignoring the interruption. "Is there any more news on Faulkner?"

"His wife Christina's been in touch again," said William. "She's asked to see me."

"Has she indeed. Any clues?"

"No, sir. I've no idea what she wants. But she makes no secret of the fact that she's just as keen as we are to see her husband behind bars. So, I don't imagine she's suggesting tea at the Ritz simply to sample their clotted cream scones."

"Mrs. Faulkner will be well aware of any other criminal activities her husband is involved in, which would be useful for us to know about," said Lamont, "in advance. But I wouldn't trust that woman an inch."

"Neither would I," said Hawksby. "But if I had to choose between Faulkner and his wife, I consider her the lesser of two evils. But only by half an inch."

"I could always turn the invitation down."

"No way," said Lamont. "We may never get a better chance to put Faulkner behind bars, and don't let's forget, however minor the offense, because of the judge's suspended sentence, it would put him inside for at least four years."

"True enough," said the Hawk. "But, DS Warwick, you can be sure Faulkner will be watching us just as closely as we're watching him, and he's certain to have a PI tailing his wife around the clock, until the divorce is finally settled. So while tea at the Ritz is acceptable, dinner is not. Do I make myself clear?"

"Abundantly, sir, and I'm sure Beth would agree with you."

"And never forget that Mrs. Faulkner's slips of the tongue have always been well rehearsed. And she's also well aware that everything she tells you will be repeated word for word the moment you arrive back at the Yard."

"Probably even before her chauffeur has dropped her off at the flat in Eaton Square," added Lamont.

"Right, let's get back to the matter in hand. There are several cases you'll have to brief the new Art and Antiques Squad on before you start work on your new assignment."

"You were about to tell us, sir, before DC Adaja joined us, how the new unit will differ from any other existing drugs squads."

"I can't tell you too much at the moment," said the Hawk, "but you will have only one purpose, and it won't be to catch low-level dealers selling cannabis on the street to pot heads." Suddenly everyone was wide awake. "The commissioner wants us to identify a man whose name we don't know, and whose whereabouts we can't be sure of, other than that he lives and works somewhere south of the river in the Greater London area. However, we do know what his day job is." The Hawk opened a file marked TOP SECRET.

2

"So, have you passed your sergeant's exam," asked his father, "or are you destined to be a detective constable for the rest of your life?"

William's expression gave nothing away, as if he were facing the eminent QC from the witness box.

"One day your son will be the commissioner," said Beth, giving her prospective father-in-law a warm smile.

"I'm still waiting to hear the results of the exam," sighed William, as he winked at his fiancée.

"I'm sure you will have passed with flying colors, my dear," said his mother. "But if your father were to take the same exam, I wouldn't be quite as confident."

"That's something we can all agree on," said his sister, Grace.

"A judgment that's made without evidence or facts to support it," said Sir Julian, as he rose from his place and began to circle the room. "Tell me, what form does this examination take?" he demanded, clutching the lapels of his jacket as if he were addressing a wavering jury.

"It falls into three parts," said William. "Physical, which includes a five-mile run that has to be completed in under forty minutes."

"Not much hope of my achieving that," admitted Sir Julian, as he continued to circle the room.

"Self-defense, where I just about held my own."

"No chance with that one either," said Sir Julian, "unless it was a verbal attack rather than physical."

"And then, finally, you have to swim three lengths of the pool in uniform, holding a truncheon, without sinking."

"I'm exhausted just thinking about it," said Grace.

"Your father's failed on all three counts so far," said his mother, "so he would certainly have to spend the rest of his life as a constable on the beat."

"Does the police force have any interest in mental acuity," demanded Sir Julian, as he came to a halt in front of them, "or is it just about who can do the most press-ups?"

William didn't admit that there wasn't actually a physical test, and he'd simply been winding his father up. But he was still determined not to let the old man off the hook.

"After that came the practical tests, Dad. It will be fascinating to see if you fare any better with them."

"I'm ready," said Sir Julian, setting off on his perambulation again.

"You have to attend three crime scenes so the examiners can see how you'd react in different circumstances. I did quite well on the first test, when I had to breathalyze a driver who'd been involved in a minor prang. The test result was amber, not red, indicating that he'd been drinking recently, but he wasn't over the limit."

"Did you arrest him?" asked Grace.

"No, I let him off with a warning."

"Why?" demanded Sir Julian.

"Because he didn't actually fail the test, and also the police national computer revealed that he was a chauffeur with no previous offenses, so if I'd arrested him, he might have lost his job."

"You're a wimp," said Sir Julian. "Next?"

"I had to follow up a robbery at a jewelry shop. One of the staff was screaming, and the manager was in a state of shock. I calmed them both down before radioing for assistance, then sealed off the crime scene and waited for back-up to arrive."

"You seem to be doing very well so far," said his mother.

"I thought so, too, until I was put in charge of a team of young constables who were attending a protest march in support of nuclear disarmament, and it started to get out of hand."

"What happened?" asked his sister.

"It appears that I didn't respond calmly enough when a protester called one of my men a fascist bastard."

"I can't imagine what they would have called me," said Sir Julian.

"Or how you would have reacted," said Marjorie.

Everyone laughed except Beth, who wanted to know how William had responded.

"I kicked him in the balls."

"You did what?" said his mother.

"Actually, I only drew my truncheon, but that wasn't what he claimed when we got him back to the station. It didn't help that I failed to mention what actually happened in my report."

"I can't pretend I'm doing any better," said Sir Julian, slumping back in his chair.

"Father, let's face it," said William, handing him a cup of coffee. "You'd have locked up the drunk driver, told the shop manager and his assistant to stop being so pathetic, and undoubtedly kicked the protester in the balls a second time. Excuse my French, Mother."

"You said there were three parts to the exam," said Sir Julian, trying to recover.

"The third part is a written exam."

"Then I'm still in with a chance."

"You have to answer sixty questions in ninety minutes." William sipped his coffee and leaned back, before indulging his father. "If you picked some wild daffodils from a neighbor's garden and then gave them to your wife, would either of you have committed a crime?"

"Most certainly," said Sir Julian. "The husband is guilty of theft. But was the wife aware that he'd taken the daffodils from their neighbor's garden?"

"Yes, she was," said William.

"Then she's guilty of receiving stolen goods. An open-and-shut case."

"I don't agree, m'lud," said Grace, rising from her place. "I think you'll find the relevant word is 'wild.' If all parties concerned were aware that the flowers were wild and had not been planted by the neighbor, my client was entitled to pick them."

"That was my answer," said William. "And it turns out that Grace and I are right."

"Give me one more chance," said Sir Julian, readjusting his nonexistent gown.

"At what age is a young person responsible for a criminal act? Eight, ten, fourteen, or seventeen?"

"Ten," said Grace, before her father could respond.

"Right again," said William.

"I confess I don't defend many juveniles."

"Only because they can't afford your exorbitant fees," said Grace.

"Have you ever defended a juvenile, Grace?" asked her mother, before Sir Julian could continue his cross-examination.

"Yes. Only last week I represented an eleven-year-old accused of shoplifting in Balham."

"No doubt you got him off, after claiming he'd come from a deprived background and his father beat him regularly."

"Her," said Grace. "Her father abandoned the family home soon after she was born, leaving his wife to hold down two jobs while bringing up three children."

"It should never have come to court," said William's mother.

"I agree with you, Mother, and it wouldn't have if the girl hadn't unfortunately been caught stealing the finest cuts of meat from her local supermarket and dropping them into a foil-lined carrier bag, to evade the store's security detectors. She then walked a hundred yards up the road and sold them to an unscrupulous local butcher."

"What did the court decide?" asked Marjorie.

"The butcher was heavily fined, and the child has been taken into care. But then, she didn't have the advantage of being brought up by loving middle-class parents, in a comfortable country cottage in Kent. She'd never strayed more than a mile from her own front door. She didn't even know there was a river running through the city she was born in."

"Should I be regarded as guilty, m'lud, simply for having tried to give my children a decent start in life?" said Sir Julian, before adding, "Am I allowed one more chance before the examiners deport me?"

"Pass him a violin," said Marjorie.

"A publican becomes aware that some of his customers are smoking cannabis in his beer garden," said William. "Is he committing an offense?"

"He most certainly is," said Sir Julian, "because he is allowing his premises to be used for the consumption of a controlled substance."

"And if one of the customers smoking the cannabis hands it to a friend, who takes a puff, is he also guilty of a crime?"

"Of course. He is guilty of both possession and of supplying a controlled drug, and should be charged accordingly."

"Madness," said Grace.

"I agree," said William. "Not least because the force doesn't have the resources to pursue every minor crime."

"Hardly minor," said Sir Julian. "In fact, it's the beginning of a slippery slope."

"What if the landlord or the customer wasn't aware it was a crime?" asked Beth.

"Ignorance of the law is no defense," said Sir Julian. "Otherwise you could murder whomever you pleased, and claim you didn't realize it was a crime."

"What a good idea," said Marjorie. "Because I would have pleaded lack of knowledge a long time ago if I could have got away with murdering my husband. In fact, the only thing that's stopped me doing so is the knowledge that I'd need him to defend me when the case came to court."

Everyone burst out laughing.

"Frankly, Mother," said Grace, "half the Bar Council would be only too willing to defend you, while the other half would appear as witnesses for the defense."

"Nevertheless," said Sir Julian, passing a hand across a furrowed brow, "am I right this time?"

"Yes, Father. But don't be surprised if cannabis is legalized in my lifetime."

"But not in mine, I hope," said Sir Julian with feeling.

"It sounds to me," said Marjorie, "that even though your father would have failed the exam hopelessly, you must have passed."

"Despite kicking a protester in the balls," said Sir Julian.

"No, I didn't," said William.

"No, you didn't pass, or no, you didn't kick the protester in the balls?" demanded his father.

They all laughed.

"You're right, Marjorie," said Beth, coming to her fiancé's rescue. "As of next Monday, William will be Detective Sergeant Warwick."

Sir Julian was the first to stand and raise his glass. "Congratulations, my boy," he said. "Here's to the first step on a long ladder."

"The first step on a long ladder," repeated the rest of the family, as they all stood and raised their glasses.

"So, how long before you become an inspector?" asked Sir Julian, before he'd even sat back down.

"Pipe down, Father," said Grace, "or I might tell everyone what the judge said about you during his summing-up of your most recent case."

"Prejudiced old buffer."

"Takes one . . ." said all four of them in unison.

"What's next on your agenda, my boy?" asked Sir Julian, in an attempt to recover.

"The Hawk is planning to shake up our entire department, now the politicians have finally accepted that the country is facing a major drugs problem."

"Just how bad is it?" asked Marjorie.

"Over two million people in Britain are regularly smoking cannabis. Another four hundred thousand are snorting cocaine, among them some of our friends, including a judge, although in his case only at weekends. More tragically, there are over a quarter of a million registered heroin addicts, which is one of the main reasons the NHS is so overstretched."

"If that's the case," said Sir Julian, "some evil bastards must be making a fortune at the addicts' expense."

"Some of the leading drug barons are coining literally millions, while young dealers, some of them still at school, can make as much as a hundred pounds a day, which is more than my commander is paid, let alone a humble detective sergeant."

"With so much cash swirling around," said Sir Julian, "the less scrupulous of your colleagues might well be tempted to take a cut."

"Not if Commander Hawksby has his way. He considers a bent copper worse than any criminal."

"I agree with him," said Sir Julian.

"So what does he plan to do about the drugs problem?" asked Grace.

"The commissioner has given him the authority to set up an elite unit, whose sole purpose will be to track down one particular drug baron and take him out, while the area drugs squads concentrate on the supply chain, leaving the local police to handle the dealers on the streets, and the users, who are committing other crimes like burglary and theft to fund their addiction."

"I've defended one or two of them recently," said Grace. "Desperate, pathetic creatures, with little purpose in life other than getting their next fix. How long will it be before those in authority realize it's often a medical problem, and not all addicts should be treated as criminals?"

"But they are criminals," interjected her father, "and they should be locked up, not mollycoddled. Wait until it's your home that's burgled, Grace, then you might feel differently."

"We've already been burgled, twice," said Grace.

"Probably by someone who can't hold down a job. Addicts begin by stealing from their parents," said William, "then their friends, then anyone who leaves a window open. When I was on the beat, I once arrested a young adult who had a dozen TVs in his flat, scores of other electrical items, paintings, watches, and even a tiara. And then there are the fences, who are making a small fortune. They set up so-called pawn shops for customers who never intend to claim the goods back."

"But surely you can shut them down?" said Beth.

"We do. But they're like cockroaches. Stamp on one of them and half a dozen more come scuttling out of the woodwork. Drugs are now an international industry like oil, banking, or steel. If some of the biggest cartels had to declare their annual profits, not only would they be among the top hundred companies on the stock exchange, but the Exchequer would be able to collect billions more in taxes."

"Perhaps the time has come to consider regulated legalization of some drugs," said Grace.

"Over my dead body," said Sir Julian.

"I fear there will be a lot more dead bodies, if we don't," said William.

Sir Julian was momentarily silenced, which Marjorie took advantage of. "Thank heavens we live in Shoreham," she said.

"I can assure you, Mother, there are more drug dealers in Shoreham than there are traffic wardens."

"So what does the Hawk plan to do about it?" demanded Sir Julian.

"Cut the head off the monster who controls half the dealers in London."

"So why don't you just arrest him?"

"On what charge? Apart from the fact that we don't even know what he looks like. We don't know his real name, or where he lives. In the trade he's known as the Viper, but we've yet to locate his nest, let alone—"

"How are your wedding plans coming along, Beth?" asked Marjorie, wanting to change the subject. "Have you finally settled on a date?"

"Unfortunately not," said William.

"Yes, we have," said Beth.

"Good of you to let me know," said William. "Let's hope I'm not on duty that day, or worse, in a witness box trying to nail a hardened criminal who's being defended by my overpaid father."

"In which case, the trial will be over by lunch," said Sir Julian, "and we'll both be able to make it on time."

"I need to ask a favor," said Beth, ignoring them both and turning to Marjorie.

"Of course," said Marjorie. "We'd be only too delighted to help."

"Because my father had to spend a couple of years in prison, and as we've—"

"A miscarriage of justice that was rightly overturned," interjected Grace.

"And as we've only recently found somewhere to live," continued Beth, "I wondered if we could be married in your local church?"

"Where Marjorie and I were married," said Sir Julian. "I can't think of anything that would give me greater pleasure."

"How about Miles Faulkner ending up in jail for four years," suggested William, "and at the same time, Booth Watson QC being struck off the Bar Council."

Sir Julian didn't speak for some time. "I'll have to ask the judge for a recess, as I might have to consider a change of plea."

"How about you, Grace?" asked William.

"I only wish I could marry my partner in the local church."

3

"Congratulations, sarge," said Jackie, joining him at the bar. She had drawn the short straw and only drank a single shandy that night, as she would be driving the newly promoted detective sergeant home. She'd already warned Beth that it wouldn't be much before midnight.

"Thanks," William replied, after he'd drained his fourth pint.

"Not that anyone was surprised."

"Except my father."

"Time, gentlemen, please," said the landlord firmly, not least because most of his customers were coppers. Although in truth, once the civilians had departed, they would often enjoy a lock-in, when the landlord would continue to serve the boys and girls in blue. There was at least one pub in every division that had a similar arrangement, which not only added to the publican's profits, but meant he had no fear of prosecution. However, Jackie still felt it was time for William to leave.

"As you've clearly had one too many," she said, "the boss has recommended that I take you home."

"But it's my celebration party," William protested. "And I'll let you into a secret, Jackie. I've never been this drunk before."

"Why am I not surprised? All the more reason for me to drive you home. It would be a pity if you were demoted the day after you'd been promoted. Although it would mean I'd probably get your job."

"My father warned me to watch out for women like you," said William, as she took him by the arm and led him unsteadily out of the pub to cries of "Goodnight, sarge," "Choirboy," and even "Commissioner," without any suggestion of irony or sarcasm.

"Don't expect me to call you 'sir' and kiss your arse until you're at least a chief inspector."

"Do you know where the expression 'kiss my arse' comes from?"

"No idea. But why do I have a feeling you're about to tell me?"

"The Duc de Vendôme, a seventeenth-century French aristocrat, used to receive his courtiers even when he was sitting on the loo, and after he'd wiped his bottom, one of them rushed forward and kissed it, saying, 'Oh noble one, you have the arse of an angel.'"

"Much as I'd like to be reinstated as a sergeant," said Jackie, "I wouldn't be willing to go that far."

"As long as you don't call me Bill," said William, as he slumped back in the passenger seat.

Jackie drove out of the car park onto Victoria Street and headed for Pimlico as William closed his eyes. Only a year ago, when Constable Warwick had first joined the team, she had been a detective sergeant, perched firmly on the second rung of the ladder. But now, following the Operation Blue Period fiasco, and the successful return of the Rembrandt to the Fitzmolean, their positions were reversed. Jackie didn't complain—she was happy to still be part of the commander's inner team. William began to snore. When Jackie turned the corner she spotted him immediately.

"It's Tulip!" she said suddenly, throwing on the brakes and startling William out of his slumber.

"Tulip?" he said, as his eyes tried to focus.

"I first arrested him when he was still at school," said Jackie, as she jumped out of the car. William could only make out her blurred figure running across the road toward an unlit alley where a young black man carrying a Tesco shopping bag was passing something to another man, whose face was well hidden in the shadows.

Suddenly William was wide awake, adrenaline replacing alcohol. He leaped out of the car and followed Jackie, accompanied by the sound of several car horns as he nipped in and out of the traffic. Horns that warned Tulip he'd been spotted. He immediately sped off down the alley.

William ran past Jackie, who was handcuffing the other man. But he already knew this wasn't going to be the night for overtaking someone about the same age as himself. Street dealers rarely drink, and few of them take drugs, because they know it could cost them their job. Even before Tulip turned the corner, leaped on a black Yamaha motorbike, and roared away, William had accepted that he wasn't going to catch him. He reluctantly came to a halt at the end of the passageway, steadied himself against a lamppost, bent down, and was violently sick all over the pavement.

"Disgusting," muttered an elderly gentleman, as he hurried by.

William was only relieved he wasn't in uniform. He eventually straightened himself up and made his way slowly back down the alley, to find Jackie reading the prisoner his rights. William followed them unsteadily across the road, and managed on a second attempt to open the rear door of the car, allowing Jackie to shove the prisoner onto the backseat.

William joined her in the front, and tried not to be sick again as the car swung around and headed for the nearest police station. Jackie knew the location of London nicks the way cab drivers know hotels. She came to a halt at the back of Rochester Row police station, grabbed her charge and was escorting him toward the custody area before William had even got out of the car.

Some prisoners scream in protest, letting out a stream of invective that would turn the night air purple, while others are spoiling for a fight and need a couple of burly coppers to keep them under control. But the majority meekly bow their heads and say nothing. William was relieved that this one clearly fell into the bowed-head category. But he'd learned after only a few weeks on the job that while users are often ashamed, dealers never are.

The custody sergeant looked up as the three of them approached the desk. Jackie produced her warrant card and told him why she had arrested the prisoner, and about his lack of cooperation after he'd been cautioned. The sergeant took a custody record and a property sheet from below the counter, so he could take down the prisoner's details before he was placed in a cell overnight. After he'd entered the words *two wraps of white powder,* he turned to the prisoner and said, "Right, lad, let's start with your full name."

The prisoner remained resolutely silent.

"I'll ask you once again. What's your name?"

The prisoner continued to stare defiantly across the counter at his interrogator, but still said nothing.

"This is the last time I'm going to ask you. What's—"

"I know his name," said William.

◄○►

"And you still remembered him, after all these years?" said Beth, as he climbed into bed later that night.

"You never forget the first crime you solve," William replied. "I was responsible for Adrian Heath being expelled from our prep school after I proved he'd been stealing Mars bars from the tuck shop. So no one was surprised when I joined the police force, though some of his friends never forgave me. I wasn't Choirboy then, just a sneak."

"I feel rather sorry for him," said Beth, as she turned off the bedside light.

"Why?" asked William. "He's obviously gone from bad to worse, just as my father predicted he would."

"It's not like you to be so judgmental," said Beth. "I'd like to know what happened during the years after you lost contact with him, before I jump to any rash conclusions."

"I'm unlikely to find out, as Lamont's almost certain to take me off the case."

"Why would he do that, when you might be the one person Adrian would be willing to talk to?"

"You can't afford to become personally involved with a suspect," William said. "It's a golden rule for any police officer."

"Didn't stop you getting personally involved with Christina Faulkner," said Beth, as she turned away from him.

William didn't respond. He still hadn't told Beth that Christina had been in touch with him again.

"I'm sorry," Beth whispered, turning back toward William and kissing the jagged red scar that had never quite faded, physically or mentally. "If you hadn't turned her into a friend, we might never have got the Rembrandt back. Which reminds me, we've got a fundraiser at the gallery tomorrow night, and although your attendance isn't compulsory, I'd like you to come. Not least because some of the older ladies rather fancy you."

"What about the younger ones?"

"They've all been banned," said Beth, as she settled into his arms. A few moments later she'd fallen asleep.

William lay awake for some time, and tried not to think about what had happened that night in Monte Carlo. And now the boss wanted him to see Christina again. Would he ever be free of her? She'd lied about everything else, and if Beth ever asked her, would she also lie about what had taken place after she'd crept into bed with him?

⤙◦⤚

"So you and the suspect were at school together, detective sergeant?" said Lamont after William had briefed the superintendent on what had happened after he and Jackie had left his celebration party the night before.

"Prep school," said William. "Adrian Heath was among my closest friends at the time. So I presume I'll be taken off the case and DC Roycroft will handle it."

"No way. This is exactly the kind of opportunity the Hawk has been looking for. We might even have a chance of getting on the inside track if you're able to turn your friend into a snout."

"But we couldn't have parted on worse terms," William reminded him. "Don't forget, I was responsible for him being expelled."

"He'll still feel safer with you than with Jackie, or any other copper for that matter." William didn't offer an opinion. "I want you to return to Rochester Row nick right now and turn Heath back into your best friend. And I don't care how you do it."

"Yes, sir," said William, although he still wasn't convinced.

"And while we're on the subject of friends, have you returned Mrs. Faulkner's call?"

"Not yet, sir," admitted William.

"Then get on with it. And don't report back until both of them are on your Christmas card list."

◄○►

"Christina?"

"Who is this?"

"William Warwick, returning your call."

"I thought you'd forgotten me," she said, with a friendly laugh.

"That's hardly likely, considering what happened the last time we met."

"Perhaps we should meet again. I might have something to tell you of mutual interest."

"Lunch at the Ritz?" suggested William hopefully.

"Not this time," said Christina, "because we wouldn't have ordered our first course before my husband had been informed I was having lunch with the young detective who'd arrested him. It had better be somewhere more discreet this time."

"How about the Science Museum?"

"I haven't been there since I was a child, but what a good idea. I have to be in town next Thursday, so why don't we meet outside the main entrance at eleven?"

"Not outside the entrance," said William. "Someone might recognize one of us. I'll meet you by Stephenson's *Rocket* on the ground floor."

"Can't wait," she said, before the phone went dead.

William wrote a report of his conversation with Mrs. Faulkner and dropped it on Lamont's desk before leaving the office and heading for Strutton Ground. During the short walk, he rehearsed several questions he would put to Adrian Heath, although he wasn't convinced that they would elicit any answers if last night was anything to go by. A few minutes later he was standing outside Rochester Row nick. When he showed the desk sergeant his warrant card, the older man couldn't hide his surprise.

"I'd like to interview Adrian Heath, the prisoner we brought in last night," said William.

"Be my guest. He's in number two," said the sergeant, filling in an empty box on the custody record. "Refused breakfast this morning. We might get him in front of the magistrate later this afternoon, so he's not going anywhere fast."

"That's good, because I was hoping to have an intel chat with him unconnected with the offense he's been arrested for."

"Fine, but keep me briefed, so all the paperwork's in order."

"Will do," said William, as the desk sergeant handed him a large key and said, "He's all yours."

William took the key, walked along the corridor and stopped in front of cell number two. He peered through the grille to see Adrian lying down, a glazed expression on his face, and looking as if he hadn't moved since last night. He turned the key in the lock, pulled open the heavy door, and walked in. Adrian opened his eyes, looked up, and said, "This place isn't much better than our old prep school."

William laughed as he sat down next to him on the thin, urine-stained mattress. *I'm innocent,* had been scratched on the wall above Adrian's head by a previous prisoner.

"I'd offer you tea and biscuits," said Adrian, "but I'm afraid room service isn't that reliable."

"I see you haven't lost your sense of humor," said William.

"Nor you your quest to be Sir Galahad. So, have you come to rescue me, or to lock me up for the rest of my life?"

"Neither. But I might be able to help you if you felt willing to cooperate."

"What would you expect in return? Because I've never believed in the old boys' network."

"Me neither," said William. "But I might have something to offer that could prove mutually beneficial."

"You're going to supply me with drugs for the rest of my life?"

"You know that's not going to happen, Adrian. But I could ask the magistrate to be lenient when your case comes up this afternoon, despite this not being your first appearance in the dock."

"That's not much of an offer. I'll probably only get six months anyway, and there are worse places to be than holed up in your own cell with a TV, central heating, and three meals a day, not to mention a ready supply of drugs."

"As this is your third offense, you're more likely to be spending Christmas sharing a cell in Pentonville with a murderer, which might not be quite so much fun."

"Come on then, Choirboy, surprise me."

It was William who was surprised. "Choirboy," he repeated.

"That's what my old friend Sergeant Roycroft called you last night. A great improvement on Sherlock, I thought."

William tried to regain the initiative. "As you clearly know what I've been up to since we last met, how about you?"

Adrian stared up at the ceiling for a long time, as if his interrogator wasn't there. An old con's trick, William knew. He was about to give up and leave when suddenly a torrent of words came flooding out.

"After my expulsion from Somerton, thanks to you, my old man used his influence to get me into one of the minor public schools. They were willing to turn a blind eye whenever I needed a quick drag behind the bicycle shed, but they drew the line when I moved on to cannabis. Can't say I blame them." He paused, but still didn't look at William, who had taken out his pocket book and begun to make notes.

"After that, my father sent me to a crammer, and I somehow got offered a place at a university a long way from home. Heaven knows how much the old man had to stump up for that little favor."

Another long pause. "Unfortunately, I didn't get beyond my freshman year after one of the postgrads introduced me to heroin. It wasn't too long before I was hooked, and spent most days in bed, and most nights wondering how I'd get my next fix. After I was rusticated, my tutor told me I could resume my studies if I kicked the habit, so my father sent me off to one of those rehab centers that are full of do-gooders who want to save your soul. Frankly, my soul was no longer worth saving, so I signed myself out at the end of the first week, and I haven't spoken to the old man since. I stayed in touch with my mother, and she kept me afloat for a couple of years. But even her patience eventually ran out, and probably her money, so I had to find other ways to get hold of the cash I needed to survive. It's quite difficult to continually try and borrow money from your friends, when they know you have no intention of ever paying them back."

William continued to take notes.

"But after I met Maria I checked myself back into the clinic, and tried a little harder."

"Maria?"

"My girlfriend. But she was never convinced I'd really kicked the habit, and one night she caught me snorting a line of coke and became my ex-girlfriend. She told me she'd had enough and would be going back home to Brazil. Can't say I blame her. Though I'd do anything to get her back. But I don't think she'd be willing to give me a third chance."

The first chink in his armor, thought William. "Maybe I could help convince her that this time you're determined to kick the habit?"

"How?" Adrian sounded interested for the first time.

"Have you ever considered becoming a gamekeeper, rather than a poacher?"

"Why would I want to be a grass? People are killed for less."

"Because together, we might do something worthwhile."

"You must be joking, Choirboy."

"I couldn't be more serious. You could help me put the real criminals behind bars. The ones who supply drugs to children in school playgrounds, and ruin young lives. That might convince your girlfriend you've turned over a new leaf."

Another long silence followed. William was beginning to fear his appeal had fallen on deaf ears when Adrian suddenly opened up.

"What would I have to do?"

"I need to find out the name of the man who controls all the drug operations south of the river, and where his main factory is."

"And I'd like a million pounds in cash and two one-way tickets to Brazil," said Adrian.

"Two one-way tickets to Brazil might be possible," said William. "Now all we need to discuss is the price."

"I'll let you know just how much I expect, Choirboy, but not before the magistrate lets me off with a warning."

4

"*Rocket,*" said a young man who was addressing a small group of schoolchildren gathered around the ancient steam engine, "was built in the 1820s by the renowned locomotive engineer Robert Stephenson."

"Robert Louis Stevenson?" inquired a piping voice from the front row.

"No," said the guide. "Robert Louis Stevenson was the distinguished children's author, who wrote *Treasure Island* and hailed from Edinburgh, not Northumbria."

William smiled as he stood at the back of the group listening to a lecture he'd first heard twenty years before, when his mother had taken him to the museum.

"Mr. Stephenson won first prize at the locomotive trials held at Rainhill in Lancashire in 1829, when—"

William's thoughts were interrupted when he felt a gloved hand touch his shoulder. He didn't look around.

"Good of you to see me, Rocket Man," said a voice he immediately recognized. "All things considered."

"My boss is still determined to put your husband behind bars," replied William, not wasting any time on small talk.

"Amen to that," said Christina. "But there's not a lot I can do while we're still in the middle of a rather acrimonious divorce, just in case you hadn't noticed, Detective Constable Warwick."

William didn't correct her.

"Five locomotives competed for the five-hundred-pound prize," continued the museum guide. "*Cycloped, Novelty, Perseverance, Sans Pareil*, and, of course, Stephenson's *Rocket*. Mr. Stephenson's 0-2-2 engine won by a country mile."

William turned around to look at Christina. She was dressed in a low-cut cotton dress that stopped well above the knees and left little to the imagination. She was clearly on the lookout for her second husband.

"Can you think of any other crimes, however minor, that he might have committed during the past five years?" he asked.

"Too many to mention, but you can be sure he will have covered his tracks more thoroughly than a Highland poacher. Though what I can tell you," she went on, "is that following the recent Rembrandt trial, Miles is no longer bothering to rob art galleries, or the homes of wealthy art collectors, as there isn't an insurance company left that will do business with him."

"He's not the sort of man to stand in line waiting for the next bus, so do you have any idea what his latest scam is?"

"I only wish I did. Though I have a feeling Mr. Booth Watson QC remains the common thread with the criminal fraternity. That man's quite happy to represent any crook who can afford his fees. In fact, I suspect he does most of his networking during prison visits."

"Following *Rocket*'s successful trial, it became the accepted prototype for all steam engines, and remains, to this day, the most significant breakthrough in the history of locomotion."

William tried a long shot. "Has your husband ever taken drugs?"

"Marijuana occasionally, but who hasn't? He's certainly not an addict."

"You can still get six months if you're caught in possession of marijuana, and added to his suspended four-year sentence—"

"If he was caught, Booth Watson would appear on his behalf, and claim you'd lit the joint for him."

"Having captured the prestigious prize, Stephenson was awarded the contract to build seven more locomotives for the Liverpool and Manchester Railway Company."

"All I can tell you is that since I've moved out of Limpton Hall, Miles has started hosting all-night parties, and I'd be surprised if one or two of his friends didn't snort coke or even worse. But you'd still have to get past the front gates to catch them at it, and so far, you're the only policeman who's ever managed that—and just in case you've forgotten, Miles was away at the time. In any case, I can't see a magistrate issuing a search warrant on such flimsy grounds as you suspecting that somebody just might be smoking pot during a private dinner party."

"At the opening ceremony of the Liverpool and Manchester Railway in 1830, *Rocket* struck a local member of parliament while he was standing on the track, and his injuries sadly proved fatal."

"Mind you, I'm still in touch with our old housekeeper, so if I hear anything, I could let you know."

"Please do," said William, turning back toward the lecturer.

"After *Rocket* completed its final run in 1862, the L and MR donated Stephenson's masterpiece to the Science Museum, where it has resided to this day."

"Anything else, detective constable?" asked Christina. "I'm already late for my lunch at the Ritz."

"If you were able to find out the date of his next party—"

"You'll be the first to hear, William," she said before slipping quietly away.

"That's the end of my little talk," said the guide. "If you have any questions, I'll be happy to answer them."

Several hands shot up as William turned to leave. But then, all his questions had been answered.

William was waiting for a train at South Kensington tube station, on his way back to Scotland Yard, when he spotted him standing on the opposite platform, looking like any commuter on his way to work. William recognized him immediately; he was even carrying the same Tesco shopping bag. The moment their eyes met, Tulip immediately turned and began running toward the nearest exit. That was his first mistake. Instead of getting on the next train, he'd made a run for it.

William charged up the escalator steps two at a time. As he approached the barrier, he saw Tulip handing his ticket to a collector, who, after checking it, looked puzzled. William didn't stop running and flashed his warrant card at the collector without breaking his stride. He began to gain on his prey, but then this time he was sober.

Each time Tulip looked back over his shoulder, William had gained a precious yard. But then he stopped to hail a passing cab and leaped inside. Tulip's second mistake. William was just a couple of yards adrift when the cab moved off, and it had only traveled a hundred yards before it stopped at a red light. William treated the chase like an Olympic final, and was only a few strides from the tape when the light turned amber. He grabbed the cab door and was still holding on when the light turned to green, causing the driver to slam on his brakes.

"What the hell do you think you're doing?" shouted the cabbie, as he got out from behind the wheel, while the cars behind angrily blasted their horns. "I've already got a customer."

"Police," said William, producing his warrant card. He jumped into the cab, only to see Tulip leaping out of the other side. But he immediately collided with a cyclist, giving William enough time to grab his arm and bend it halfway up his back, before dragging him inside the cab.

"Drop us off at the nearest police station," said William firmly. "And leave your meter running."

The cabbie drove off without another word, while William kept Tulip's nose pressed up against a side window.

A few minutes later they pulled up outside Kensington police station, where the driver even opened the back door to let his passengers out.

"Don't move," said William to the cabbie, before frogmarching Tulip into the nick, only letting go of his arm so he could produce his warrant card for the desk sergeant.

William began to empty Tulip's pockets, placing the contents on the counter along with the Tesco carrier bag. He grabbed Tulip's wallet and extracted two pound notes.

"What the hell do you think you're doing?" demanded the desk sergeant.

"He forgot to pay his taxi fare," said William, as he turned to leave.

"And what's this?" said the sergeant, pointing to the bag.

"The evidence," said William. "Enter it on the charge sheet. I'll be back in a minute." He left the station and handed the two pounds to the cabbie, who smiled for the first time. "One more thing before you leave," said William. "Where did he ask you to take him?"

"The Three Feathers pub in Battersea."

Tulip's third mistake.

A grin crossed William's face as he made his way back into the station. But it soon disappeared when he saw the desk sergeant devouring the evidence.

"What are you up to?" he asked in disbelief.

"Removing any damning evidence we found in the shopping bag," said the sergeant. "Care for a slice?"

<o>

"I wonder if I might seek your advice on a private matter, Sir Julian," said Beth, as they sat in the corner of the drawing room after lunch.

"I do wish you wouldn't call me Sir Julian, my dear. It makes me feel so old. But how can I help?"

"Some of my colleagues at the Fitzmolean feel our director Tim Knox should be awarded a knighthood, but we have no idea how to go about it. After all, we've been voted Museum of the Year for the past two years, ahead of the Tate and the National Gallery, and both of their directors have been honored. I thought as you had a knighthood, you might be able to point me in the right direction."

"Don't tell anyone what you're up to, would be my first piece of advice, because if it were to leak out, his rivals might try to scupper the whole idea."

"Tim's such a decent and kind man, I can't believe he has any rivals."

"Anyone who's hoping to be knighted has rivals, not least those who think they're more deserving of an honor than him. But on a more practical level, you'll need a sponsor, preferably someone whose reputation is like Caesar's wife, beyond reproach. Who is the gallery's chairman?"

"Lord Kilholme."

"Fine fellow," said Sir Julian. "A former cabinet minister whose reputation has grown since leaving office, and that's a rare thing." He paused while his wife handed them both a coffee. "However, Kilholme will still need several letters of support from leading figures in the art world, and not all from the same political party. But Kilholme is an old pro, so he'll know exactly how to go about it."

"And surely he'll also know who sits on the honors committee?" said Beth.

"No one knows who sits on the committee. If people did, imagine the pressure they'd come under. It's a more closely guarded secret than the contents of the next budget. They're simply referred to as the great and the good."

"How interesting," said Beth. "Is that how you got your knighthood?"

"Certainly not, I was simply born in the right cot. I succeeded my father, who succeeded his father, who switched parties when Lloyd George became prime minister."

Beth laughed. "Does that mean that one day William will be Sir William?"

"And you will be Lady Warwick, which—"

"What are you two whispering about?" asked William, as he walked across to join them.

"The arrangements for our wedding," said Beth.

"You'd make a rather good member of the honors committee," whispered Sir Julian.

◄○►

"Care for a slice of Black Forest gâteau, superintendent?" asked Commander Hawksby.

"Don't mind if I do," said Lamont.

"How about you, DC Roycroft?"

"Always been one of my favorites," said Jackie, as the commander cut her a thick wedge.

"Have to make sure we destroy all the evidence," said the Hawk, after handing Paul a second slice, "because I hear Tulip is considering suing the Met for wrongful arrest, using unnecessary force while dealing with a law-abiding citizen, and racial prejudice."

"Pity it wasn't me who arrested him," said Paul. "Then at least he would have had to drop one of the charges."

"He's also demanding that the officer concerned be suspended while an inquiry into police brutality takes place."

"All the more reason to destroy the evidence," said Lamont, scraping up the last few crumbs.

"Sorry we couldn't offer you a slice, DS Warwick," said the Hawk, "but then we would have to add accepting a bribe to the long list of charges against you."

Jackie tried not to smirk.

"But—" began William.

"Fortunately for you," said the commander, "the drugs in question had been shoplifted from a local Tesco store, but as the evidence has now been destroyed, we were left with no choice but to caution him, and release the suspect with a warning."

"But—" repeated William.

"Hardly the six-to-eight-year sentence you'd been hoping for, DS Warwick."

"And what's more," said Jackie, "the address Tulip gave us, surprise, surprise, doesn't exist."

"But the pub does," said William.

"What pub?" demanded the Hawk, sounding serious for the first time.

"The Three Feathers in Battersea. That's where he told the cabbie to take him."

All four officers were suddenly alert.

"Perhaps I should stake it out," said William. "Try to find out who his fellow dealers are?"

"That's the last thing you're going to do," said Hawksby. "They'd spot a choirboy like you a mile off. No, this is a job for one of our more experienced undercover officers. You just make sure you don't go anywhere near the place."

"Do I know the officer you have in mind?" asked William.

"Even his own mother doesn't know him," said the Hawk.

5

"Detective Sergeant Warwick," he said, after picking up the phone on his desk.

"I now know the name of the person you're looking for," said a voice he immediately recognized. "But it's going to cost you a ton for starters."

"A hundred pounds?" said William. "For that, I'd expect him to be sitting at my desk signing a confession."

"Not this time," said Adrian. "And for another hundred, I'll tell you where you can find him every Friday afternoon at five o'clock."

"Where shall we meet?" said William, as another phone began to ring.

"The lower room of the Salt Tower in the Tower of London. Next Wednesday at eleven."

"You're needed on this line," shouted Jackie, cupping a hand over the receiver. "Sharpish!"

"And I'll expect to see the cash before I even consider revealing his name, or where you'll find him on a Friday afternoon at five."

"I don't think she'll hold on much longer," said Jackie.

"Otherwise all you'll be seeing is the Crown Jewels, and that'll cost you fifty pence." The line went dead. William slammed down the receiver, shot across the room, and grabbed the phone from Jackie's outstretched hand.

"Detective Sergeant Warwick," he repeated.

"Detective Sergeant?" said a voice that sounded as if she didn't expect to be kept waiting.

"Christina?" said William, trying not to sound surprised.

"Miles will be hosting a dinner party for nine close friends at Limpton Hall on May the seventeenth. Eight o'clock."

"Do you know the names of any of these *close friends*?" asked William, as he opened his pocket book.

Another line went dead.

"You hang about for ages waiting for a bus to appear," said William, "and then two turn up at the same time."

"I'm all ears," said Lamont.

"My contact claims he knows the name of the Viper, and where he goes at five o'clock every Friday afternoon, but he expects a couple of hundred for the information."

"Worth every penny," said Lamont to William's surprise, before adding, "if, one, he's telling the truth, and two, his information turns out to be kosher."

"Do you want to risk it, guv'nor?"

"It's your call, DS Warwick. But if you decide to go ahead, I'll have to get clearance from the commander before I can release that kind of money. And he'll want to be sure you don't hand over a penny before your snout's given you the information. Never forget, your old school chum isn't your friend, and he never will be. But that doesn't mean you don't stick to your side of the bargain. You'll have to, if you're going to secure his trust. And the other call?"

"Christina Faulkner. She says her husband's planning a dinner party for nine guests at Limpton Hall on May the seventeenth."

"I'd like to be a fly on the wall for that little soirée," said Lamont. "But even you won't be able to pull that off."

"No, but we could be somewhere nearby to check out the guest list."

—◦—

"What are you up to today, dare I ask?" said Beth as William climbed out of bed.

"I'm visiting the Tower of London."

"Are you expecting someone to steal the Crown Jewels?"

"No, but I am hoping to come away with a couple of gems," he replied, before disappearing into the bathroom. He turned on the hot water as he prepared to shave. He planned to be at the Tower by ten thirty, so he would be waiting for his old school chum long before he appeared. But first he would have to call in at the Yard and collect the two hundred pounds Hawksby had reluctantly authorized.

"If you fail to come back here with a name and address, or it turns out to be a false lead, I'll deduct every last penny from your pay packet."

As a detective sergeant's salary was less than three hundred pounds a week, the thought wasn't exactly appealing. He would like to have said, "You must be joking," but he knew the Hawk didn't joke about money.

After breakfast, he and Beth caught a bus to Kensington before going their separate ways: Beth on foot to the Fitzmolean, while William took the tube to St. James's Park. He glanced at the *Daily Mail* front-page photograph of Princess Diana with her two young sons before disappearing down the steps into the underground. As he sat on the train he thought about Beth, and couldn't wait for her to be pregnant. But at the moment, she considered the Fitzmolean her first priority.

The super was sitting at his desk when William walked into the office. Two neat piles of ten-pound notes were stacked in front of him. William was surprised by how slim the two cellophane packets were. He sat down opposite Lamont, who slowly counted out the notes, ". . . eighteen, nineteen, twenty," then placed them back in their packs, opened a drawer in his desk, and extracted the inevitable form, which he handed to William.

William read the carefully worded document twice, before returning to a paragraph that was highlighted in bold capitals: ANY CHARGE OF MISUSE OF FUNDS COULD RESULT IN A PRISON SENTENCE OF UP TO TEN YEARS. He signed the release form, and DC Adaja added his signature as a witness. Lamont retained a carbon copy for his records before handing over the cash.

William tucked the money into an inside pocket of his jacket and left without another word. Once he was on the move, he found himself regularly touching the pocket to be sure the money was still there.

During the underground journey to Tower Hill, he sat at the far end of the carriage and reread the official guide to the Tower of London, glancing up each time another passenger came anywhere near him. Jackie had warned him that only the most seasoned pickpockets worked the London underground.

After twenty minutes he emerged into bright sunlight. William stood on the pavement for a moment to admire the ancient fortress, perched incongruously on a grassy mound surrounded by modern glass buildings that he doubted Sir Christopher Wren would have approved of. Sir Thomas More, Guy Fawkes, and Anne Boleyn had spent the last nights of their lives in the Tower's cells before being executed. If he returned to the Yard with nothing to show for his two hundred pounds, he might have to join them. He was only relieved he could no longer be drawn and quartered.

William walked the short distance to the Tower's walls, where he joined a queue of eager tourists waiting at the East Gate entrance. When he reached the front, he handed over fifty pence in exchange for a ticket. The small group of visitors joined their guide, a Yeoman Warder, dressed in his traditional navy and red tunic and wearing the distinctive Beefeater's hat. He shepherded his flock out onto the battlements while giving a running commentary. He informed them that work on the Tower had been started in 1078 by William the Conqueror, to keep his Norman invaders safely out of reach of the vengeful locals. A squawking raven landed nearby to remind them that as long as there were ravens resident at the Tower, England would be safe from invading infidels. As they approached the Jewel House, the guide declared, as if reading their thoughts, "Now for the moment you've all been waiting for, a chance to see the twenty-three thousand five hundred seventy-eight precious gems of incalculable value which make up the Crown Jewels."

"Who owns them?" someone asked.

"Her Majesty the Queen," came back the immediate reply.

"Not the people?" inquired an American voice.

"No," said the warder. "They pass from monarch to monarch, so no politician will ever be able to get their hands on them."

The first thing William noticed as they headed for the jewel room was that there wasn't a guard in sight, while their guide must have been over sixty, and was somewhat portly. But then, as the guidebook confidently stated, no one had escaped from the Tower in almost a thousand years.

But William wasn't a tourist, and today was not one for admiring state treasures, so he discreetly peeled off from the group and followed the signs for the upper and lower Salt Tower. He walked down the slope toward the Queen Elizabeth Arch and slipped into an unlit vault that had been added in the late 1230s as part of Henry III's curtain wall that surrounded the fortress. The small octagonal stone room was empty, and of little interest to anyone except the most ardent historian.

William knew that Bess of Hardwick had been imprisoned in the Salt Tower for supposedly practicing witchcraft, and wondered if that was what Adrian had in mind. He sat down in a stone alcove that afforded him a good view of the entrance, so he wouldn't be taken by surprise.

One or two tourists stuck their heads inside but, after a glance, quickly moved on to more promising possibilities. William heard the tower clock strike eleven, but then he'd never expected Adrian to be on time. He patted the two wads of notes in his breast pocket once again as he waited for his informer to appear.

He looked up to see a familiar figure standing in the archway. His eyes darted around the room like a cornered animal, until he spotted William. He walked quickly across to join him, and before he'd even sat down, said, "Did you bring the money?"

"Every penny," said William, extracting the corner of one of the cellophane packets to reveal the crisp new notes, which brought a smile to Heath's face. He blinked as the money disappeared back into William's pocket.

"First, the name," said William calmly.

"Khalil Rashidi."

"Have you ever met him?"

"No."

"Then how can you be sure he's the one they call the Viper?"

"Maria had a brief fling with him. That's how we met."

"And you trust her?"

"She's the only person I do trust."

William recalled Lamont's words: *Never forget, your old school chum isn't your friend, and he never will be. But that doesn't mean you don't stick to your side of the bargain. You'll have to, if you're going to secure his trust.* He extracted one of the cellophane packets and handed it to Heath. It disappeared instantly.

"What about the other hundred?" said Heath.

"Not before you tell me where Rashidi goes at five o'clock every Friday afternoon."

"Number 24 The Boltons."

"Is that where he lives?"

"No idea. That wasn't part of our bargain. Pay up."

William extracted the second package and handed it over. "If your information isn't kosher," he said, "I'll personally drag you back here, put you on the rack, and I'll be the one tightening the screws."

"That's not very friendly," said Heath, "considering I'm working on something even bigger for my old school chum."

"Any clues?" said William, trying hard not to sound excited.

"Not yet. But if I pull it off, I'll need enough money for me and Maria to disappear."

"Disappear to where?" asked William. But Heath, unlike Bess of Hardwick, had already escaped.

6

"Brazil would be my bet," said William.

"Why Brazil?" asked Lamont.

"Heath let slip during our first interview that his girlfriend came from there."

"Two and two don't always make four," said the Hawk. "But if his first two pieces of intel turn out to be accurate, your old school chum might prove invaluable in the long run."

"And expensive."

"Not if Khalil Rashidi turns out to be for real," said Lamont.

"He's real enough," said William. "However, according to Interpol, that's not the name on his birth certificate, but it's certainly the one he goes by nowadays."

"You still need to convince me that it was money well spent," said Hawksby. "What else do we know about him?"

"He was born in Marseilles in 1945," began William, checking the Interpol report. "His father was an Algerian farm laborer who fought alongside the French Resistance during the Second World War, and was killed by the Germans only weeks before hostilities ended."

"And his mother?"

"The daughter of a local politician from Lyons, who didn't

acknowledge his grandson until he was awarded a place at the Sorbonne, from which he graduated with honors."

"And after that?"

"He attended business school in Paris, and like so many second-generation immigrants—" Adaja raised an eyebrow—"he worked a damn sight harder than his indigenous rivals, which resulted in him being snapped up by the Lyons tea importers, Marcel and Neffe. After just three years, at the age of twenty-seven, he was posted to the company's Algiers office as regional director, the youngest in the firm's history."

"How did that work out?" asked Hawksby.

"He resigned without explanation after a couple of years, and no one at Marcel and Neffe was quite sure why, because he'd doubled the company's profits during that period."

"So did he resign or was he sacked, and they simply didn't want to explain how he managed it?" said Lamont.

"With that in mind, I've asked the fraud squad to carry out a full Companies House investigation on our behalf. See if they can throw any light on his unexpected resignation."

"Even more mysterious," said Adaja, "is that five years later he returns to Lyons unannounced, takes over the company and appoints himself chairman. No one knows where he got the money from. And if anyone asked, they were either sacked, or were never seen again."

"I'm pretty sure," said William, "that Marcel and Neffe is nothing more than the respectable front for what Rashidi's really importing, and it's not tea. After Britain joined the EEC in 1973, Rashidi and his mother moved to London. She now lives in The Boltons, and my old school chum assures me that he visits her every Friday afternoon at five o'clock."

"Do you think she's aware that her son is leading a double life?" asked Lamont.

"I don't think so," said Jackie, coming in on cue. "I've been keeping an eye on Mrs. Rashidi for the past few days, and she gives every impression of being a model citizen. She does the ladies who lunch circuit, attends the occasional concert at Cadogan Hall, likes Debussy and Strauss, sits on the local committee of Médecins Sans Frontières, and never misses Sunday-morning mass at the Brompton Oratory. It's either an elaborate smoke screen, or she has no idea what her son's up to."

"I presume," said Hawksby, "her house is now under constant surveillance?"

"Night and day," said Lamont. "But other than a few local tradesmen, and the occasional visit from the parish priest, no one else has darkened her doors."

"Does she employ any staff?" asked Hawksby.

"A chauffeur, who used to be a corporal in the Guards, a cook, and a housekeeper, who've been with her for years," said Adaja.

"I assume you'll all be out in force waiting to see if Rashidi turns up at five o'clock next Friday? Not that visiting one's mother is a crime."

"Yes," said William. "A retired solicitor who lives across the square was only too happy to allow us the use of his top-floor flat, and more important, he didn't ask any questions."

"Then let's hope that Rashidi's weekly visit to his mother is something we can rely on, in which case it will have been two hundred pounds well spent."

"And it's possible there's more to follow," said William. "OSC hinted that he was working on something even bigger."

"Like what?" asked Lamont.

"No idea, but he says it's going to cost us a damned sight more."

"Then it had better be a damned sight bigger," said the Hawk.

"It has to be one of two things," said Lamont. "Information concerning a large shipment of drugs coming from abroad . . ."

"Or he's discovered the location of Rashidi's slaughter," suggested Paul.

"Slaughter?" said William.

"Where they cook up the drugs, and prepare the cling film wraps, before selling them on," explained Paul. "Also known as the boiler room or hothouse."

"If it turns out to be a large shipment from overseas," said Hawksby, "don't arrest everyone in sight at the port of entry. Try to follow the cargo all the way to the slaughter. The commissioner is more interested in locking up Rashidi than a bunch of minnows, so it will be fascinating to see who locates the hothouse first, William's old school chum or Jackie's undercover officer."

"Don't put your money on DS Warwick," said Jackie, "because my UCO contacted me again last night."

Suddenly the team's attention was focused on DC Roycroft.

"Thanks to DS Warwick's intel," Jackie continued, "Marlboro Man has taken a part-time job behind the bar of the Three Feathers."

"Where no doubt he'll work hard enough to ensure it will end up a full-time job," suggested Paul.

"But not so hard that anyone becomes suspicious," threw in Jackie.

"How did he manage to get the job so quickly?" asked William.

"DC9 supplied him with a reference from a pub in Wiltshire that would have impressed any landlord. He's playing the innocent West Country bumpkin who's just arrived in the big smoke."

"Is the landlord also involved?" asked Lamont.

"MM doesn't think so," said Jackie. "But he's happy to turn a blind eye while the cash keeps flowing across the counter. In fact, our man tells me he's making more in tips as a part-time barman than he earns as an undercover DS."

"Which no one would begrudge him," said Lamont.

William frowned but didn't comment.

"Has he come up with anything substantial yet," asked the Hawk, "or is it still too early?"

"The Three Feathers turns out to be a regular haunt for several well-known dealers, including Tulip, so he suspects the slaughter can't be too far away. But so far he's made no attempt to speak to Tulip."

"That makes sense," said the Hawk. "Patience has a whole new meaning when you go undercover. If Tulip suspected for one moment that MM was a copper, he'd slit his throat and leave him to bleed to death while he ordered his next pint."

"Why would anyone even consider becoming involved in anything quite so risky?" asked William.

"My UCO watched his younger brother die from a heroin overdose," said Jackie, "so for him, it's personal."

◄○►

Jackie and Paul took it in turns to focus their binoculars on the front door of No. 24, while William was in constant touch with his team on the ground. He'd told them they needed to blend in with the natives if Rashidi wasn't going to become suspicious. At the same time he kept Lamont informed back at the Yard.

They had been expecting a chauffeur-driven car to appear at the far end of the square, and were taken by surprise when a black cab pulled up outside No. 24 just before five o'clock. The police photographer focused his long lens and started clicking from the moment the cab door opened. An elegantly dressed man of average height, wearing a hat, a long black coat, a scarf, and leather gloves, despite it being a warm afternoon, stepped out onto the pavement, opened the gate, and walked up the short path to the front door. He knocked once.

By the time Rashidi's mother had opened the door and embraced her son, the photographer had shot thirty-nine frames, but he wasn't feeling optimistic. When the front door closed, William gave the order for the Yard's unhailable taxi service to be on standby, as he couldn't risk a squad car tailing Rashidi if he left on foot. He radioed the Yard and brought the super up to date.

"Be careful," Lamont said. "We're in no hurry now we know where Rashidi's likely to be every Friday afternoon. If he suspects we're on to him, he'll disappear into thin air. Remember, we're playing the long game."

"Understood," said William.

Jackie's and Paul's eyes never left the front door.

William heard a crackle on the radio.

"I'm at the top of Tregunter Road," said a voice on the other end of the line.

"Stay out of sight," said William, "but the moment I give you the word, switch on your 'For Hire' sign and drive into The Boltons. Don't pick anyone up unless they're wearing a hat, a long black coat, scarf, and gloves."

"Understood."

It was almost two hours before the front door opened again and Rashidi reemerged. His mother gave him an even longer hug and, according to the lip reader, said, "See you next Friday, Khalil." Once again, the photographer went about his business.

William picked up his radio as Rashidi began to walk down the path. "Stand by, subject one is on the move."

The taxi appeared as Rashidi opened the gate and stepped out onto the pavement, its FOR HIRE light glowing in the early evening dusk. Rashidi ignored the cab and kept on walking.

"Shit," said Jackie, as Rashidi turned the corner and disappeared out of sight.

"Get moving, Adaja," said William. "Grab the taxi."

"On my way, sarge," said Paul, who bounded down the stairs and out onto the street, to find the cab waiting, its engine running. He jumped in and the driver immediately took off, throwing him onto the backseat. As they turned the corner, Paul spotted Rashidi getting into another taxi coming toward them, making him wonder why he'd ignored theirs.

Rashidi's taxi turned left at the end of the road, just as the traffic light changed to red. If a lorry hadn't stopped in front of them, Constable Danny Ives would have jumped the light.

"We've lost him," said Danny.

"Are you going to tell DS Warwick, or will I?" asked Paul.

"Silly question."

◄○►

"You lost him?" said the Hawk, once they were all seated around the table in his office back at the Yard.

"I'm afraid so, sir," said William. "But now we know he has his own taxi, in future we'll follow the vehicle, and not the man."

"Then be sure to change your number plates every week, and to switch taxis if it turns out to be a long journey. I don't care how many Fridays it takes to locate his slaughter, as long as we eventually do."

"Agreed," said Lamont. "Did we learn anything worthwhile from the photographs?" he asked as he flicked through them.

"Only that we're dealing with an extremely cautious man," said

William. "As you can tell from how little we can see of his face. But the lab did pick up something interesting."

"Enlighten me," said Hawksby, using one of his favorite expressions.

"Take a close look at his gloves. Our experts have studied all of the photographs, and they're convinced that Rashidi is missing part of the third finger of his left hand."

"What makes them think that?"

"Look carefully at the enlargement of frame number forty-six, where he's embracing his mother on the way out."

Hawksby took his time studying the blown-up image of a gloved hand.

"You can see that three of the fingers and the thumb of his left hand are touching his mother's back, while the third finger of the glove is loose, and not touching anything. If you then look at the enlargement of his right hand on frame fifty-two, all four fingers and the thumb are clearly holding his mother's arm."

"Clever," said the Hawk.

"So is he," said William. "So we can't afford to make the slightest mistake."

"What are you getting at, DS Warwick?" asked Lamont.

"It's obvious we're dealing with an exceptionally cunning and cautious man, so we'll need to always be on our guard, otherwise he'll lead us up the garden path every Friday afternoon."

"Your point, Warwick?" said the Hawk.

"We know Rashidi's a very wealthy man, but he doesn't turn up to see his mother in a chauffeur-driven car, but in his own anonymous taxi. He has no bodyguards, because he doesn't want to draw attention to himself or make his mother suspicious. Let's face it, we're up against a man who could have chaired a public company, been a cabinet minister, or lectured at the LSE, but preferred to pursue a life of crime."

"More profitable than the other three put together," said Lamont.

William looked around the table. "Remind you of anyone else we know?"

"We're up against another Faulkner," said the Hawk, letting out a deep sigh.

"Let's hope they never come across each other," said Jackie.

"Unless it's in Pentonville."

7

Every weekday morning around seven thirty, Jackie would take the tube to St. James's Park station, then walk across the road to Scotland Yard. But not on a Thursday.

On a Thursday, she would get off one stop earlier, at Victoria, and make her way up Victoria Street. After a couple of hundred yards she would turn sharp right and cross an open paved square to the south entrance of Westminster Cathedral. She always followed a small group of tourists inside, to be sure no one noticed her.

This Thursday morning, on entering the cathedral she encountered the usual handful of worshippers scattered around the pews, heads bowed, all praying to a God she no longer believed in. Jackie walked slowly down the left-hand aisle, not wanting to draw attention to herself as she admired Eric Gill's Stations of the Cross stone reliefs, aware that if the great sculptor were alive today, she would have to arrest him. But as the pope had pardoned Caravaggio for murder, why wouldn't the Cardinal Archbishop forgive Gill for his indiscretions? After all, there's no mention of his particular sin in the Commandments.

Jackie stopped when she reached an offertory box placed below a portrait of the Virgin Mary that was illuminated by a dozen recently lit candles. She looked around to make sure no one was watching her before she took a key from her handbag and unlocked the small wooden box, to find a few coins scattered on the bottom. *Even less than last week*, she thought. Checking once again that no one was watching, she removed an empty Marlboro cigarette packet that was propped up in the corner of the box, and slipped it into her handbag. She then locked the box and strolled on toward the altar. She bowed to the cross, before turning into the right-hand aisle, and passing the remaining Stations of the Cross before she left the cathedral.

Having completed her task, which took less than five minutes, she continued on her way to work. But when she entered the Yard, she didn't take the lift to her office on the fourth floor, but made her way down to –1, where the darker arts are practiced.

Jackie didn't break her stride as she walked along a well-lit corridor until she reached a door on which CONSTABLE BECKWORTH was printed in neat black letters on pebbled glass.

Jackie knocked on the door and, not waiting for a response, entered, walked across to join PC Beckworth and placed the cigarette packet on her desk. The young constable looked up, showing no hint of surprise. She said nothing, but simply flicked the packet open, deftly removed the inner layer of silver paper, laid it flat on her desk and carefully smoothed out a few creases with the palm of her hand. She then took it across the room to a machine standing in the corner, the top of which she opened before placing the silver paper onto a copper plate. She closed it, turned on a switch, which caused a bright light to glow inside the machine, and waited for a moment before lifting the top again. She watched patiently, as apparently random letters began to appear on the silver paper. She then copied the short message onto a small white card, slipped it into an envelope, and sealed it before handing it to her once-a-week visitor. Jackie bowed, using the only sign language she knew. PC Beckworth returned the compliment more fluently, before going back to her desk.

As she turned to leave, Jackie gave the young constable a final thumbs-up, but she was already preoccupied, putting the silver paper in a filing cabinet next to her desk.

Jackie took the lift to the fourth floor, where Angela ushered her straight through to the commander's office. She was surprised to find William already sitting there with the Hawk, both of them clearly waiting for her. She handed the sealed envelope to her boss, who opened it and studied the contents for some time before saying, "Although I can't share everything that's on this card, I am able to pass on some information that impacts on a case you're both working on."

Jackie sat down next to William.

"Every Thursday morning at around seven our UCO drops an empty cigarette pack in an offertory box at Westminster Cathedral, which Jackie picks up an hour later. That's how he supplies me with his latest intel."

"How do you contact him?" asked William.

"Jackie drops an empty Marlboro pack in the same offertory box on her way home on Wednesday evenings. I presume PC Beckworth didn't show you today's message?" he said to Jackie.

"No, sir."

"Six names. But only three of them are directly connected with cases you're working on. Adrian Heath, user, we already knew that. Tulip, dealer, no surprise there. But occasionally the gods give us a small reward: Miles Faulkner, occasional user, does come as a surprise, and could be a real breakthrough. If Faulkner's hoping to get a supply of drugs for his dinner party at Limpton Hall on the seventeenth, you might need to call your OSC and find out if he can supply us with any details."

"I can't call Heath," said William. "He only ever contacts me."

"Then we'll have to wait for him to run out of money," said the Hawk. "The one thing you can rely on with any drug addict."

"Heath might be able to find out if Faulkner's a user, even who his supplier is, but whether he'd be willing to give evidence in court is quite another matter."

"You told me his girlfriend was desperate to return to Brazil, and he wants to go with her. If we were able to make that possible, maybe he'd agree to turn Queen's evidence."

"Then we'd have to hope his love for Maria is greater than his fear of Rashidi."

◄○►

"Now you put the black ball back on its spot," said William, chalking his cue.

Paul leaned over the edge of the snooker table and lined up the white and red balls before taking his next shot. "Hopeless," he said, as the red failed to fall into the corner pocket and careered back into the middle of the table, leaving William with a simple pot.

William took his place and made a break of 32, leaving Paul needing too many snookers to bother returning to the table.

"Do you have time for a quick drink?" asked William, as he placed his cue back in the rack.

"Sure, sarge," said Paul.

"It's only 'sarge' when we're on duty," said William after they'd sat down at a table in the corner of the recreation room. He took a sip of his pint before asking, "How are you enjoying your new assignment?"

"Delighted to have been transferred to Scotland Yard," said Paul. "I dreamed about it, but never thought it would happen."

"We're lucky to have you on the team," said William. "I may know the odd thing about stealing Rembrandts, but I'm still a complete novice when it comes to drugs you can't buy in a high street chemist."

"You'll know as much as any dealer before long," said Paul. "And by then you'll want to lock them all up and throw away the key."

"Including the addicts?"

"No. You'll end up feeling sorry for them."

"I already do. So how are you settling in?" asked William, changing the subject.

"Fine. I already feel like a member of the team."

"Any problems?"

"None that I can't handle."

"No strange looks when people come across you for the first time?"

"Only from some of the older guys, who frankly were never going to accept me. But the younger ones are fine."

"Anyone in particular giving you trouble?"

"Lamont's obviously finding the idea hard to come to terms with, but that's only to be expected. He's old school, so I'll just have to prove myself."

"If it's any consolation, I had the same problem with Lamont when I first joined the team. Don't forget he's Scottish, so he considers us both illegal immigrants."

Paul laughed. "I don't think it would make any difference with him if I'd been born in Glasgow rather than Lagos."

"Have you worked out yet what the common thread is between the commander, Jackie, and their UCO?"

"No," said Paul, putting down his glass. "I hadn't given it a thought."

"They're Romans."

"Roman Catholics?"

"In one. Whereas Lamont is a Freemason, so watch out for the strange handshake. And they're all a bit suspicious of us because we've come through the accelerated promotion scheme. So we'd better stick together. Anyway, what made you want to join the force in the first place?"

"Too much Conan Doyle as a kid, and not enough Thackeray. It didn't help that my father's a schoolteacher, and thinks that if I don't make at least commander, it will have been a waste of a good education."

"I've got the same problem," said William, raising his glass. "Although in my father's case, nothing less than commissioner will do. But don't tell anyone."

"Everyone already knows," said Paul, laughing. "But I still intend to give you a run for your money."

"I look forward to that. Do you feel like another game?"

"No thanks. I've been humiliated enough for one night."

"Why don't you come around to my place for supper, then you can meet Beth."

"Another time perhaps, William. I've got a date tonight, and I know you'll find this hard to believe, but I think she rather fancies me."

"Must be a first date," said William.

◄○►

William was fast asleep when the phone by the bed rang. No one from the gallery would be calling Beth in the middle of the night,

59

so it had to be for him. He grabbed the receiver, hoping the shrill noise hadn't woken her.

"I need to see you urgently," said a familiar voice.

Me too, thought William, but satisfied himself with, "Where? When?"

"The Tate at eleven o'clock tomorrow."

"Why the Tate?"

"There are unlikely to be many dealers hanging about in an art gallery on the off chance of finding a customer. As I recall, art was your favorite subject at school, so you can decide where."

"There's a large Henry Moore in gallery three."

"Who's Henry Moore?"

"You won't be able to miss her."

"Then I'll see you there at eleven tomorrow."

"Today," William said, but Adrian had already put down the phone.

"Who was that?" said Beth.

◄◦►

"Josephine Hawksby."

"Good afternoon, Mrs. Hawksby. My name's Beth Rainsford. I'm sorry to bother you, but—"

"You've invited Jack and me to your wedding next month, and we're both looking forward to it."

"That's kind of you to say so," said Beth. "William and I are delighted you'll be able to make it. But that wasn't why I was calling. I was hoping you'd be able to advise me on a personal matter, but preferably not over the phone."

"Of course. Why don't we have tea next Friday, say five o'clock at Fortnum's? That's one place I can be fairly confident we won't be overheard by any nosy policemen."

◄○►

After briefing Lamont on his early morning phone call, William left Scotland Yard and set off for the Tate to catch up with his OSC. He was anxious to discover why Adrian wanted to see him so urgently, and had several questions prepared long before he climbed the steep flight of steps that led up to the gallery entrance.

Although he was early, William headed straight for gallery three, where he found a small group of visitors admiring Moore's *Reclining Figure*. While he waited for Heath to appear, he tried to relax by walking around the room, familiarizing himself with some old friends, while making new ones. He occasionally glanced back at the Moore, but once again Heath was late, so he circled the room a second time, even more slowly.

Heath strolled into gallery three at twenty past eleven, possibly imagining that being late gave him the upper hand. William had drifted across to Eric Gill's *Crucifix*, where Heath joined him a few moments later.

"Let's talk on the move," said William, "then we won't be overheard."

Heath nodded as William walked on to stand in front of Millais's *Ophelia* floating in a river surrounded by flowers. He tried to concentrate on the man and not the woman. "Why did you want to see me so urgently?"

"Do you remember Tulip?"

"Your dealer."

"Not any longer."

"How come?" William asked. Someone had joined them to drool over *Ophelia*, so they quickly moved across to Stubbs's *Horse Attacked by a Lion*.

"Tulip ended up in hospital after swallowing a cling film wrap of cocaine just before he was arrested."

"An occupational hazard," said William, without emotion.

"Which I intend to take advantage of, because he's asked me to service his customers while he's away."

William thought about the significance of these words while pretending to concentrate on a Norfolk river scene by Constable.

"Constable and Turner were born only a year apart," he said, as someone else joined them. "But they couldn't have been more different: one old-fashioned and traditional, the other genuinely original and rebellious. Which is probably why they were never friends."

"Sounds a bit like us," said Heath, before walking away and pretending to look at another picture. "But let's get down to business. I need a favor," he said once William had rejoined him.

"What do you have in mind?" William asked, as one of them took a closer look at Morland's *The Fortune Teller.*

"While Tulip's away, it's my big chance to make some real money so I can finally escape, but I'll need your boys to give me a free run for a few weeks, no more."

"Why would we agree to do that?"

"Because as soon as Tulip's back, I'll give you the names of every one of his contacts."

"He'll kill you."

"Not if I'm on the other side of the world before he finds out, he won't."

"It's not enough," said William, as two members of the public paused to admire the Morland.

"What more do you want?" asked Heath, as they walked on to the next painting.

"The location of Rashidi's slaughter."

"Even Maria doesn't know that. But I'm working on it."

"Then let's start you off with something a little easier as proof of your goodwill."

"What do you have in mind?"

"We know that one of Tulip's customers is a man called Miles Faulkner."

"I've seen his name on Tulip's list, but he's not a regular. Always expects the purest gear, and pays top whack. But he hasn't been in touch recently."

"He will be," said William without explanation. "And when he is, I need to know exactly which drugs he orders and where he wants them delivered."

"And if I tell you that, you'll let me get on with my job until Tulip gets back?"

"Only my guv'nor can sanction that, but if he agrees, and you fail to deliver, I'll personally visit Tulip in hospital and tell him what you've been up to in his absence."

"You wouldn't do that to an old friend."

"Like Turner, you're not an old friend," said William, as they arrived back at Gill's *Crucifix*.

"I must admit," said Heath, "Moore's good."

8

"It's a different number plate, but the same taxi," said Jackie, lowering her binoculars.

"How can you be sure?" asked William, as they watched a black cab drive slowly into The Boltons.

"Same box of Kleenex on the back shelf."

"Well spotted," said William. They continued to watch as Rashidi stepped out of the cab and opened the front gate of No. 24.

"Same hat, gloves, coat, and scarf," said Paul. "Clearly a man of habit."

"Which might well turn out to be his downfall," said William.

The photographer had begun snapping away as soon as Rashidi stepped out of the taxi, although he'd warned William that because he was so well covered up, he didn't expect the results to be any different from last week.

The door opened before Rashidi had a chance to knock. The same hug, allowing the photographer to zoom in on the left-hand glove, before mother and son disappeared into the house.

William turned on his radio, which connected him straight to the Yard. "All units stand by, stand by, subject one has arrived at the known address," he announced. "The subject has now entered the house. If last week's anything to go by, he won't be coming back out for at least a couple of hours."

"What's your back-up looking like?" asked Lamont.

"I've got three taxis covering all the exits out of the square, ready to move at a moment's notice."

"And on the ground?"

"Two plainclothes officers in the back of each cab, detailed to follow the target the moment he gets out of his taxi."

"Cars?"

"Four unmarked cars stationed in the area between The Boltons and Earls Court, ready to move at a moment's notice."

"Let me know the minute he reappears."

"Will do, sir."

Lamont flicked off his receiver. "Don't you wish it was the two of us out there giving the orders," he said, "and not just watching from the sidelines?"

"Of course," admitted the Hawk, "but don't tell my wife."

◄○►

"Milk and sugar?"

"Just milk, thank you, Mrs. Hawksby."

"Please call me Josephine," she said, handing Beth a cup of tea. "I've already given a great deal of thought to our recent telephone conversation."

"But I didn't explain why I needed to see you."

"That wasn't too difficult to work out. I assumed you wanted to know what it's been like being married to a policeman for the past thirty years."

"Was it that obvious?" said Beth.

"Hell on earth, is the simple answer. The late nights, the last-minute cancelations, questions you can never ask, and, worst of all, the fear that one day he might not come home. But it's helped that I've never stopped loving Jack."

"But there are so many divorces in the force," said Beth. "Superintendent Lamont for example, and Jackie for another, and that's just in our department."

"True. But you will learn to accept the fact that the police are expected to keep the same hours as criminals, although the criminals get longer holidays in more exotic places." Beth laughed. "It was never going to be a nine-to-five job, and from what Jack tells me, William doesn't have the problem a lot of coppers suffer from." Beth put down her cup. "Too much testosterone and too many WPCs."

"Can you ever be sure?" asked Beth.

"No you can't, but Jack tells me you've found an exceptional young man, who's clearly devoted to you."

"And I'm devoted to him, but he'll need an exceptional woman as his partner, and I'm only an assistant curator at the Fitzmolean, who does work from nine to five."

"Thank goodness one of you is normal," said Josephine, as she selected a cucumber sandwich.

"But I worry that he's already married."

"To the job?" Beth nodded. "Every good copper is, my dear. But if I could go back thirty years, and he asked me again, I'd still marry Constable Jack Hawksby."

"Can I ask you a personal question, Josephine?"

"Anything."

"Have you ever considered divorcing your husband?"

"Divorce never. Murder several times."

◄○►

"Have you been invited to the wedding?" asked Lamont.

"Yes. Josephine and I are looking forward to it, although I expect there will be far too many criminal barristers on the guest list who I've only ever met while standing in the witness box."

"And possibly the odd criminal."

"No," said Hawksby. "Sir Julian Warwick QC isn't a man who mixes business with pleasure, so Booth Watson won't have been invited."

Lamont chuckled. "Have you met Beth?"

"Only at the Fitzmolean for the unveiling of the Rembrandt. It wasn't hard to see why William fell for her."

"Heaven help the poor lass."

"What makes you say that, Bruce?"

"I've been divorced three times, and DC Roycroft once. In fact, you're the exception that breaks the rule."

"I have a feeling William will last the course. My only worry is that Beth might try to get him to leave the force."

"All three of my wives tried," said Lamont, "and look where that got them. Each time I was promoted, my latest wife left me but not before she'd cleaned out my bank account."

"I'm pretty sure William won't be going down that path," said the Hawk. "However, I'm still relying on you to remove the last vestments of the latent choirboy before I'll even consider making him a detective inspector."

"And Adaja?"

"If he can handle the racial prejudice he's bound to come up against on the street . . ."

"Not to mention inside this building," said Lamont. "I realize I'm not exactly blameless myself. When I first joined the force the only thing that was black was the coffee."

"Did you ever watch *The Sweeney*?" asked the Hawk.

"Never missed an episode. Saw myself as John Thaw."

The Hawk smiled. "But did you spot the mistake in last week's rerun?"

"Remind me."

"The old Black Marias, DI Regan claimed, were named after a woman who always attended court hearings wearing a black dress. But DC Adaja informs me that in fact the term originates from a woman called Maria who kept an unruly boardinghouse in Boston, which the police had to visit far too regularly."

"Adaja's as bad as Warwick when it comes to plying us with useless information," said Lamont.

"And just as bright," said the Hawk. "In fact, William could have a genuine rival, and by 2020, the Met might even be ready to appoint its first black commissioner."

"Well, at least that would be better than its first woman commissioner."

The Hawk was about to comment when the radio crackled back into life.

"The subject's on the move," said William.

◄o►

The same hug, the same slow walk back down the path; the only difference was that when he stepped out onto the pavement this time, he turned left, not right.

"Stand by first. He's heading toward Bolton Gardens. Stand by," repeated William.

"Contact, contact," said a voice over the radio. "Target is getting into a taxi that doesn't have its light on. Off, off. Heading west on Brompton Road."

"Contact—I have the eye," said Danny.

"Stay with him," said William, "but only for about another mile. I've got an unmarked car just behind you ready to take over."

"Understood," said Danny, who kept his distance, but never let the target out of his sight. "Subject's moved into the outside lane," he reported a few moments later. "Could be turning right."

"Or carrying straight on," said William. "In which case we might find out where he lives."

"I'd rather find out where he works," said Lamont. "But I don't expect we'll get that lucky."

"Drop back, Danny," was William's next command, "and let the patrol car take over. But stand by, as I may need you again later."

It amused William that his four unmarked cars were all five-year-old Austin Allegros, in standard colors but with souped-up engines that could do 120 miles per hour if required. No one gave them a second glance as they proceeded down the middle lane of the Great West Road, never exceeding 40 miles per hour.

"Target has reached the Courage roundabout. Looks like he might be heading for the M4."

"Where do taxis usually end up after they hit the M4?" asked William rhetorically.

"The airport," said Danny.

"That's all we need."

"It's definitely looking like the motorway," said the driver of the patrol car, "because he's running out of turnoffs."

"Peel off at the Hammersmith flyover and let Danny take over. Another cab will be less conspicuous on the motorway, especially if Rashidi's heading for the airport. But, Danny, if his cab stays in the outside lane, let another car take over, while you slip off the motorway at the Heathrow exit and then return to the Yard."

"Will do, sarge."

"Target's moved back into the middle lane and is slowing," said Danny. "I think you're right, sarge. It has to be Heathrow."

"Damn," said William. "I haven't got enough back-up to cover all three terminals."

"It's terminal one, domestic."

"Keep your distance," said William. "Paul, be ready to follow him into the terminal."

"On the edge of my seat, sarge."

A short period of silence followed, while William paced around the room, fearing that if this became a weekly exercise, he'd wear out his shoes before they worked out where the subject was going.

"He's getting out of the taxi and heading for departures," said Danny. "Paul's tailing him."

"Is he carrying anything?"

"Nothing, sarge."

"Then he's unlikely to be flying anywhere."

"Could be meeting someone?" suggested Jackie.

"Not in departures. I suspect it's just another ploy to lose anyone who might even consider following him."

"Paul's entering the terminal," said Danny.

"What about Rashidi's taxi?" asked William.

"It's on the move again. Do you want me to follow him?"

"No. If the driver's a pro, he'll have spotted you by now. Wait until Paul tells us where Rashidi ends up."

"I've lost him, sir," said Paul, sounding embarrassed. "There must be a dozen entrances and exits in departures, while there are a thousand passengers roaming around in every direction."

"My fault," said William. "I should have told Danny to follow the taxi."

"Just make sure you have all three terminals covered next week," said Hawksby, who had been following every word.

"What makes you think he'll turn up at his mother's again next week?" said William, trying to keep the frustration out of his voice.

"Mr. Rashidi and I have one thing in common," said the Hawk. "We're never late for our mothers."

9

Beth's father tapped on the bedroom door. "The car's arrived."

"We're almost ready, Arthur," said his wife. "Just give us a few more minutes."

Arthur checked his watch. The chauffeur had done a dry run to the church earlier that morning, and reported that it had taken him eleven minutes. Of course, Arthur understood that everyone would expect the bride to be fashionably late, but not so late that the groom would become anxious, not to mention their two hundred guests.

Beth looked at herself in the mirror once again. Nothing had changed. She couldn't have imagined a more beautiful dress, and knew she would never be able to thank her father properly for the sacrifices he'd made so that this day would be one she would never forget.

"Does every bride have misgivings on the day of her wedding?" she said, almost to herself.

"I did," admitted her mother, as she readjusted Beth's veil. "So I expect the answer is yes."

Another tap on the door.

"I'm afraid this is one of those rare occasions when they can't start without you," Arthur reminded them, before walking back downstairs, opening the front door and pacing up and down the path.

A few moments later his daughter appeared at the top of the stairs and, like every father of the bride, he was the proudest man on earth. He left the house and opened the back door of the Rolls-Royce—even that had been rehearsed—and waited for Beth to climb in before he joined her in the back. The Rolls drifted sedately off and Arthur wondered if he should tell the driver to speed up, but thought better of it.

"You look sensational," he said, as he turned to admire his daughter once again. "William's a very lucky man."

"I'm so nervous," said Beth. "I hope it doesn't show."

"And so you should be, young lady. You're about to sign a partnership contract for life, with no get-out clause."

"I don't know how to thank you, Dad. None of this would have been possible without your extraordinary kindness and generosity, not just today, but for so many years. I know there must have been times when I drove you mad."

"Fairly regularly," replied Arthur with a chuckle, "but I'm happy to pass on that responsibility to the man who got me out of jail and back to work when no one except you believed that was possible." He took her hand. "Fathers are always convinced that nobody's good enough for their daughter, especially an only daughter, but I couldn't be more delighted to have William as a son-in-law. Of course he's not good enough for you, but he'll do!"

Beth laughed. "Mother tells me you went to his stag night at the local pub."

"Not for long."

"That's not what she says."

"Don't worry. Half the Met police force were there to keep an eye on him. Apart from a few unrepeatable jokes, and some dreadfully out-of-tune singing, he was still sober when I drove him home. Do you know his nickname?" he asked, as they turned into the High Street, and the ancient parish church of St. Anthony's came into view.

"Choirboy," she said, but she didn't tell her father her private name for William.

She and William had attended a couple of rehearsals during the week, and the parish priest, the Reverend Martin Teasdale, such a venerable old gentleman, had taken them slowly through the service, placing great emphasis on the importance of the marriage vows made in the presence of the Almighty. He ended by warning them that something would go wrong on the day, it always does.

When the Rolls drew up outside the church, Arthur checked his watch once again. They were seven minutes late, and he suspected that William would be getting quite nervous. But he knew his anxieties would be dissipated the moment a peal of joyous bells rang out and he saw his bride coming up the aisle.

Arthur stepped out of the car and held open the back door to allow his daughter to join him. The maid of honor rushed forward to straighten Beth's train, then nodded to the bridesmaids, who quickly fell in line. Beth linked her arm in her father's, and they entered the church to the sound of Mendelssohn's "Wedding March."

The congregation rose as one, as Beth made her way slowly up the aisle. On her left were friends from her schooldays and Durham University, sitting among a large contingent from the Fitzmolean.

When she glanced to her right, she saw that the pews were filled with what looked like a police convention or a visiting rugby team, interspersed with William's friends from his schooldays and King's College London. She smiled when she spotted Gino, reminding her of their first date.

As she continued up the aisle, Beth saw Jack and Josephine Hawksby, Grace and Clare, who were holding hands, Jackie Roycroft, Paul Adaja, and Tim Knox, who gave her a bow. And then she saw William standing on the top altar step, looking so handsome in his long tailcoat, white shirt, and silver tie, with a pink carnation in his buttonhole. He gave her that same nervous smile she'd first noticed when he'd come to the Fitzmolean to hear a lecture that should have been given by the museum's director. If Tim hadn't fallen ill, Beth wouldn't have been asked to step in at the last moment, and they might never have met. Beth hadn't admitted to anyone, not even William, that it had been hard enough having to deliver a lecture in public for the first time, and it hadn't helped that an extremely handsome young man wasn't always looking at the paintings.

When they reached the altar steps, Arthur Rainsford released his unmarried daughter for the last time, took a step back, and joined his wife in the front pew.

Beth climbed the steps to join William, who was staring at her as if he couldn't believe he'd got so lucky.

"Can't wait to remove the seventh veil," he whispered.

"Behave yourself, Caveman," she replied, glad he couldn't see her blushing.

When the last chord had been struck, and the organ fell silent, the vicar began by welcoming the bride and groom. He then looked down at the packed congregation and declared, "Dearly beloved, we are gathered together here in the sight of God, and in the face of this congregation . . ."

Beth knew the marriage ceremony almost by heart, like a young actress waiting for the curtain to rise so she could give the most important performance of her life. So when the vicar intoned, "Therefore if any man—" *Why not any woman*, she had thought during the rehearsal—"can show just cause why these two may not be lawfully joined together, let him speak, or else hereafter forever hold his peace."

The vicar had told them during the rehearsal that he would, as tradition demanded, pause for a moment before saying to William, "Will you take this woman to be thy lawful wedded wife." He paused, and a voice rang out, "I can show just cause!"

The congregation were momentarily stunned, and every head turned to search for the source of the lone voice. A man Beth had only ever met once before stepped out into the aisle and began striding purposefully toward her soon-to-be husband. When he reached the altar steps, he said, "This man," pointing at William, "is having an affair with my wife, and it has caused the breakdown of our marriage. He has no intention of being faithful to this woman, and I can prove it."

A shocked babble of voices turned into a chorus as Beth burst into tears. William took a stride toward Faulkner, and it took his best man and two of the ushers to keep them apart.

In over forty years as a minister the Reverend Martin Teasdale had never experienced an intervention during the marriage service. He tried desperately to recall what he was meant to do in the circumstances. He could hardly phone the bishop.

It was Sir Julian who came to his rescue. "Perhaps the two families, along with Mr. Faulkner, should accompany you to the vestry so this can be sorted out," he whispered from the front pew.

"Would the two families and the gentleman concerned, please join me in the vestry," the minister said, "in the hope that this matter can be resolved?"

William and Beth reluctantly left the altar steps and followed the vicar into the vestry. Once the parents of the bride and groom had joined them, they waited in silence for William's accuser to appear. Faulkner took his time before he entered the room.

"What is your name, sir?" asked the vicar.

"Miles Faulkner," he announced, with the same confident air he'd recently displayed in the witness box.

"A man who is currently serving a four-year suspended sentence for fraud," said Sir Julian. "My son was the arresting officer. This is clearly nothing more than a vexatious man seeking revenge."

"Is it true you have been convicted of fraud, Mr. Faulkner?" asked the minister.

"It is," replied Faulkner. "But I have something to say that was not revealed during the trial, and will prove Sir Julian's assertion that I am motivated by revenge is nothing more than an attempt to silence me, whereas in fact I am simply carrying out my Christian duty."

Everyone began talking at once, except the minister who, when the torrent of accusations and counter-accusations had subsided, said simply, "We will hear what you have to say, Mr. Faulkner. This may not be a court of law, but we are in the presence of a far higher authority, who will pass the final judgment."

Faulkner bowed, to suggest that he had taken in the gravity of the situation.

"In the sight of God," he said solemnly, "I accuse this man of having an affair with my wife while he was engaged to this woman. An act of infidelity that caused the irretrievable break-down of my marriage."

It sounded a little over-rehearsed to Sir Julian, who wasn't in any doubt who'd penned the script, although he wasn't sure how William would be able to prove his innocence.

"I have met Mrs. Faulkner on three occasions," protested William, "and then only in my capacity as a police officer."

"Can you deny that on one of those occasions, you spent the

night with my wife at our home in Monte Carlo, while I was safely out of the way on the other side of the world?"

"We spent the night in the same house," said William firmly, "but not in the same bed."

"Are you going to deny in the presence of God my wife joined you in bed that night?"

William didn't respond, and this time Sir Julian was unable to come to his rescue.

"I'm afraid that's true," said a voice from the back of the vestry. Everyone looked around to see who had spoken these words. Christina Faulkner stepped forward. "When William was staying as a guest in my home, after he'd gone to bed, I crept into his room uninvited, and slipped in beside him."

She couldn't have had a more attentive audience if she'd been giving an opening-night performance at the Albert Hall.

"No woman likes to be rejected," she said quietly, "but William did just that, and quite literally showed me the door. I shall not forget his words to my dying day. 'I'm in love with a remarkable woman,' he told me, 'and even the promise of you returning the stolen Rembrandt to the Fitzmolean wouldn't tempt me to be unfaithful to her.' If you think that must have been humiliating," said Christina, "just imagine what I'm going through now in the presence of God and this congregation." She paused once again before delivering her final riposte. "Two other simple facts may interest you, vicar. I had begun divorce proceedings long before I met Detective Sergeant Warwick, and perhaps more important, we haven't met since, as I'm sure my husband's private detective will confirm."

Beth took William in her arms and kissed him gently on the lips. "It's nice to know you consider me more valuable than a Rembrandt," she said. "I can't think of a better wedding present."

Everyone except Faulkner burst into warm applause. Arthur, who hadn't spoken until then, stepped forward, grabbed Faulkner by the arm, and twisted it halfway up his back with all the skill of a former amateur wrestler, and marched him to the back door. He opened it with his free hand and, with the help of a well-polished shoe, kicked him out into the graveyard.

Faulkner stumbled forward, falling on one knee before he recovered his balance. As he walked away he could hear Arthur shouting, "I've been arrested for murder once. Don't give me an excuse to make it twice!" He slammed the door and rejoined the others, to hear the vicar pronouncing, "Vengeance is mine, sayeth the Lord."

The bride and groom filed back into the body of the church and retook their places on the altar steps to a warm round of applause, revealing the fact that the vicar had forgotten to close the vestry door.

"Where were we before I was so rudely interrupted?" said the vicar, which was greeted with laughter and further applause. "Ah, yes. Will you take this woman to be your wedded wife?"

After William and Beth had exchanged vows, the vicar declared, "I now pronounce you husband and wife. You may kiss the bride." A standing ovation accompanied Mr. and Mrs. Warwick as they proceeded back down the aisle.

The reception gave everyone a chance to air their opinions on Faulkner's tasteless intervention, while the speeches that followed made no mention of it. When four o'clock struck, Arthur started to grow anxious once again, worried that if Beth took any longer changing into her going-away outfit, Mr. and Mrs. Warwick would miss their flight and would have to spend their first night as husband and wife in the back of a hire car.

He'd told her several times that the journey to Gatwick would take at least an hour, and once again she'd ignored his warnings. But when she reappeared in a navy and red cashmere outfit, complemented by a red silk scarf and small beige handbag, all was forgiven. Arthur tipped the cabbie ten pounds and told him to make sure they didn't miss their flight.

"Hold on tight, sarge," said the driver, as they climbed into the backseat. "I may have to break the speed limit."

"Oh, no, not you, Danny," said William. "What else can go wrong today?"

They reached the airport forty-six minutes later, and as the newlyweds dashed into the departure lounge, they were greeted with an announcement over the tannoy: "This is the final call for flight 019 to Rome. Would all passengers please make their way to gate thirty-one?"

Mr. and Mrs. Warwick were among the last to board the plane, and didn't relax until it had begun to taxi down the runway. William was squeezing Beth's hand as they waited to take off, when an announcement came from the flight deck. "This is your captain speaking," said a friendly voice. "I'm sorry to have to report that our engineer has identified a minor fault in the starboard engine, and we will therefore have to return to the gate where you will be required to disembark and wait until we locate an available aircraft to take you to Rome."

A loud groan went up in the cabin, followed by a hundred questions, none of which the aircrew were able to answer.

"May I assure you," continued the captain, "that your safety is our first priority. I hope it won't be too long before you are able to resume your journey."

"I wouldn't be surprised," said William, as he took Beth's bag down from the overhead locker, "if Faulkner turned out to be the engineer." Beth didn't laugh.

The passengers were escorted off the plane and back into the terminal, where they were offered tea and biscuits in the lounge while they waited for a further announcement. The promise that "It shouldn't be too long now," regularly repeated by solicitous staff, became less and less convincing, until finally there was an official announcement from the airline.

"I'm sorry to say that no replacement aircraft is available at this time. All passengers will be offered a seat on the first scheduled flight to Rome in the morning."

"It looks, Mrs. Warwick, as if we'll be spending our first night together as man and wife in an airport lounge," said William, taking Beth in his arms.

"At least it will give us something to tell your son," she said.

"My son?"

"Or daughter perhaps, Mr. Warwick. I'm pregnant."

10

"Mr. and Mrs. Warwick?"

William wondered how long it would take him to get used to that. He blinked and looked up, to see a stewardess he recognized from the plane.

"Yes?"

"Would you and your wife be kind enough to follow me?"

"What's happening?" asked a sleepy voice, as William gently woke Beth. "I'd just fallen asleep."

"I have no idea, but I imagine that if we follow this lady from the airline, all will be revealed."

Beth stood up, stretched her arms and yawned like an animal emerging from hibernation before reluctantly accompanying her husband.

"Maybe she's taking us to the first-class lounge," whispered William.

"A better class of sofa not to sleep on."

"Plus free food and drink."

"Wrong again, oh great detective," said Beth, as they walked straight past the first-class lounge and out of the terminal.

A driver opened the back door of a waiting courtesy car displaying the airline's livery.

"Curiouser and curiouser," said William, as they climbed into the back.

"Where do you think they're taking us?" asked Beth.

"Not Rome, that's for sure," said William, as the car moved off.

"Nor London," said Beth, as the driver ignored the signs for the motorway and turned left down a country lane.

They drove for a couple more miles, before the car slowed and passed through a set of wrought-iron gates onto an even smaller road that had been carved through a dense forest. They must have traveled for about another mile before a beautifully proportioned Georgian mansion of honey-colored stone clad in ivy loomed up in front of them. When they came to a halt outside the entrance, a young man dressed in a smart green uniform rushed forward and opened the back door of the car.

"Welcome to the Lakeside Arms Hotel, Mr. and Mrs. Warwick," he said, as they stepped out onto the gravel drive. "Would you be kind enough to follow me?"

The vast oak door opened while they were still several paces away, and a tall, elegantly dressed man wearing a dark jacket, striped trousers and a silver-gray tie awaited them. He looked as if he'd just come from their wedding.

"Good evening, Mr. and Mrs. Warwick," he said. "My name is Bryan Morris, and I am the manager of the hotel."

Without another word he led them up a wide, thickly carpeted staircase to the first floor before stopping outside a set of double doors with the words NELL GWYNNE SUITE painted in gold leaf on a panel. He took out his passkey, opened the door, and led them into a suite of spacious rooms that was bigger than their flat in Fulham.

"This is the bridal suite, which overlooks the lake," the manager said, as he walked across to a large bay window. "I do hope the peacocks won't disturb you." He paused for a moment by a dining table that was laid for two, and straightened a napkin before leading them through to the master bedroom, which boasted a vast bed that could have comfortably slept four without any of them meeting. He still hadn't finished his guided tour; the next room he took them into was a bathroom that boasted a Jacuzzi as well as a walk-in shower that could have accommodated a football team.

Speechless, they followed him back into the bedroom to find that their suitcases had mysteriously appeared, and their nightwear had been unpacked and laid out on the bed. A bottle of champagne was standing in an ice bucket. The manager uncorked it, poured two glasses and handed them to his guests.

"Please pick up the phone and order dinner whenever it suits you," he said. "You'll find the menus on the dining table."

"Can I stay here for the rest of my life?" asked Beth.

"Not if you're still hoping to fly to Rome in the morning, madam," said the manager. He bowed, retreated, and closed the double doors quietly behind him.

"Am I dreaming?" said Beth, as she raised her glass. "Because I can't believe the airline does this for every customer who's held up overnight."

"Don't let's ask too many questions, or we may find ourselves back in the airport lounge," William said, as he looked at the double bed and began to unbutton Beth's jacket.

"Caveman," she said.

"Some cave," he replied.

◄○►

"She wants what?" said Faulkner.

"Limpton Hall, with all the fixtures and fittings. That includes the seventy-three oil paintings, although she says you can keep the statue of yourself."

"Anything else, dare I ask?"

"Twenty thousand a year to pay for her staff," said Booth Watson, "as well as a final settlement of one million pounds."

"I presume that's it?"

"Not quite. She keeps all her personal belongings. Jewelry, clothes, etc., plus the Mercedes and Eddie, your chauffeur, who'll remain on your payroll."

"Tell her to get lost."

"I already have, if not in precisely those words."

"Don't forget she slept with Warwick in Monte Carlo, and they're still lovers."

"I don't think so, Miles. As you found out first-hand when you turned up at a wedding I advised you not to attend."

"You wrote my script, in case you've forgotten," Faulkner reminded him.

"Reluctantly," said Booth Watson.

"But I wasn't to know Christina would be there."

"Because unlike you, she'd received an invitation, which would rather suggest they're not lovers."

"In any case, it's still her word against mine."

"If a jury had to choose between a tearful, wronged wife and a man serving a suspended sentence for fraud, which side do you imagine they'd come down on?"

"It wouldn't matter, because as you've so often told me, a jury can't be informed about any previous convictions I've received."

"A ridiculous rule, but one that I admit works in your favor. Unless of course any of them have read a national newspaper during the past year."

"You think it might end up in court?"

"Bound to, if you're not willing to settle."

"I'm not going to let go of any of my pictures without putting up a fight," said Faulkner. "It's taken me a lifetime to build the collection."

"If you want to hold on to them, Miles, she's going to expect something in return. And unfortunately the collection's worth more than all three houses, the yacht, and the plane put together, none of which she has shown any interest in."

"Delay the settlement for as long as you can, BW. I might just have another card up my sleeve."

◄○►

Breakfast was served in their suite at ten o'clock the following morning, with copies of the The Times and Telegraph on a side table.

"Their first mistake," said Beth with a grin. "But I don't suppose they have many guests who take The Guardian."

"Or the Sun for that matter," said William, as he began to tuck into a full English breakfast, while Beth sipped her freshly squeezed orange juice and read about Prince Andrew's engagement to Sarah Ferguson.

At 10:20 there was a gentle tap on the door and, like the fairy godmother, Mr. Harrison reappeared.

"I hope you both enjoyed a good night's sleep," he ventured.

"Couldn't have been better," said William, after he'd drained his coffee.

Not much chance of that when you're married to a caveman, Beth wanted to tell him, but kept her thoughts to herself.

"I only ask because you didn't order dinner last night."

"We were both full of crisps and peanuts," Beth blurted out.

"Unfortunately you missed the early morning plane for Rome.

However, we managed to book you onto the twelve thirty-five flight, and the airline has upgraded you to business class. A limousine will be waiting outside to take you back to the airport."

"Of course it will," said Beth.

"I beg your pardon, madam?"

"My wife simply meant that this has been a truly unforgettable experience, and you couldn't have done more to make our stay memorable."

"How kind of you to say so, sir. I'll leave you now and send a porter to pick up your bags in a few minutes' time," said Mr. Harrison, who once again bowed before leaving the room.

"Detective Sergeant Warwick," said Beth, taking her husband in her arms, "you're going to have to get promoted fairly regularly."

"Why?" asked William innocently.

"Because I could get used to this." William was about to protest when she added, "But for now, I'll settle for spending our wedding anniversary in this room once a year for the rest of our lives."

◄○►

"They've just left, sir," said the manager, looking out of the window in his office as the limousine disappeared down the drive. "I think you'll find we carried out your instructions to the letter."

"You did indeed, Mr. Harrison. My daughter phoned a few minutes ago to tell me that they'd been grounded because of an engine problem, but the airline went out of its way to make up for it."

"That's most gratifying to hear, sir. Where shall I send the bill?"

"To my office in Marylebone. Mark it personal, for the attention of Arthur Rainsford."

◄○►

Detective Superintendent Lamont picked up the phone on his desk to be greeted by a public-school accent that grated on his Scottish ear.

"Reporting in, sir."

"Are you enjoying being in charge, DC Adaja, even if it's only while DS Warwick is away on his honeymoon?"

"Every minute. I don't suppose there's any chance of delaying his return, sir, as I was rather hoping to solve the case before he gets back?"

"No chance," said Lamont. "Not least because Warwick's just called from Rome and all he wanted to know was if we'd found out where Rashidi lives."

"Why am I not surprised?"

"Any developments on that front?" asked Lamont, ignoring the comment.

"You were right about having all three airport terminals covered, sir. Rashidi was dropped off at terminal three this time, but ended up back at terminal one."

"And where did he go from there?"

"A dark blue BMW picked him up and drove him to Little Charlbury, a village in Oxfordshire."

"Have you located his house, just in case DS Warwick phones back?"

Paul laughed. "It's not so much a house, sir, more like a castle. It even has its own moat and drawbridge. The grounds must be over a thousand acres, and the nearest neighbor is at least a mile away."

"Then you'd better be wary of briefing the local police about what we're up to. With that much money washing around, he might have one or two of them on his payroll, or at least wary of annoying him."

"There's just a village bobby, and the only thing that's older than him is his bicycle."

"Security?"

"State of the art, plus some personal touches. The entire estate is surrounded by a ten-foot wall topped with electrified barbed wire."

"Criminals always take more stringent precautions when it comes to their own safety and possessions than honest people," said the Hawk, coming on the line for the first time. "Do you think it's possible his drugs factory could be situated somewhere in the grounds?"

"It seems unlikely, sir," said Paul, "not least because it would make a lousy distribution center. Everyone in the village would see the gear coming in and going out. But I'll stay put for now and see if I can pick up anything on the local grapevine."

"Good," said Lamont. "Meanwhile, I'll arrange to fly over the property in the Met's helicopter tomorrow morning. Though from what you say, I don't expect to find anything incriminating. I suspect the place is all part of his public front, as the chairman of a successful tea company."

"And the taxi that took him to the airport—where did it end up?" asked the Hawk.

"Back at the driver's home in Chiswick," said Jackie. "He turns out to be a licensed black cab driver. But on Friday afternoons he only has one customer, who he picks up in the City at four twenty p.m. and drops off in The Boltons around five. He then drives him on to Heathrow a couple of hours later, dropping him at a different terminal each week. I've already fitted a tracking device to his taxi so we don't always have to cover every terminal."

"I've only just authorized that," said the Hawk, "so did you attach the device before or after you had my permission?"

"It may have been a few hours before," admitted Jackie.

"Don't make that kind of mistake again, DC Roycroft. It's the sort of thing that could trip us up in court and scupper the whole operation. In future, play it by the book, or you might find yourself back on the beat."

"Yes, sir," said Jackie. After she'd put the phone down she added, "But the criminals are working from a different book, in case you haven't noticed . . . sir."

◄○►

"I wonder if they've discovered where the factory is?" said William to a large marble lady.

"I'm sure they'll somehow manage to survive without you for a couple of weeks, detective sergeant," said Beth, as she checked her guidebook.

"So what have you got planned for this afternoon?" asked William, feeling a little guilty.

"A visit to the Borghese, where you'll have a chance to see three of the finest Berninis, an unforgettable Raphael, and—"

"Titian's *Sacred and Profane Love*."

"Painted in which year?"

"1514."

"I sometimes forget that you read Art History at King's, between running around a cinders track all day and reading Agatha Christie at night."

"Simenon, actually. In French. So when do we get to see Da Vinci and Michelangelo?"

"Patience, Caveman. We still have another week to view the works of arguably the two greatest artists who've ever lived."

"I'm more of a Caravaggio man, myself."

"Then you probably already know that there are eleven of his works in galleries or churches right here in Rome. But tell me, DS Warwick, if you had been given the opportunity to arrest Caravaggio and have him hanged for murder in 1606, following a barroom brawl, what decision would you have made?"

"Hanged the damned man," said William. "Unlike that greedy hypocrite Pope Paul the Fifth."

"I'm glad you weren't pope at the time," said Beth, "otherwise we wouldn't be able to see nine of those eleven masterpieces."

◄○►

"Do you think the Hawk knows we're having an affair?" said Jackie.

"Of course he does," said Ross. "That's why he chose you as my liaison officer."

"But most people think you've left the force."

"Including my mother. But that was all part of Hawksby's plan. So many young officers resign in the first couple of years, they're quickly forgotten."

"But it's still a hell of a decision to become a long-term UCO, considering all the risks that involves."

"I've always been a loner," said Ross. "The Hawk spotted that early on in my career, and took advantage of it."

"So are you getting anywhere, or just claiming lots of overtime?"

"That's for others to decide. But I've already established that Tulip is a regular at the Three Feathers, as are several other dealers whose names I'll be able to add to fairly soon. But it's not something I can afford to hurry. For a UCO patience isn't a virtue, it's a necessity. That is if you hope to survive. If just one of those bastards suspected for a moment that I was a member of the drugs squad, the next time you saw me I'd be floating up the river on the early morning tide." He placed a hand on the inside of Jackie's thigh.

"Not yet," she said, removing his hand.

"But I haven't had sex for weeks."

"Who do you think you're kidding? The Hawk got your latest report, and even asked me to congratulate you. But now he wants you to find out where Rashidi's slaughter is."

"That could take a little longer, because the Viper doesn't invite you into his nest until you've proved yourself, and I'm still only a runner, the lowest form of life. So I doubt that's going to happen overnight." He took Jackie in his arms and began to kiss her gently on her breasts.

For a moment she forgot what the other question was that the Hawk wanted answered, as her lover's tongue moved hungrily down her body. She lay back and didn't think of England. Soon after they'd made love, Ross slipped out of bed and began to get dressed.

"Aren't you going to take a shower?" she asked.

"Doesn't go with the territory," said Ross unashamedly.

And then she remembered. "The boss wants you to keep an eye out for a dealer called Adrian Heath. He was on your last list. Try and find out what he's up to and keep us informed."

"Did he give you any clues why the guy's so important?"

"The Hawk doesn't give clues, just commands."

"Silly question," admitted Ross, as he pushed open the window.

"And next time you turn up without warning, make sure you knock."

"Why?" said Ross, as he climbed out onto the fire escape.

"You might find I'm in bed with someone else."

11

Sir Julian looked up from the other side of his desk and smiled at his client.

"Your husband is offering you Limpton Hall—but not the paintings—the Eaton Square flat, which has only nine months left on the lease, ten thousand pounds a year to cover your staff expenses, and a settlement of half a million pounds."

"So how should I respond?" asked Christina.

"Accept Limpton Hall and the flat in Eaton Square, but ask for sixteen thousand a year, and nothing less than eight hundred thousand pounds as a settlement. After all, it's your husband's moral and legal responsibility to ensure that you continue to live in the style you've grown accustomed to after so many years as his dutiful wife."

"I do believe, Sir Julian, you are enjoying yourself."

"Certainly not, madam. I am simply carrying out my fiduciary duties on behalf of a client. No more."

"And certainly no less."

Sir Julian allowed himself a wry smile. He didn't care much for Mrs. Faulkner, but he had to admit he always enjoyed her company. "I need to ask," he continued, "how strongly you feel about the paintings being part of the final settlement?"

"I couldn't feel more strongly about it," she said. "In fact, it's a deal breaker."

"May I ask why, Mrs. Faulkner, when you've made it abundantly clear you have no particular interest in art?"

"The moment the decree absolute is granted, I'll be putting them all up for auction. Miles won't be able to resist buying them back, and I intend to make sure he doesn't get them cheaply."

Sir Julian avoided asking the obvious question, and simply said, "Then I shall insist the paintings at Limpton Hall are part of the settlement."

"All seventy-three of them," said Christina. "And you can tell Miles not to bother trying to foist me off with copies or fakes, because if he does, my next call will be to Commander Hawksby."

Sir Julian suppressed a smile. "Do you have any other questions concerning the settlement, Mrs. Faulkner?"

"Just one. Did the other side agree to pay your fees?"

"They did."

"Then I will be calling on you for advice fairly regularly, Sir Julian, and it may not always be about Miles. But it will always concern him."

◄○►

Jackie walked quickly across to the other side of the room when the phone on William's desk began to ring.

"DC Roycroft." The line went dead.

"Probably William's old school chum," said Lamont. "Unfortunately he's unlikely to talk to anyone else."

"What if he calls again?"

"We'll have to hope Warwick's back by then."

"And if he isn't?"

93

"Then you'll have the unenviable task of deciding whether to interrupt his honeymoon."

—◁◦▷—

William stared up at the ceiling of the Sistine Chapel that, according to the guidebook, scholars considered had changed the history of Western art.

"How long did Michelangelo take to complete the fresco?" Beth asked.

"He worked on it tirelessly from 1508 to 1512," replied William. "The poor man spent most of that time lying on his back on the top of a crudely constructed scaffold. By the time he'd finished he was virtually a cripple. It didn't help that Pope Julius the Second never paid him on time."

Beth was mesmerized by the sheer ambition of the project, and didn't stop staring up at the ceiling until her neck began to ache.

"You could have used one of the large mirrors provided," suggested William.

"I could also have bought a postcard. If Rome wasn't littered with masterpieces, I'd visit the chapel every day until you had to drag me away!"

"Even though you'd have to join a long queue of fellow worshippers early each morning?"

"Michelangelo lay on his back for four years to achieve this unique masterpiece, so I'd be only too happy to queue for a couple of hours to pay homage to his memory."

—◁◦▷—

The phone on William's desk was ringing again. If it hadn't been the third time that morning, Lamont would have ignored it.

"Answer it," he said in exasperation. "But don't tell whoever it is that William's still on his honeymoon."

Jackie picked up the receiver and said, "DS Warwick's not available at the moment."

"I need to speak to him urgently."

"Can I pass on a message?"

"Tell him Faulkner has placed his dinner order."

"Anything else?"

"I'll call back in an hour's time, when I'll expect him to be on the other end of the line. I can't believe he's got anything more important to do than catching Faulkner in the act."

"That won't be possible," said Jackie, but the line had already gone dead.

⃟

The phone began to ring just as William finished shaving. He grabbed the bathroom extension in the hope it hadn't woken Beth.

"Good morning," he said quietly.

"William, it's Jackie. Your OSC has just called, to say that Faulkner's placed his dinner order, whatever that means. He needs to talk to you about it urgently. Do you want me to give him your number when he next rings?"

"Yes, of course. Tell him to get in touch as soon as possible," whispered William, before putting the phone down.

"Another woman?" said Beth sleepily when he returned to the bedroom.

"That's never going to be your problem," William said, as he sat down on the bed beside her and gently rested an ear on her stomach. "I can hear something."

"A little boy?"

"No, it's a little girl."

"How can you be so sure?"

"She's grumbling."

"About their father wanting to desert both of us and go home, rather than spend another day with the other man in my life."

"So is that what you have planned for today?"

"Yes. I want to go back to the Sistine Chapel."

"Fine by me. But we'll have to queue."

"I'll queue and get the tickets, and you can join me there in a couple of hours' time. That should give you enough time to take any messages from the office without me finding out who's been calling you," she said before disappearing into the bathroom.

◄○►

"I'm delighted to report, Mrs. Faulkner," said Sir Julian, "that the other side have accepted our latest terms unconditionally, so I can now draw up a final settlement."

"Miles agreed that I could keep all of the paintings at Limpton Hall?" asked Christina, not sounding convinced.

"Without exception. They've even sent an inventory so you can check they're all accounted for," he said, handing her a two-page document.

Christina studied the list carefully, and long before she'd reached the Vermeer, she said, "They have to be copies."

"I thought you might say that," said Sir Julian, "so as you instructed, I warned Booth Watson that a specialist from Christie's would have to authenticate every one of the works before we'd agree to sign a binding document."

"What did he say?"

"No more than my client expected."

"I don't believe it," said Christina. "Miles never rolls over that easily." It was some time before she added, "He's up to something."

◄○►

An hour passed, and Adrian hadn't called. But then, he always felt the need to make a point. William continued to check his watch every few minutes, but the phone remained resolutely silent. He was trying to decide if he should skip the Sistine Chapel, and face Beth's wrath, or go and join her and live happily ever after. He was just putting on his jacket when the phone rang. He picked it up before the second ring. "William Warwick."

"You wanted to know what would be on the menu for Saturday's dinner party at Limpton Hall." William didn't interrupt. "For starters, top-shelf cannabis, nothing but the best, followed by the finest wraps of ninety-six percent pure Colombian cocaine for the main course." He paused. "I think you owe me another two hundred."

"You'll be paid in full," said William, "but only after you've delivered the goods."

"I'll be traveling down to Limpton Hall at seven o'clock on Saturday. I could report back to you around eight and collect my money."

Not from me, thought William, but satisfied himself with, "Would you be willing to testify in court that you'd sold the drugs to Faulkner?"

"Possibly. But we'll need to discuss terms, because if I agree to do that, I'll never be able to work in England again. Everything comes at a price." He didn't bother to say good-bye.

After making a hurried phone call to brief Superintendent Lamont, William headed quickly for the door. He was confident he could still make it in time, even if he might find it hard to concentrate on *The Creation of Adam,* rather than the downfall of Miles.

◄○►

"William's just called from Rome," said Lamont. "He briefed me on the conversation he had with his OSC, and I'm recommending we go ahead with a full-scale operation on Saturday night. Just a pity William will miss out on the raid."

"I'd ask him to cut short his honeymoon," said the Hawk, "if I didn't think Beth would kill him first, and then come looking for me. Take me through your plan, Bruce, so I can brief the commissioner."

"I've already obtained a search warrant for Limpton Hall . . ."

◄○►

"Perhaps you should fly home a couple of days early?" suggested Beth as they walked back into the hotel.

"Certainly not," said William. "I'm only going to have one honeymoon in my life, and I don't intend to spend a single day of it with Miles Faulkner."

"But you might not get another opportunity like this, and you've somehow managed to survive ten days with the phone only ringing once." William didn't respond. "Why do I get the distinct impression that you'd rather be spending Saturday night at Limpton Hall with Faulkner, than eating another spaghetti in the Campo de' Fiori with me?"

"Certainly not," repeated William, but not with quite the same ringing conviction.

"It may come as a shock to you, Detective Sergeant Warwick, that after Faulkner's pathetic attempt to stop us getting married, I wouldn't be unhappy to see him behind bars."

"Despite the fact you're still hoping to get some other pieces from his collection once the divorce has been settled."

"Only one painting in particular," admitted Beth. "I confess it would enhance the gallery's collection, but I won't believe it until I see it hanging on the museum's wall."

"What have you been up to behind my back?"

"My new best friend, Christina Faulkner, has promised the Fitzmolean first choice of any of the seventy-three paintings in Limpton Hall once her divorce has been settled. I've got my eye on a small but exquisite Vermeer, *The White Lace Collar*, which would grace the south entrance of the museum."

"What makes you think she's any more likely than her husband to keep her word?"

"Because your father is her lawyer and Clare has drawn up the agreement, so we're all on the same team now."

William stopped at the concierge's desk.

"*Si, signor,* how can I help?"

"I need to catch the first available flight back to London."

◄○►

Once the flight attendant had opened the plane door, William shot through the gap like a greyhound out of the slips. He didn't stop running until he reached a row of public phones.

"Where are you?" asked Lamont.

"Gatwick. Should be with you in about an hour."

"How does Beth feel about that?"

"It was her idea. In any case, there's a gentleman with a back problem whose work she wants to visit one more time."

"Then ask her to fall on her knees and pray, because we may need the intervention of the Almighty to pull this one off. Meanwhile, get back here as quickly as you can."

William went straight to the front of the queue at passport control and produced his warrant card. An officer checked his passport and he was ushered quickly through. Thanks to Beth having agreed to take care of his luggage, he was able to skip the baggage hall and head straight for the Gatwick Express. When the train pulled into Victoria station thirty minutes later, he was the first to hand his ticket to the collector at the barrier, before running all the way to Scotland Yard. Once the automatic doors had opened, he ignored the lifts, bounded up the stairs to the fourth floor, and headed straight for the commander's office.

As he ran along the corridor, William noticed the odd looks he was getting from his fellow officers as he passed them, and realized he was still wearing an open-neck floral shirt, jeans, and slip-on sandals. But they weren't to know that only hours before, he'd been strolling around Rome enjoying temperatures in the nineties. He knocked on the commander's door and waited for a moment to catch his breath before he walked in. The team rose as one when he entered the room, and began to bang the palms of their hands on the table.

"Take a seat," said the Hawk after the clamor had died down. "Thanks to you, the assistant commissioner has green-lit the operation, and authorized a full-scale raid on Faulkner's home tomorrow evening. I know exactly the role I have in mind for you, DS Warwick, but arresting someone wouldn't be appropriate dressed in that outfit, even in Italy."

12

William sat in the back of a taxi, and waited for the super to join him.

The final briefing in the commander's office had lasted for over three hours, and only broke up after every detail had been thrashed out for a third time.

Over lunch at a corner table in the canteen, Lamont continued to double-check the plan for any flaws while his soup went cold. William was aware that his boss couldn't afford to be involved in another Operation Blue Period. Not how he hoped to end his days at the Yard.

Just after five o'clock, Lamont joined William in the cab. Danny Ives, waiting behind the wheel, didn't need to be told where to go. He'd done a dry run the day before, and even selected the dropping-off point. DC Adaja, DC Roycroft, and a photographer were in a second taxi, waiting for Danny to move off.

The two cabs left the Yard and headed west toward the M4. Five miles from Limpton Hall, Danny pulled into a petrol station. He hadn't run out of petrol, he was far too professional for that. But the advance party needed the sun to go even farther west before they set out on the final part of the journey.

Jackie got out and stretched her legs, while William bought a Kit Kat from the shop, not because he was hungry, just to kill time.

He had paced around the perimeter of the petrol station several times before Lamont finally said, "Let's get going."

William had never felt so nervous. He knew that everything now depended on the credibility of his contact. If Heath didn't turn up, the whole operation would be aborted and they would have to return to Scotland Yard and face the wrath of the Hawk, who would be sitting waiting for them. William was all too aware that there would only be one person to blame. The word "detective" would be erased from his warrant card and the mothball removed from his uniform.

After a short drive along the motorway, Danny turned down a country lane, and a mile or so farther on the two cabs swung off the road and parked in a copse, from which they had a clear view of the house. Lamont was quickly out of the lead car, and immediately trained his binoculars on the front gates.

"Perfect, Danny," he said. "We can see them, but they can't see us."

A photographer got out of the second car and climbed up into the branches of a nearby oak tree. He only needed a clear view of the road, and would have nothing to show them until they met up in the commander's office the following morning for the debriefing. No one else was thinking about tomorrow.

Lamont turned his attention to a farmyard on the other side of the road. Officers in four squad cars and two large black windowless vans were well hidden behind the barn, awaiting their orders.

"How did you manage that?" asked William.

"The farmer sits on the bench, and he hasn't, how shall I put it, formed a high opinion of Faulkner over the years. He was only too happy to help."

Jackie joined Lamont, a radio in her hand. "The taxis have all arrived at the local railway station, and are parked and ready, in case any of Faulkner's guests should arrive by rail."

"Unlikely," said Lamont. "Criminals rarely travel by train. They don't want to be in a situation where they can find themselves trapped. They like to be able to make themselves scarce at a moment's notice, which is difficult on a moving train."

"What about the commander?" asked William.

"He'll be behind his desk waiting impatiently for any news. It took all my powers of persuasion to convince him he shouldn't join us."

"Winston Churchill had the same problem with King George the Sixth on D-Day," said William.

"That's a comfort to know," said Lamont, his dry Scottish humor getting the better of him. They returned to the car. Only Danny seemed to be relaxed.

"So in theory, DS Warwick, the next car to come over that hill will be driven by your OSC, who'll be on his way to deliver the gear to Faulkner. Should he fail to make an appearance," Lamont added, his tone changing, "the Hawk's orders couldn't have been clearer. Abort. We're not going to raid Faulkner's house unless we can be sure the evidence we need to convict him has been delivered."

"No pressure," whispered Jackie as William checked his watch: 18:47.

No one spoke as they all stared intently in one direction, willing a car to appear. Heath might have been casual about his meetings with William, but surely he'd be on time for an important customer like Faulkner. Several more minutes passed before William breathed a sigh of relief, when he spotted a red MGB heading toward them. The binoculars confirmed that it was Heath at the wheel. He drove past them a few minutes after seven.

Lamont followed the car's progress all the way to the front gates, where it came to a halt. A guard stepped out of the gatehouse, clipboard in hand. He spent a few moments talking to

Heath before the gates swung open and the MGB proceeded up the long drive before disappearing from view.

Lamont picked up his radio and pressed the red button. "OSC has arrived and entered the grounds."

"Call me the minute he comes back out," responded the Hawk.

"Will do, sir."

Lamont began to pace around among the trees, uncomfortably aware that the success or failure of the operation was now in the hands of others. "Did you remember the sandwiches, Jackie?" was all he had left to say.

"Yes, sir. Cheese and tomato, or ham?"

"Cheese and tomato."

"William?"

"No, thank you," he said, recalling that less than forty-eight hours ago he had been with Beth, sitting in a restaurant in the Campo de' Fiori, enjoying linguine alle vongole and a bottle of Barolo from a vineyard in Piedmont.

Twenty-six minutes later, the gates opened and Heath's car reappeared. They all watched in silence as it came closer and closer, until he drove past their hiding place and disappeared back over the hill. Lamont radioed the commander and brought him up to date.

"In theory," said Hawksby, "the next car should be the first of the dinner guests. Maintain radio silence until they're all accounted for."

They didn't have to wait long before a green Jaguar sailed past them, the passenger in the back completely hidden behind gray-smoked windows.

"If the windows in the back are clear, the passenger has nothing to hide," remarked Lamont.

"I can't imagine many of Faulkner's friends having nothing to hide," said William, as he recorded the number plate in his pocket book. Three more cars followed in quick succession, and three more number plates were noted by William, before the radio crackled to life again. It was the temporary porter at the local railway station.

"Yes, DC Adaja?" said Lamont.

"One of the guests has just arrived on the seven thirty-two from Waterloo and is on his way to Limpton Hall in the first of our cabs."

"That means we'll get someone past the gates and up as far as the house, if only for a few minutes."

"I told him to report to you when he comes back out."

"Good thinking, Paul. Keep sweeping the platform."

A few minutes later a black cab passed them and flashed its headlights twice. The photographer smiled for the first time as he had a clear view of the passenger. Lamont followed the taxi's progress all the way to the front gates; a stopwatch in one hand, binoculars in the other. Two minutes and eighteen seconds later, the guard finished checking the invitation and the gates swung open once again.

"With any luck," said Lamont, as another large chauffeur-driven car sped by, "our man should be back with us in a few minutes' time, and I'll be able to ask him some questions we don't yet have an answer to."

"Crooks seem to prefer Rolls-Royces," observed William, jotting down the latest number plate as another Silver Cloud purred by.

"And not last year's model," remarked Danny.

"Nothing more than vulgar status symbols to show their place in the criminal pecking order," snarled Lamont.

William took a sip of water, but still ignored the last of the ham sandwiches. He was wondering if his heart could beat any faster, when the taxi reappeared and, moments later, pulled off the road to join them. Jackie took over binocular duty, while the cab driver joined them in the car.

"Did you pick up any worthwhile information about your passenger?" was Lamont's first question to the driver.

"He's a banker, but I couldn't find out which bank. His accent would suggest he's from the Middle East. I slowed down as I passed you, so the photographer could get some decent shots. I can tell you, my taxi's back windows have never been so clean. Just like you see in films."

"How long did it take you to get from the gates to the front door of the house?"

"One minute and forty seconds, but I didn't hurry, so you could knock at least twenty seconds off that."

"And the guests' cars, are they parked in the driveway outside the house?"

"No, sir, in a paddock behind the conservatory. To judge from the noise that was coming from there, I think the drivers are having a party of their own."

"But they won't be drinking. And we can be sure there will be one or two of the heavy brigade among them, whose driving skills aren't the reason they're here tonight. Well done, constable. Get back to the station, but hang about, because we might need some back-up later."

"I hope so, sir," he said, causing them all to laugh.

"Nine guests accounted for," said Jackie, as another large car swept past them.

Lamont watched as the final guest pulled up outside the gatehouse, and the driver presented his invitation. He kept the binoculars trained on the car until it could no longer be seen.

"A full house," he said, before picking up his radio to bring the commander up to date. Next, he briefed the inspector in charge of the squad cars, and finally DC Adaja, who was still sweeping the platform while he waited for the next train. "Now let's concentrate on how we get past the gatehouse," he said. "The guard looked to me like a professional, and you can be sure he has plenty of bells and whistles in case of an emergency, so we'll have to take him out before he realizes that, unlike Cinderella, we don't have an invitation to the ball."

"When are you thinking of moving, sir?" asked William.

"Just after ten. That should give them more than enough time to finish dinner and be sampling the desserts before we move in."

"Their just desserts?" said Jackie. Both men groaned.

William spent the next hour repeatedly glancing at his watch, but it didn't make the minute hand move any faster.

Just before ten, Lamont announced over the radio, "Stay alert, people." Not that William was sure how much more alert he could be. "I'll be giving the order to move in about five minutes." And he would have done so, if the radio hadn't started crackling.

"What the hell are you playing at, Adaja?"

"I thought you ought to know, sir. Ten scantily dressed young women arrived on the last train from London, commandeered all three of our cabs, and are on their way to Limpton Hall."

"Radio the drivers and tell them to go slowly through the gates. That will give the squad cars an opportunity to follow them in, which will solve one of our biggest problems."

"Understood, sir. They should be passing you in about ten minutes."

The superintendent's next call was to the commander. He listened to the latest news with interest, and his next command took Lamont by surprise. "Put the operation back by at least an hour, Bruce."

"Why, sir?"

"Because then you'll catch them with their trousers down."

13

"Have you ever fancied yourself as a madam?"

"Oh no, sir," said Jackie. "That would be above and beyond the call of duty."

"Not if you're still hoping to be reinstated as a sergeant, it wouldn't," said Lamont.

William tried not to smile when the superintendent briefed Jackie on what he had in mind.

"I could drive Jackie in my taxi, sir," said Danny, once the superintendent had fully explained what he expected DC Roycroft to do. "Then the guard will think we've come from the station."

"Good idea, Danny," said Lamont. "But leave Jackie to do the talking. Never been your strong suit."

"Thank you, sir," said Danny.

"Right, let's go over the plan one more time," said Lamont. "Jackie will . . ."

◄○►

Fifteen minutes later Danny drove his black cab out onto the road with a single passenger in the back. He made his way slowly toward Limpton Hall, and came to a halt in front of the closed gates. The guard emerged from the gatehouse and slowly approached the taxi. Jackie wound down her window, adjusted her skirt, and greeted him with her most seductive smile.

"Can I help you, madam?"

"Well, at least you got that right," said Jackie, glad to see his eyes settling on her legs. "You can call me Blanche. I've come to make sure my girls arrived safely. All part of the service."

The guard checked his clipboard. "But you're not on my list."

"Neither were they," said Jackie, taking a risk. "But then that's the way Miles prefers it, as I'm sure you know."

He didn't look convinced. "Where have you come from?" he asked politely.

Danny gripped the handle of the cab door.

"From the station," said Jackie. "Like my girls."

"But the last train to Limpton Hall was over an hour ago," said the guard. "I'll have to call the Hall and check with Mr. Makins that you're expected. Could you give me your name again, madam?"

Danny thrust open the cab door and rammed it into the guard, who fell unceremoniously to the ground, as Jackie leaped out, shot past him, and headed for the gatehouse. She had just located the switch marked FRONT GATE by the time the guard had recovered, rushed back into the gatehouse, and brushed her aside with one sweep of an arm. He was about to hit the red panic button when a knee landed in his groin with all the force Jackie could muster.

The guard doubled over and grabbed his crotch, momentarily stunned, and didn't see the fist swinging toward his chin. A referee wouldn't have had to count to ten to confirm he'd been knocked out.

Danny sat on the guard as Jackie quickly flicked up the switch and the vast wrought-iron gates swung slowly open.

Seconds later four squad cars that had been waiting around the

109

corner, engines idling, shot past them and headed up the long drive. No lights, no sirens, the drivers thankful for a half moon.

"How are you going to explain that?" said Danny, looking down at the prostrate figure laying on the ground.

"Resisting arrest," said Jackie.

"Then you'd better pray they find enough evidence of a crime once they get inside the house. Because if they don't, it won't be promotion you'll be looking forward to, but—" said Danny, as the first of the squad cars screeched to a halt outside the hall seventy-two seconds later.

Lamont leaped out and ran up the steps to the front door. He kept his thumb pressed on the bell while two of the cars swung left into the paddock, blocking the exit for the eight drivers and assorted bodyguards, several of whom were quietly dozing or listening to their car radios.

Lamont was about to give the order to break down the door when it was opened by possibly the only person in the house who was still fully dressed.

"Good evening, sir," said Makins, as if greeting a late guest. "How may I help you?"

"I am Superintendent Lamont, and I have a warrant to search these premises." He held up the legal authority, before barging past the butler and into the hall. He was followed by sixteen drugs squad officers and two sniffer dogs, all of whom immediately went to work. None of them could have failed to notice the stench of cannabis in the air.

Lamont stationed himself in the middle of the hall while his officers spread through the house, ignoring the guests, some of whom were zipping up their trousers, others looking somewhat flustered, while one elderly man appeared to have passed out.

William was among the last of the team to enter the house. The first thing he noticed was that the Constable landscape was still hanging in the hall, but then he was distracted by something that hadn't been there when he'd first visited the house over a year ago. He stared in disbelief at a large bust of Miles Faulkner with a falcon on his arm, lit by a single spotlight. He was about to offer his unfettered opinion of its vulgarity, when a voice from above him shouted, "What the hell is going on?"

William looked up to see Faulkner standing at the top of the stairs in a red silk dressing gown, glaring down at them. He walked slowly down the sweeping marble staircase and stopped directly in front of Lamont. Their noses almost touching.

"What exactly do you think you're doing, chief inspector?"

"Superintendent," said Lamont. "I have a warrant to search these premises," he added, holding up an official-looking document.

"And what were you hoping to find, superintendent? Another Rembrandt perhaps? Not that you'd know one if it was staring you in the face."

"We have reason to believe that you are in possession of a large amount of illegal drugs," said Lamont calmly. "And not just for your personal use, which is contrary to the Misuse of Drugs Act 1971."

"I'm sure it is," said Faulkner, "but I can assure you, superintendent, you will not find any drugs on these premises, as my guests are all law-abiding citizens." He crossed the hallway and picked up the phone.

"Who are you calling?" demanded Lamont.

"My lawyer, which is no more than my legal right, as you well know, superintendent."

"Just be sure it's only your lawyer you're calling," barked Lamont. He didn't take his eyes off Faulkner, as his officers spread through the house.

After he made the call, Faulkner sat down in an armchair and lit a cigar, while Makins poured him a brandy. By the time his goblet had been refilled a second time, and his cigar was no more than a glowing ember, all the intruders had to show for their troubles was a couple of joints and an Ecstasy tablet. The dogs' tails, which had previously been wagging eagerly, were now between their legs. William couldn't resist looking at the paintings that lined the walls as he walked along the corridor and entered Faulkner's study. No books. Just photos of Faulkner with so-called celebrities. It was then that he spotted it on the desk, and wondered if it was possible.

He returned to the hall to hear Faulkner asking Lamont, "May I be allowed to get dressed, superintendent, while this charade continues?"

Lamont didn't respond immediately, but then reluctantly agreed. "I don't see why not. But DS Warwick will accompany you. Don't let him out of your sight, Warwick."

"Otherwise, like Peter Pan, I might fly out of the window and never be seen again?" said Faulkner. He rose from his place and began walking up the stairs, with William only a pace behind, this time not even glancing at the pictures on the wall.

Once they reached the first floor, William followed him along a corridor and into what could only have been the master bedroom. His eyes settled on a Vermeer that hung above the bed, the one Beth had told him had been promised to the Fitzmolean, once Faulkner's divorce had gone through.

"Enjoy it while you can," he said. "Although I have a feeling you may have seen it before," Faulkner added as the bathroom door opened and a young girl appeared, wearing only her knickers.

"You didn't tell me there would be two of you," she said, giving William a warm smile.

"Not this time," said Faulkner. "But I won't keep you waiting much longer," he added, as he pulled on a clean shirt.

The girl looked disappointed, grinned at William, and disappeared back into the bathroom.

By the time William had recovered, Faulkner was zipping up his jeans and strapping on the Cartier Tank watch William remembered from the first time he'd arrested him. Once he was dressed, Faulkner marched out of the bedroom, headed back downstairs, and returned to his seat in the corner of the hall.

"Found anything worth reporting back to Commander Hawksby?" he asked Lamont, as Makins refilled his brandy glass. He didn't receive a reply.

Lamont was beginning to wonder if Choirboy had been set up by his OSC, who might have recently transferred his allegiance to a new paymaster, someone who was now lighting another cigar. His thoughts were interrupted when the front doorbell rang.

"Good evening, sir," said the butler as Mr. Booth Watson strode into the hallway. The QC took his time surveying the carnage around him before he offered an opinion.

"I can see you've had a fruitful outing, superintendent," he said when his eyes settled on the two small plastic bags, one containing a couple of joints, the other an Ecstasy tablet, both marked *Evidence*. "No doubt you'll be calling Commander Hawksby to inform him of your spectacular triumph."

Faulkner laughed, stubbed out his cigar, and strolled across the hall to join his lawyer.

"Hardly a hanging offense," continued Booth Watson. "My client, as you well know, superintendent, is a model citizen, who lives a quiet life, devoting a great deal of his time to supporting worthy causes, not least the Fitzmolean Museum, with which I believe you are familiar. So may I suggest, as much for your reputation as my client's, that the least you can do is release his dinner guests and allow them to return to the bosom of their families, unless of course you feel that any of them might be suppliers of illegal substances, and should be arrested and carted off to the nearest police station." He paused, staring at the evidence once again. "Although I can't imagine what the charge would be."

Lamont nodded reluctantly, and a few minutes later every one of the guests had quietly left the house, one or two of them accompanied by someone they hadn't arrived with. Several of them shook hands with Faulkner on the way out, and one even said, "You can call me as a witness, Miles." Booth Watson made a note of his name and telephone number.

Once all the guests had left, Booth Watson turned his attention back to Lamont. "You have without doubt, superintendent, caused my client considerable embarrassment, not to mention the damage you've done to his relationships, both personal and professional, with some of his oldest friends and most respected colleagues. I cannot begin to imagine what this unwarranted intrusion has already cost the taxpayer. But let me assure you, it is nothing compared to the amount I will be claiming on behalf of my client in compensation for the damage you have done to his beautiful home and his priceless possessions."

One or two of the officers looked embarrassed by the sight of the ripped sofas and upended antique furniture sprawled across the floor. Booth Watson graced them with a smile he usually reserved only for juries, while Makins began taking photographs of the wreckage.

"Keep him talking," murmured William, as he walked past Lamont and made his way quickly back down the corridor, before disappearing into Faulkner's study.

"You have to appreciate, Mr. Booth Watson," said Lamont, "that we were acting in good faith on information received."

"Clearly from an unreliable source, which I think you'll agree, superintendent, is becoming a hallmark of your investigations when dealing with my client."

Lamont tried to remain calm.

William looked up the number in his pocket diary and began to dial. He started to pray, and to his relief, the call was answered a few moments later.

"Who's this?" a voice demanded.

"William Warwick. I apologize for disturbing you at this time of night, Christina, but an emergency has arisen and I have a feeling you're the one person who might be able to help."

"You're lucky to catch me, William. I've only just walked in after enjoying a rather lengthy getting-to-know-you dinner. Let me guess, it has to be Miles who's causing you so much trouble. How can I help?"

William hurriedly explained the problem he was up against, and when she supplied him with the answer, he felt a complete fool, because it had been staring him in the face the whole evening.

"Thank you," he said. "I'll give you a call in the morning and let you know how it all worked out."

"Not too early," said Christina. "My dinner companion is considerably younger than I am."

William laughed for the first time that evening. "Have a good time," he said before replacing the receiver. He took a moment to compose his thoughts, and was about to leave the room when he once again spotted the rolled-up twenty-pound note on the desk, which now made him feel more confident. He picked it up and left Faulkner's study to head back down the corridor toward the hall.

"Well, look who's rejoined us," said Booth Watson as William reappeared. "None other than our newly appointed sergeant—I do apologize, detective sergeant. Not for much longer, I suspect." Only Faulkner laughed.

"Well, detective sergeant," said Booth Watson, glancing dismissively at the twenty-pound note William was holding. "Apprehended one of the Great Train Robbers, have we?"

"Far better," said William without explanation, as he placed the note in a plastic bag and labeled it *Evidence*. He then strolled slowly over to the bust of Faulkner. "Only someone with an oversized ego would allow such a grotesque object to be seen in a house full of masterpieces," he said, turning to Faulkner.

"I hope you have another job lined up, detective sergeant," said Booth Watson, "because I have a feeling your days as a police officer are numbered."

"No, I haven't," William replied. "But it shouldn't be too difficult to get a job identifying fake works of art." He lifted the bust off its stand.

"Put that down!" yelled Faulkner. "It's extremely rare!"

"Unique, I would hope," said William. "But if that's what you want, Mr. Faulkner, I'm only too happy to oblige." William allowed the bust to slip from his fingers and crash onto the marble floor, where it shattered into a hundred pieces.

Everyone stared, not at what was left of the broken statue, but at a dozen small paper wraps, each containing a white substance, that lay strewn across the floor.

The dogs' tails began to wag excitedly, while the photographers immediately set about their task. Once they'd finished, a dozen officers began to gather up the evidence.

"I suspect it doesn't get any purer than this," said a senior drugs officer, holding up one of the bags. "I'll get this lot back to the lab for testing, superintendent, and have a report on your desk first thing on Monday morning."

Lamont stepped forward, thrust Faulkner's arms behind his back, and handcuffed him. "I've been looking forward to this for some time, Mr. Faulkner," he said. Booth Watson made a note. "I'll leave you to do the honors, DS Warwick."

William walked up to Faulkner and stood directly in front of him. He was so nervous he nearly forgot the words of the caution.

"Miles Faulkner, I am arresting you on suspicion of being in possession of a Class A substance with an intent to supply. You do not have to say anything unless you wish to do so, but what you say may be given in evidence."

He accompanied the prisoner out of the house, and bundled him into the back of a waiting squad car. He couldn't resist waving good-bye as he was driven away.

Lamont picked up the phone in the hall and began dialing. "I think I'll take your advice, Mr. Booth Watson," he said with a smile, "and give Commander Hawksby a call to tell him about my spectacular triumph."

14

When William and DC Adaja entered the small interview room in the basement of Scotland Yard, they found Adrian Heath already seated on the other side of the table. He looked anxious, and displayed none of his usual self-confidence.

"Is Faulkner safely out of the way?" were his first words, even before the two police officers had sat down.

"For the time being, yes," said William. "He's currently locked up in a local police station, but will be applying for bail on Monday afternoon, and the magistrate may well release him from custody, which means he could be out there looking for you long before the trial takes place."

"He will be," said Heath, "even if he's locked up. What are you going to do about it?"

"All in good time," replied William. "First, we need to ask you some questions, and your answers will determine how much help we're willing to offer you."

"But I kept my side of the bargain," protested Heath, who began to shake uncontrollably.

"You did indeed," said William. "But there's one thing that still puzzles me. After you supplied Faulkner with twelve wraps of cocaine, you say he handed over eight hundred pounds in twenty-pound notes."

"Yes, but first he opened a wrap, cut a line, and snorted it through one of the notes to test the quality, and only after he was satisfied did he finally hand over the cash."

"But when the police picked you up after you'd left the house, Mr. Heath," said DC Adaja, "you were only in possession of seven hundred and eighty pounds."

"He must have forgotten to put the one he used for snorting back in the pile."

"This one?" said William, holding up the twenty-pound note he'd found on the desk in Faulkner's study.

"If you say so," said Heath. "Now when do I get my money?"

William handed over two cellophane packets containing Heath's latest addiction—cash.

"And don't forget the eight hundred you took off me. That's also mine."

"That's now part of the Crown's evidence," said Paul. "But we'll make sure you're properly compensated." He paused. "That's assuming you continue to keep your side of the bargain. You'll get the full amount back the moment the trial is over."

"So, what happens next?" asked Heath.

"You'll appear as the Crown's principal witness when Faulkner comes up for trial in about six months' time," said William. "You'll be questioned in the witness box, and be expected to tell the truth under oath. No more and no less."

"I've written out the statement you volunteered earlier," said Adaja. "DS Warwick and I have witnessed it, so all you have to do is sign it."

"Before I do, I want to know what I'm getting in return."

"Ten thousand pounds in cash, two one-way tickets to Rio de Janeiro for you and Miss Maria Ruiz—"

"Business class. Plus a passport under a new name."

"That shouldn't be a problem," said Adaja.

"What about the six months before the trial takes place? I'll be a sitting duck if I'm found roaming around without police protection," said Heath.

"We can do better than that," said William. "You and Maria will enter our witness protection program, and be housed at a secret location. After you've given your evidence, you'll be driven straight to Heathrow. So, while Faulkner is in a Black Maria on his way to Pentonville, you and Maria will be flying business class to Rio."

"I wouldn't be so sure of that," said Heath. "That man's found more ways to escape than Houdini."

"The choice is yours," said William. "Sitting duck or safe house?"

"Put like that, I don't have a lot of choice. So where do I go from here?"

"There's a car outside waiting to take the two of you to the safe house."

"Where's that?"

"Even I don't know," said William.

◄o►

"If you'll come with me, sir," said the desk sergeant, "I'll take you to see your client."

The officer led Booth Watson down a dimly lit brick-walled corridor, past a couple of cells, before stopping outside a door with a young constable stationed outside. The sergeant selected a key from his chain, unlocked the heavy door and pulled it open. The two officers stood aside to allow the senior silk to enter. The constable closed the door behind him and remained in his place, while the sergeant returned to his desk.

Booth Watson found his client seated on the end of the bed, clearly impatient to see him. He was still dressed in the clothes he'd been wearing at the party on Saturday night but he now looked tired, disheveled, and badly in need of a shave.

"Get me out of here," Faulkner mumbled, before his counsel had spoken a word.

"Good morning, Miles," said Booth Watson, as if this was a normal consultation taking place in his Middle Temple chambers. He sat down on the other end of the bed, placed his briefcase to one side and an overnight bag on the other.

"I've spent the night in this hellhole," said Faulkner, not displaying his usual bravado. "I've already been booked in, fingerprinted, and questioned. So I'm bound to ask, what's the point of you?"

"Did they question you under caution?" asked Booth Watson, ignoring the outburst.

"Yes. But as I didn't say a word, all they've got is a lot of questions, and no answers."

"Good," said Booth Watson, pleased his client had carried out his instructions to the letter.

"What happens now?"

"We're up in front of the magistrate tomorrow afternoon, when I'll be making an application for bail on your behalf."

"What are my chances?"

"Depends who's on the bench. If it's a local councilor who's looking for fifteen minutes of fame, you'll be placed on remand. However, if it's one of the more experienced JPs, you're in with a chance. We'll find out soon enough."

"And if the application fails?"

"I'm afraid you'll be detained in prison while the Crown prepares its case."

"How long could that take?"

"Six or seven months, but don't waste any time worrying about that. Just try to focus on your bail application."

"What will I be expected to do once I'm in the magistrates' court?"

"Not a lot, other than to state your name and address."

"That's it?"

"Not quite. It's important that you look like a decent law-abiding citizen, and not as if you've just emerged from a drunken orgy. So I took the liberty of picking up a change of clothes from your home that I felt would be more appropriate for the occasion." He opened the overnight bag and laid out on the bunk a dark blue suit, white shirt, a pair of pants and socks, and an old Harrovian tie. He finally placed a monogrammed washbag by the side of the toilet.

"I'm going to need a damn sight more than that if I end up inside."

Booth Watson didn't tell him that he'd already packed a larger suitcase for that eventuality, which he'd left in his office.

"The next time you'll see me, Miles, will be in court," said Booth Watson as he stood to leave. "If the magistrate should ask you anything, don't forget to call him sir." He banged on the door, which didn't have a handle on the inside, and waited for it to be opened to allow one of them to escape.

◄o►

"I have to be in court by two o'clock," said William, as he sat down opposite his father and began unloading his tray.

"Faulkner's bail application?" asked Sir Julian, picking up his knife and fork. "I wouldn't want to put money on which way that will go."

"He ought to be safely locked up until the trial takes place."

"Possibly, but unfortunately you won't have any influence on that decision, whereas Booth Watson will."

"More's the pity," said William. "That man should be sharing the same cell as Faulkner."

"Behave yourself. Try to remember you're lunching at Lincoln's Inn, where we're all meant to treat each other as brothers." William had to smile. "By the way, when you were at Limpton Hall, were you able to establish if Faulkner's art collection are still all originals, or has he replaced them with copies as his wife fears?"

"All I can tell you is that while my colleagues were searching Faulkner's home for drugs, I took a close look at as many of the paintings as I could."

"And?"

"I'm not an expert, but I'd say every one was an original. They must be worth a small fortune."

"That's good to hear, because along with the house and the flat in Eaton Square, they're due to be handed over to my client as part of her divorce settlement. Mrs. Faulkner told me that, with one exception, she'll be putting the entire collection up for auction as soon as the decree absolute has been granted. She's convinced that Miles will want to buy them all back for far more than he'd be willing to pay her."

"Cunning woman," said William.

"To do her justice," said Sir Julian, "which is difficult at times, Mrs. Faulkner has agreed to donate a Vermeer to the Fitzmolean. The museum has Beth to thank for that."

"Another cunning woman."

"Which reminds me," said Sir Julian. "Your sister will be representing the Crown at the magistrates' court this afternoon, and opposing Faulkner's bail."

"Does that mean she'll get the main gig?"

"If you're referring to the trial, my boy, not a chance. They'll want a QC of equal standing to take on Booth Watson and cross-examine Faulkner. In fact, the Department of Public Prosecution rang me this morning and asked if I'd consider representing them on this occasion. Desmond Pannel reminded me that I owed him a favor, so I told him I'd sleep on it."

"If you agreed to take the case, you could appoint Grace as your junior."

"Not if I want to win."

"Father, they're already talking about her becoming a QC."

"I don't approve of women QCs."

"Wait until you come up against her, then you might change your mind."

—◦—

The magistrates' court at Guildhall, which usually dealt with drunk and disorderlies, shoplifters, and the occasional application for a liquor license, was packed long before Mr. Joseph Lanyon OBE JP and his two colleagues took their places on the bench that Monday afternoon.

Mr. Lanyon looked down into the well of the court and feigned not to be intimidated by the presence of some of the most distinguished barristers in the land, along with their solicitors, a bevy of Fleet Street reporters, and a public gallery so packed that the clerk had informed him there'd been a queue outside the courtroom when he'd arrived that morning.

The magistrate looked across at the defendant standing in the dock. A tall, handsome man with a fine head of wavy fair hair that added to the film-star looks the press so often referred to. He was dressed in a dark suit, white shirt, and navy-blue tie with thin white stripes, making him look more like a successful stockbroker than a man facing a serious drugs charge.

Mr. Lanyon nodded to the court bailiff who turned to face the defendant and said firmly, "Will the prisoner please stand?"

Faulkner rose unsteadily from his place and gripped the rails of the dock.

"For the record, will the defendant please state his full name and current address?"

"Miles Adam Faulkner, Limpton Hall, Hampshire, sir," he said, looking directly at the magistrate, with an assurance that belied his true feelings.

"You may sit down."

"Thank you, sir," said Faulkner, having delivered the seven words Booth Watson had prescribed.

"No doubt you wish to apply for bail, Mr. Booth Watson," said the magistrate, turning to face the defendant's legal team.

"I do indeed, sir," said Booth Watson, heaving himself up from the bench. "I would like to begin by reminding the court that my client has an unblemished record—"

"Forgive me for interrupting you so early in the proceedings, Mr. Booth Watson, but am I not right in thinking that your client is currently serving a four-year suspended sentence for a previous fraud charge?"

"He is indeed, sir. However, I can assure you that he has carried out the court's directive to the letter. I would also point out, with respect, that my client has pleaded not guilty to the present charge, and as he has no previous record of violence, and is a man of considerable means, he could hardly be described as a danger to the public. I find it hard to believe that the Crown would even consider opposing this bail application."

"What do you say to that, Ms. Warwick?" asked the magistrate, turning his attention to the other end of the bench.

Grace rose slowly from her place.

"The Crown will most certainly be opposing this application, on several grounds. As you rightly reminded the court, Mr. Lanyon, the accused is currently serving a four-year suspended sentence on a charge of fraud. However, that is not the sole reason why the Crown opposes bail. As my learned friend has pointed out, his client is a man of considerable means, but what he failed to tell you is that he is no longer domiciled in this country, but has recently become a tax exile, and spends most of his time in Monte Carlo. So I would suggest, sir, that in view of the fact that he owns both a private jet and a yacht, the likelihood of his absconding should be taken into consideration."

"I would remind the court," said Booth Watson, rising a little more quickly this time, "that my client also owns a large estate in the country, as well as an apartment in Eaton Square."

"Both," countered Grace, "are currently part of his wife's divorce settlement, the terms of which have been agreed in principle by both sides."

"In principle, but not yet signed by both sides," said Booth Watson, who remained standing.

"But your client has already signed the agreement," said Grace.

"That may be so, but he still retains a lease on the apartment in Eaton Square."

"Which he's recently put on the market."

"How can you possibly know that?" barked Booth Watson.

"Because it was advertised in last month's *Country Life*," responded Grace, producing a copy of the magazine from below the bench, and waving it in Booth Watson's face. William barely resisted the temptation to applaud.

"Mr. Booth Watson, Ms. Warwick," interjected the magistrate, "this is not a Punch-and-Judy show, but a court of law. Kindly treat it as such."

Both counsel looked suitably chastised and resumed their places on the bench, while the three magistrates put their heads together and consulted for a few moments.

"Well done," whispered Clare, who was sitting in the row behind Grace. "You've certainly given them something to think about."

"What do you think?" William asked Lamont from his seat at the back of the court.

But Mr. Lanyon began addressing the court before the superintendent was able to offer his opinion. "We have listened most carefully to the arguments presented by both learned counsel," he began, "and have come to the conclusion that the defendant is not a danger to the public."

Booth Watson allowed himself a wry smile, while William frowned.

"However, I take seriously Ms. Warwick's point that he is in possession of sufficient funds to make it possible for him to abscond while on bail. With that in mind, I am willing to grant the application on two conditions. One, Mr. Faulkner hands in his passport to the court. And two, he provides a surety of one million pounds, which will be forfeited should he fail to appear in court for his trial."

A hubbub of whispered conversations emanated from the press benches. Booth Watson sat impassively, arms folded, like Buddha. Clare put a tick and a cross on her yellow notepad, then leaned forward and whispered to Grace, "Score draw."

"Until those two conditions are met," continued the magistrate, "the defendant will remain in custody."

The press had their headline, and Mr. Lanyon his fifteen minutes of fame. William left the court disappointed, while Faulkner was well satisfied. After all, he needed to be on the outside if he was to carry out the next part of his plan.

15

"I always enjoy breakfast at the Savoy," said Faulkner, "even if the circumstances could be better."

"They couldn't be much worse," said Booth Watson, as he dropped another sugar lump into his coffee.

"But you got me out on bail. And you said they couldn't even do me for possession on that evidence."

"When I said that, the evidence was a couple of joints and an Ecstasy tablet, not twelve grams of pure cocaine. No judge will believe they were for your personal use, so possession in this case is nine-tenths of the law."

"It was planted by the police," said Faulkner, as a bowl of corn-flakes and strawberries was placed in front of him.

"That won't wash, Miles, and you know it. The Crown's star witness will swear blind that he sold you the drugs earlier that evening for eight hundred pounds, and don't forget that both the money and the evidence are in the police's possession."

"Did you find out who it was that set me up?"

"Not yet, but I'm working on it. All I can tell you is that he's been spirited away to a safe house somewhere, so we may not even find out who's responsible until he steps into the witness box."

"That's assuming he ever makes it to the court."

"Now listen to me carefully, Miles. Don't do anything you'll later regret."

"Like what?"

"Like turning up to a wedding you weren't invited to."

"A clerical error."

"And that's not your only problem."

"What else?" asked Faulkner, as a waiter whisked his bowl away, and another refilled Booth Watson's coffee cup.

"Christina is refusing to sign the divorce settlement until the trial is over."

"What's her game?"

"She obviously thinks that if you're safely locked up, she'll be able to drive a harder bargain."

"Well, she can think again. Because by the time I've finished with her, she won't have a pot to piss in."

The waiter reappeared by his side.

"Can I take your order, sir?"

"I'll have the full English breakfast."

◄O►

They were all seated around the table waiting for the commander to appear. No one, not even Lamont, had ever known him to be late. Then suddenly the door was thrown open and in swept the Hawk. It was as if a force nine gale had hit them.

"I apologize," he said while he was still on the move. "I've spent the last half hour with the commissioner, telling him all about my triumph on Saturday night at Limpton Hall." They all burst out laughing and started banging the table.

"Many congratulations, Bruce," said the Hawk, as he sat down. "Twelve grams of pure cocaine and the dealer willing to give evidence on behalf of the Crown. I do believe we've got Faulkner bang to rights this time."

"Thank you, sir, but it was DS Warwick's ability to think on his feet that saved the day."

"Good thing you didn't stay in Rome, William, checking out less important statues. Have the lab reports come in yet, DC Roycroft?"

"Yes, sir," said Jackie. "The cocaine is of the highest quality, and probably originated in Colombia. They intercepted a similar batch recently in Manchester."

"What about Faulkner?"

"Handed in his passport, deposited the million with the court, and is out on bail," said William.

"Do you think he might make a bolt for it?" asked Paul.

"Unlikely. But if he does, the Director of Public Prosecutions will bank the million and we'll have seen the last of the bastard. So it won't be all bad."

"I'd rather see him behind bars," said William, "than enjoying the high life in Monte Carlo."

"Your wish may well be granted," said Hawksby. "The DPP believes there's a strong possibility that Faulkner might change his plea to guilty on the lesser charge, once Booth Watson has had time to consider Heath's evidence."

"He'll never plead guilty," said William. "Not while he thinks he has the slightest chance of getting away with it."

"You're beginning to think like Faulkner," said the Hawk. "That's good. But the trial's months away, and we still have other cases to work on, not least making sure Rashidi joins Faulkner in the dock. And one thing's for sure, Rashidi won't be granted bail in any circumstances."

"But if he was," said William, "he could pay the million in cash."

"Are we any nearer to locating his factory?" asked the Hawk.

"So near, and yet so far," said Lamont. "All I can tell you for certain, sir, is that it's not at Charlbury Manor. A police helicopter flew me over the estate last Friday, and there was no sign of any vehicles other than a dark blue Mercedes parked in the drive and a post office van making a delivery."

"Paul?" said the Hawk.

"I've spent the last few days nosing around the village," said Adaja, "and the post mistress told me Rashidi keeps himself to himself. Attends the occasional village fete to which he donates generously, but is otherwise rarely seen in public. It's beginning to look as if he leads two completely separate lives. He poses as the country squire at weekends, while becoming a ruthless drug baron during the week. The transformation from Hyde to Jekyll seems to take place on a Friday afternoon when he visits his mother." Paul paused for a moment, to make sure he had the full attention of the team.

"Stop grandstanding," said Lamont, "and get on with it."

"Every Monday morning he's driven by his chauffeur from Charlbury Manor to an office in the City. He arrives around eight, and spends the morning carrying out his responsibilities as chairman of Marcel and Neffe, a small but reputable tea company that had a turnover last year of just over four million pounds, and declared a profit of three hundred forty-two thousand six hundred pounds."

Paul handed out copies of Marcel and Neffe's annual report to the rest of the team.

"Marcel and Neffe is the perfect front for Rashidi," said William, "because it allows him to live a lifestyle that a casual observer wouldn't question while he can travel to countries where tea isn't their main export."

"However," continued Paul, "his home in the country is lavish by any standards, but because it's surrounded by a thousand-acre estate, few people know just how lavish. And that's only for starters."

"At Heathrow," said William, picking up the story, "he has a Gulf Stream jet with two pilots on standby night and day so he could disappear at a moment's notice. He has a seventy-meter yacht called *Sumaya*, named after his mother, with a crew of eighteen, moored at Cannes, as well as homes in Saint-Tropez, Davos, and a duplex apartment on Fifth Avenue in New York overlooking Central Park. He retains a large staff in each of the residences to look after his every need."

"Which he couldn't possibly afford on three hundred forty-two thousand six hundred pounds a year," commented Lamont.

"Well done, DC Adaja," said the Hawk. "Dare I ask how you came across such a fund of information?"

"I applied for a job as a second gardener on the estate, which was advertised in the village post office. I learned more about what goes on behind those walls than they did about me. But in truth, I discovered little of interest because that's his 'on the record' life. I even had a pub lunch with the head gardener to discuss my salary, and when I'd be able to start."

"Did they offer you the job?" asked the Hawk.

"Yes, sir. I promised I'd get back to them."

"What do you know about gardening, Paul?" chuckled Lamont.

"Only what I picked up in last month's copy of *Gardener's Weekly*, but they still offered me a better starting salary than I'm getting here, more days off and three weeks' holiday a year."

"We'll miss you," said the Hawk. "DS Warwick, perhaps you could tell us what you've been up to this week."

"While Paul was gallivanting around the countryside, I've been concentrating on Rashidi's office in the City. As we know, he arrives there on a Monday morning at eight, but then disappears around midday, and doesn't return to Marcel and Neffe until Friday afternoon, just before leaving to visit his mother in The Boltons. Like Paul, I'm none the wiser as to his movements in between."

"At least we now know where his workplace is, even if it's only a front."

"Which floor is Marcel and Neffe on?" asked Lamont.

"The tenth and eleventh. I've visited the company offices a couple of times, but I've never got past reception. What makes it worse," continued William, "is that I'm not wholly convinced that the man who leaves the building at midday on Mondays is the same person who's picked up outside the entrance of Tea House by his personal black cab on Friday afternoons."

"Do you think he has a double?"

"No, I think he must be well disguised. Either that, or he's entering and leaving Tea House by an exit I haven't come across. For all I know, he could be abseiling out of the building."

"What a pro," said Lamont, a hint of admiration in his voice.

"You have to be if you're making over a hundred thousand pounds a week in cash, breaking every law in the book, while not bothering to pay any tax."

"That's how they ended up nailing Al Capone," Lamont reminded them.

"There has to be a fault in his routine," said William, "but I haven't identified it yet."

"Don't sleep until you do," said the Hawk. "Right, unless there are any more questions, let's all get back to work."

"I have a question, sir," said William.

"Of course you do, DS Warwick."

"Has your UCO come up with any fresh intel recently?"

The Hawk glanced at Jackie, who remained silent. "No. Sometimes he doesn't surface for several weeks. But the moment he does, DS Warwick, I'll be sure to let you know."

"Thank you, sir."

Lamont suppressed a smile at the commander's gentle rebuke of William.

"And I have a question for you, DS Warwick," said the Hawk. "Now that Tulip's discharged himself from hospital, is there any way he could find your OSC?"

"No, sir. Even I can't tell you where Heath's holed up, because I don't know myself."

"Be sure it stays that way, because he's our one hope of sending Faulkner down when the case eventually comes to court. Right, lads, back to work. Faulkner was yesterday's triumph. Don't forget that Rashidi's still out there, destroying people's lives."

◄○►

"Will you marry me?" asked Adrian.

"Of course I will," said Maria, throwing her arms around his neck.

"This is the moment when I ought to drop on one knee and present you with an engagement ring to seal the deal, but that's not possible while we're cooped up in here. They won't even let me out for long enough to look for one."

"It won't be for much longer," said Maria. "And the ring can wait until we're safely in Rio, when we can finally put all of this behind us."

"I can't wait to get to Rio," admitted Adrian. "But I'm worried what your parents will say when they find out I used to be a drug addict, and haven't had a proper job for years."

"That's all in the past, Adrian. In any case, I've already told them you're the son of a successful banker—"

"Well, at least that's true, even if he has disowned me."

"And he's given you ten thousand pounds to start up a new business. In Rio, ten thousand pounds is a fortune, so there'll be endless opportunities."

"Which I intend to take full advantage of. But I'll never forget that without your help, I'd still be a hopeless junkie with no future."

"It's not just me you have to thank," said Maria.

"I know. Choirboy has played his part, and once Faulkner's safely behind bars I'll have kept my side of the bargain."

◄o►

"When is the trial expected to begin, Sir Julian?"

"Not for a couple of months, Mrs. Faulkner. Why do you ask?"

"I need you to take your time over the settlement. Try and slow things down."

"Why would you want me to do that, when we've got almost everything you asked for?"

"I still want to be Mrs. Faulkner when my husband goes to jail."

"May I ask why?"

"It's better you don't know the reason, Sir Julian, as I may need you to represent me should things not turn out as planned."

◄o►

William took the tube into the City and got out at Moorgate. A few minutes later he walked into Tea House, confident that Rashidi wouldn't be around on a Wednesday afternoon. He avoided the front desk, as he didn't want to be remembered, and headed for the bank of lifts where he joined a waiting group. He stepped out on the eleventh floor and took a seat in Marcel and Neffe's reception, picked up a copy of the *Financial Times,* and checked his watch every few minutes, as if he was waiting for someone to join him. The receptionist was constantly on the phone, dealing with visitors, or signing for deliveries, so he hoped he could hang around for some time before she became suspicious.

William listened attentively to the conversations taking place at the reception desk, while pretending to read his newspaper. It quickly became clear that Marcel and Neffe was not merely a front for another business; it was exactly what it claimed to be, a small, successful tea company, even if its chairman only dropped in briefly on Monday mornings and Friday afternoons.

When the receptionist gave him a third quizzical look, William decided it was time to go. A young woman emerged from one of the offices, and he stood up and joined her as she left. They got into the lift together, and when they reached the ground floor William headed for the front door while his erstwhile companion disappeared down a corridor to her right.

Back out on the street, William checked his watch and began walking toward Moorgate station. He needed to drop into Scotland Yard before going home. Not that he had anything to report. He was going down the steps into the station when he spotted the young woman he'd shared the lift with heading for the ticket barrier. William was puzzled. How could she possibly have overtaken him without him noticing?

He paused at the bottom of the steps and looked in the direction she had come from. As he did, an inconspicuous door that he hadn't noticed before swung open, and a smartly dressed older gentleman appeared, carrying a briefcase and a rolled umbrella. William ran across to the door, but it closed before he could reach it.

He didn't have to wait long before it opened again, and this time he managed to slip through the gap before it closed, to find himself in a well-lit corridor. He walked cautiously along the passageway, passing a gym and a training center on his left, before climbing a short flight of steps to another corridor, at the end of which he found himself back in the reception area of Tea House, now well aware how the woman had overtaken him. He retraced his steps to the tube station, knowing exactly where he'd be waiting for Rashidi next Monday morning.

◄○►

"The CPS have given us a date for the Faulkner trial," said Sir Julian. "November the twelfth at the Old Bailey."

Grace turned the pages of her diary, and crossed out the three weeks following November 12. "Less than a month away," she said. "I still need to take Heath through his evidence one more time."

"You can do that when they move him back to London just before the trial."

"Will you be putting William on the stand?"

"No point. Superintendent Lamont will carry considerably more weight in the eyes of the jury, and Dr. Lewis is such a highly respected expert witness on drugs that I expect the defense won't even bother to cross-examine her. In fact, I have a feeling it won't be long before Booth Watson gets in touch and tries to make a deal on behalf of his client."

"And if he does, how will you respond?"

"I'll tell him to get lost."

"The Crown," said Grace, "sees no reason to make any concessions at this particular time, but thank you for calling, BW."

Grace smiled as she watched her father write down her words.

◄○►

William and Paul watched from the other side of the road as Rashidi stepped out of his Mercedes and entered Tea House at ten minutes past eight the following Monday morning. He was dressed like the chairman of a City company, and the doorman saluted him. DS Warwick then made his way back to Moorgate tube station, but he didn't head for the escalator and return to Scotland Yard.

Jackie had taught him to remain focused during a stakeout. Lose concentration for even a few seconds, and you could lose your mark. He stood in the concourse for the next four hours, and although he occasionally paced up and down, his eyes never left the well-disguised door. Several people had emerged through it and headed straight for the ticket barrier, but he was confident Rashidi hadn't been among them. If he did leave by the front entrance of Tea House that morning, Paul was stationed on the other side of the road, and would radio William immediately. He redoubled his concentration when the hands on the station clock both reached twelve.

A few minutes later a man came through the door wearing a baggy, dark gray tracksuit, with a hood pulled over his head that kept his face well hidden. He'd passed William before he'd been able to take a closer look at him without staring. The walk was familiar, but William couldn't risk it on that alone, and it wasn't until the man presented his ticket at the barrier that William noticed he was wearing black leather gloves. His eyes moved instinctively to the third finger of the left hand.

By the time William had passed through the barrier and stepped onto the escalator, the tracksuited man was already turning left and heading for the southbound platform of the Northern Line.

Once the anonymous tracksuit had disappeared out of sight, William jogged down the escalator, only slowing down when he turned left. He could now see his prey as he reached the platform just as a train emerged from the tunnel, expelling a gust of warm air. He got into the carriage next to Rashidi's, only once glancing in his direction. He carefully watched the disembarking passengers at each station, until the tracksuit, head still covered, got off at Stockwell.

William remained in his seat. Not part of the overall plan. That would have to wait for another week. The Hawk's words were ringing in his ears: *Take no risks. We're in it for the long game.*

◄○►

There were six minders in charge of the safe house, all of them on eight-hour shifts. Their instructions were simple. Keep the witness and his girlfriend safe, well fed, and, if possible, relaxed. It wasn't easy to relax when they were never allowed out for more than a short walk around a nearby park, always accompanied by two officers and a German shepherd. It was several days before Adrian or Maria even discovered which city they were in.

As the weeks passed, Adrian got to know one of his minders quite well, bonding over their mutual support for West Ham. But it wasn't until a fortnight before the trial that he discovered who he really supported.

◄○►

Back at Scotland Yard, William handed in his report on the trip to Stockwell.

Lamont studied a map of the London underground for a few moments before saying, "If Rashidi gets off at Stockwell next Monday, DS Warwick, you'll be waiting for him outside the station. But if he changes lines and heads for Brixton, you'll have to cover for him, DC Adaja."

Both officers nodded and made a note.

"And, Jackie, now that you're no longer on the game, what have you been up to?"

"We have a two-bus problem, sir," Jackie said after the laughter had died down. Suddenly the team's attention switched to DC Roycroft. "Marlboro Man is convinced that a large shipment of drugs is on its way from Colombia to Zeebrugge. Loose talk by a couple of dealers at the bar, who'd had a little too much to drink."

"Any idea of the quantity we're talking about?" asked Lamont.

"He can't be sure. All he knows for certain is that last time it was ten kilos of cocaine."

"That must be the shipment that ended up in Manchester," said Lamont. "Does he know where it's heading for after Zeebrugge?"

"He has no idea."

"Felixstowe would be my bet," said the Hawk.

"What makes you say that, sir?"

"Anti-corruption has two customs officers there under surveillance, and they tell me they're expecting to make an arrest in the near future."

"Then DS Warwick and DC Roycroft had better get their arses down to Felixstowe sharpish," said Lamont. "And keep an eye on every ship that arrives from Zeebrugge. Well done, DC Roycroft."

"I've got more," said Jackie, looking rather pleased with herself.

"Spit it out," said Lamont.

"A word MM heard several times that night was 'caravan.'"

"We're either being set up, or that man's worth his weight in gold."

"But it's not all good news," said Jackie. "Now Tulip's back on the streets again, he's been back to the Three Feathers looking for Heath."

"That's all we need," said the Hawk.

16

"The second day of any stakeout is always the worst," said Jackie.

"Why?" asked William, keeping his binoculars trained on the entrance to the harbor.

"On the first day it's easy enough to keep your concentration, but by the second, the thrill of the chase and the sense of antici- pation are beginning to wear off."

"And by the third?"

"Boredom sets in. Your eyelids get heavier and heavier, and you struggle to stay awake. But at least that's better than having to listen to your dreadful stories, which would send an insomniac to sleep. I'll bet Beth doesn't have to count sheep at night."

"At least this time we know exactly what we're looking for," said William, ignoring the barb. "Unlike your trip to Guildford in search of a stolen Picasso that turned out not to exist."

"Don't remind me," said Jackie. "On this occasion the harbormas- ter couldn't have been more helpful. There are only two vehicle ferries arriving from Zeebrugge today, both Townsend Thoresen, and as we're looking for a car with a caravan in tow, it shouldn't be too difficult to identify, although we'll still need to check the number plate of every car, just in case."

"Where did the three caravans we spotted yesterday end up?"

"One went to a caravan park in the New Forest where its owner lives. The second is on its way to Scotland, and according to the Police National Computer the third is owned by the Reverend Nigel Oakshot of The Rectory, Sandhurst, Berkshire. We decided to give him the benefit of the doubt."

William laughed. "When's the first ferry due today?"

"The *Anthi Marina* should dock around eleven twenty, and will be unloading at RoRo one or two. We won't go anywhere near the dockside until she comes into view. We don't want to be spotted by one of the customs officers under surveillance with the anti-corruption unit. What are you reading?" she asked, looking down at the book resting in William's lap and wondering if he had been listening to a word she was saying.

"The history of Felixstowe docks."

"I bet that's a page-turner."

"Did you know that the surrounding land is owned by Trinity College, Cambridge, and is one of its most valuable assets?"

"Fascinating."

"The college bursar at the time, a Mr. Tressilian Nicholas, purchased the thirty-eight-hundred-acre site on behalf of the college in 1933, along with a road that led to the then-derelict docks. His successor, a Mr. Bradfield, spotted its potential, and it's now the largest port in Britain, and makes the college a small fortune."

"I can't wait to hear the end of this story," said Jackie.

"Lord Butler."

"Who he?"

"A former cabinet minister, and master of Trinity," replied William, who began reading directly from the book: "'Butler asked Bradfield at a finance meeting if he realized that the college owned a tin mine in Cornwall that hadn't shown a return since

142

1546, to which the bursar famously replied, "You'll find, master, that in this college, we take the long view.""

"I'm also taking the long view," said Jackie, as she spotted the *Anthi Marina* coming over the horizon. "If yesterday's anything to go by, she should be with us in about forty minutes. We'd better get going if we're to secure our preferred lookout point."

William put on his seatbelt as Jackie switched on the car engine and drove slowly down Bath Hill toward the docks. She parked at the same spot in which they'd spent so many fruitless hours the previous day. At least the last ferry had docked shortly after ten, making it possible for them to check in to a seedy little B&B on the seafront before midnight. The landlord had seemed surprised when they booked separate rooms.

Once Jackie had parked the car well out of sight, the two of them sat in married silence, as they watched the ship inch its way slowly into the port.

They didn't have to wait long for the first vehicle to emerge onto the dockside. Jackie, binoculars in hand, read out each number plate to Paul who had been patiently waiting for their call in the basement of Scotland Yard. William, being a belt and braces man, also wrote them down in his notebook. There was no sign of a caravan by the time the last car had cleared customs. Jackie lowered her binoculars and asked, "What time is the next ferry due in?"

"Two fifty," said William, running a finger down the schedule. "*Saxon Prince.*"

"More than enough time for lunch. Fish and chips?"

"Not again. That's what we had yesterday."

"And will tomorrow, if I have my way," said Jackie. "Golden rule. When you're stuck in a port doing surveillance, always eat the local catch. It's a lot fresher than the cod fricassee that ends up at the Ritz. And you should know, you go there often enough."

"Only twice," said William. "But what if we're stuck here for the rest of the week?"

"I'll settle for a kebab," replied Jackie, as she swung the car around and headed for the chippy that had been recommended by the desk sergeant at the local constabulary.

"Always a good sign," said Jackie, as she parked the car and they joined a long queue waiting outside the shop.

◄○►

DC Adaja spent his lunch break checking all the number plates Jackie had supplied on the PNC. A few parking fines, some speeding tickets, one drink-driving offense, and a woman who'd been caught going through a red light, been fined twenty pounds and had two penalty points added to her license. When Paul radioed to tell Jackie the results, she poured some more vinegar on her cod and said, "Naughty girl."

Once they'd finished their lunch—eaten out of a newspaper as they walked along the seafront—Jackie and William drove back to their vantage point on the clifftop.

After they had been staring out to sea in silence for half an hour, Jackie drew her sword from its sheath a second time. "Are you still hoping to make inspector?" she asked.

"Why ask me that question when you already know the answer?"

"Because there are only two types of sergeant in the Met, and you obviously fall into the second category, those who hope to be promoted."

"And the first category?"

"By far the larger of the two," said Jackie. "Old sweats, who've worked out that if you're promoted to inspector you can no longer claim overtime. That's why the Met has so many forty-to-fifty-year-old sergeants serving out their time. A lot of them are making far more than their superiors, and at the same time they're causing a logjam that prevents others like me from getting off the bottom rung of the ladder. Truth is, it's easier to be promoted to inspector than sergeant."

It was the first time William had heard Jackie sounding bitter about anything. "If we put Rashidi behind bars," he said, "I'm sure it won't be long before you're sewing three stripes back on your uniform." He immediately regretted his words, as they would only remind Jackie that he had been made up to sergeant following her demotion.

"Mind you," said Jackie, "I must admit that overtime allowances have made it possible for me to enjoy a few of life's little luxuries. Although I sometimes wonder if the public are aware just how many officers are sitting around in coaches parked in backstreets just in case a protest march gets out of hand."

"It's a price worth paying," said William. "Perhaps you haven't noticed Russian riot police don't sit around in coaches if the public even think about protesting."

"And on that note, Choirboy, I'm going to try and grab some kip. Wake me up when our next ship comes in."

She leaned back in her seat, closed her eyes, and had fallen asleep within minutes. William wished he could do that, but his mind refused to rest even at night. He stared out at the empty gray sea, and thought about Beth. God, he'd been lucky, and it wouldn't be long now before they were a family of three. Even more reason to hope that the promotion Jackie had hinted at wasn't too far away. He thought about becoming a father. If it was a boy he could open the batting for England, while his daughter could be the first woman director of the National Gallery.

His mind turned to Miles Faulkner whose trial would open at

the Bailey next week. So much rested on Adrian Heath's evidence. William had been interested to hear from his sister that Booth Watson had phoned their chambers earlier in the week offering to plead guilty to the lesser charge of possession, if the Crown would drop the more serious offense of intent to supply. He wasn't surprised when Grace told him that their father had politely rejected the offer. His thoughts turned next to Khalil Rashidi. After he'd left Tea House at midday that Monday, he'd taken the tube to Stockwell, and then changed onto the Victoria Line ending up in Brixton, where DC Adaja was waiting for him. Paul had made no attempt to shadow him when he'd emerged from the station, but returned to the Yard on the next train. When Lamont demanded to know why, Paul explained that Rashidi had been met outside the station by half a dozen heavies who kept checking in every direction to make sure no one was following him. At least they now knew which borough Rashidi's slaughter must be in, but they were no nearer to locating it in what was virtually a no-go area, although the police would never admit it. Perhaps Jackie's UCO would finally be able to solve that particular problem.

Next, William thought about Lamont, whose wavelength he still hadn't managed to get onto. The superintendent didn't bother to disguise the fact that he still thought of him as a choirboy, and Paul as an immigrant. And finally, the Hawk, who soared above them all.

William snapped back into the real world when he spotted a dot on the horizon. He waited until he could make out the name *Saxon Prince* on its bow before he woke Jackie. She was wide awake within moments, as if she'd never been asleep, something else he wished he could do.

"*Saxon Prince* is making its way into the harbor," he said.

"Do please be on this one," muttered Jackie plaintively, as she switched on the car engine.

They drove back down Bath Hill and returned to their favored surveillance point, which allowed them a perfect view of the ship as it entered the harbor, without being too conspicuous. It wasn't long before the first vehicle drove down the ramp.

Once again Jackie, her binoculars focused on the cars as they headed toward customs, passed the details of each number plate on to Paul back at the Yard.

Suddenly she said in a far more animated voice, "I don't believe it! Get the guv'nor on the radio, Paul, sharpish."

She handed the binoculars to William, who focused on a Volvo as it proceeded slowly along the dockside. He now had the answer to his unanswered question, and wondered how Lamont would react. He passed the binoculars back to Jackie.

The next voice they heard over the radio said sharply, "What's the problem, Jackie?"

"A Volvo towing a caravan has come off the ferry and is heading toward customs, sir."

"And?" said Lamont impatiently.

"You're not going to believe this, sir, but MM is behind the wheel, and Tulip is sitting next to him in the passenger seat."

"Where are they now?"

"In the queue waiting to clear customs. But as I'm his liaison officer, I'm not quite sure what I should do next?"

"Hold on. Don't let them out of your sight while I have a word with the boss."

The encrypted radio was silent for so long that, if it hadn't been for the occasional crackle, Jackie might have thought she'd lost contact. At last they heard the unmistakable voice of the Hawk. Brief and to the point.

"Are you certain, DC Roycroft?"

"Yes, sir," she said firmly, her binoculars still focused on the Volvo.

"Are they still in the queue?"

"No, sir. A customs officer is checking the car, and another one is chatting to Tulip. Now they're smiling and waving the car through." She paused for a moment. "A couple more minutes, sir, and we'll lose them," she said, trying to keep her foot off the accelerator.

"Stay put, DC Roycroft," said the Hawk. "We can't afford to compromise a UCO, and if the gear is being delivered to Rashidi's slaughter somewhere in Brixton, that could help us fill in one of the last pieces of the jigsaw. I repeat, stay put."

William snatched the radio out of Jackie's hand. "What if your UCO has been turned, sir? In that case we'll be none the wiser as to the location of the factory, and we'll have lost ten kilos of cocaine and a chance to put Tulip out of business."

"That's just not possible," said Jackie, almost shouting. "Ross would never switch sides," she added, breaking a cardinal rule.

"Perhaps your UCO is only telling us half the story," said William calmly. "As you never stop reminding us, sir, there's a vast amount of money involved with these drug cartels, which must be a temptation for even the most scrupulous officer." This silenced Jackie, not least because she'd never heard anyone speak to the commander like that.

"You're quite right, DS Warwick," said the commander equally calmly. "It's possible that, as DC Roycroft and I are running this particular UCO, we're too personally involved. I'll leave the final decision to you, Bruce."

Lamont came back on the line immediately. "I don't know the officer personally, sir, but he's never let you down in the past, so there's no reason to believe he's suddenly changed sides. In any case, if they were to charge in, we might even put his life in danger. I'd advise we stand DS Warwick and DC Roycroft down. And another point, sir. It won't help our colleagues if those are the two customs officers they have under surveillance."

"Good point. All the more reason for both of you to return to the Yard immediately."

"Yes, sir," said William, not sounding convinced.

He and Jackie sat and watched as the Volvo drove onto the main road, and disappeared out of sight.

"Thank you, Bruce," said the commander as he switched off the radio and broke contact with Felixstowe.

Once he had returned to his office, Hawksby picked up the phone on his desk and said, "Angela, do you have an empty Marlboro packet to hand?"

"Yes, sir."

"Could you bring it through?"

Angela fished a packet out of a drawer, took it in to her boss, and left it on his desk without a word passing between them.

Twenty minutes later, the commander picked up the phone again. "Angela, should anyone call, I'll be out of the office for about thirty minutes." He returned the silver paper to the empty cigarette packet before slipping it into an inside pocket. He then took the lift to the ground floor and headed in the direction of Westminster Cathedral.

17

The evening before the trial, Adrian and Maria were driven from Lincoln down the A1 back to London. They were booked into a small, discreet hotel not far from the Old Bailey. Two guards were stationed outside their room.

Maria slept well, despite Adrian tossing and turning throughout the night as he went over his well-rehearsed responses to every one of Sir Julian's questions, like a nervous actor waiting for the curtain to rise. Maria only had a walk-on part. As soon as Adrian stepped into the witness box, she would be driven to Heathrow, where she would check in and wait for him to join her.

Sir Julian stayed at his flat in Lincoln's Inn overnight. In the morning he rose early and went over his opening address one more time, making the occasional emendation, crossing the odd word out, even one whole paragraph. He then read it out loud, with only the morning chorus as his audience. They seemed to appreciate it.

Booth Watson also rose early, and enjoyed a large breakfast before taking a taxi to the Old Bailey, arriving only half an hour before proceedings would commence. But then, he was unlikely to be on his feet until later that afternoon, as he suspected the Crown's first witness would give evidence for at least a couple of hours before he had the chance to cross-examine him. Although he had prepared several traps to ensnare Mr. Heath, none of them looked all that promising, and he feared that if his client was found guilty on both charges, he would, with a four-year suspended sentence already hanging over him, be spending several Christmases doing cold turkey.

He had dined with Miles at the Savoy the evening before, and found him remarkably calm, even resigned to his fate. But then he could never fathom out what really went on in that impenetrable mind.

Grace took the tube to the Central Criminal Court, aware that her father wouldn't want to be distracted before he rose to address the jury. She accepted that as his junior, hers was a supporting role, ready to assist should a point of law arise or to check any statement the defense claimed as fact, as she couldn't allow Booth Watson to ambush her father while he was in full flow. At a more menial level, she even had to make sure his glass of water was always half full, and not half empty. Grace was more than happy to act as her father's junior, and although she didn't mention it to anyone, even Clare, she hoped he would allow her to cross-examine one of the less important witnesses.

Like his QC, Miles Faulkner enjoyed a hearty breakfast, having taken an early run around the park. His park. BW had told him he was unlikely to be called to give evidence until after all the Crown's witnesses had been heard, and only then if he was convinced it would assist his cause. At the moment BW wasn't convinced that anything would assist his cause.

His chauffeur dropped him outside the Old Bailey, where he found himself surrounded by a pack of journalists and photographers who had been wondering if he'd even turn up, as he clearly could afford to sacrifice a million pounds to remain a free man. He swaggered toward them, giving the photographers more than enough time to take as many snaps as they wanted, which only convinced the reporters he must be confident he would be leaving in the same car he'd arrived in.

Court number one at the Old Bailey was packed long before Mr. Justice Baverstock entered his workplace at ten o'clock that morning. He bowed to the packed courtroom and took his seat in the center of the raised podium. On the Crown's bench, Sir Julian was making sure that the pages of his opening statement were numbered and in order. Grace had already double-checked, and they were.

Booth Watson was slumped at the other end of the bench, a yellow pad resting on his knee, pen already poised in case Sir Julian made even the slightest error. His junior, Mr. Andrews, sat attentively by his side, waiting to pick up any tidbits his leader might have missed.

Miles Faulkner stood in the dock, dressed once again in a Savile Row suit and sporting an Old Harrovian tie. He smiled at the seven men and five women as they filed into the jury box, but only one of them glanced in his direction.

The judge waited for the jury to be sworn in, and once he was satisfied that everyone was settled he nodded to the clerk of the court, who rose and read out the two indictments on the charge sheet, before looking up at the defendant and asking portentously, "How do you plead, guilty or not guilty?"

"Not guilty," declared Faulkner on both counts, sounding amazed that anyone might doubt his word.

"You may be seated," said the clerk.

Once Faulkner had taken his place, Mr. Justice Baverstock turned his attention to the Crown's leader. "Are you ready to deliver your opening statement, Sir Julian?" he asked.

"I am indeed, m'lud." He rose from his place, and tugged at the lapels of his long black gown before firmly gripping the sides of the stand on which his statement rested.

"M'lud," he began, "I represent the Crown in this case, while my learned friend, Mr. Booth Watson QC, appears on behalf of the defense." The two men reluctantly exchanged perfunctory bows. "There are two counts on the indictment, My Lord, that relate to the possession and supply of an illegal substance, in this case, cocaine. On the evening of Saturday, May the seventeenth this year, the defendant was found to be in possession of a large quantity of the drug while hosting a dinner party for nine other guests. But it is not only what took place at the dinner party that night that will be of interest to the jury. Of even more significance is what happened before Mr. Faulkner's first guest arrived." He looked up to see that the jury were hanging on his every word.

"A few minutes after seven that evening, a man arrived at Mr. Faulkner's home to keep an appointment he had made some days before. On arrival, that man, Mr. Adrian Heath, was escorted through to the defendant's study in order to conduct a business transaction. He provided Mr. Faulkner with twelve grams of cocaine in exchange for eight hundred pounds in cash. The price was above the going rate, but Mr. Faulkner was a customer who demanded only the best. In this case, ninety-two-point-five percent pure, as an expert witness will later testify.

"Once the deal was closed and Mr. Heath had been paid—and we will produce the cash as evidence—he drove back to London, from where he was immediately taken, in the highest secrecy, to a safe house, because Mr. Faulkner was unaware that Adrian Heath was a police informant."

Booth Watson made his first note—*agent provocateur.*

"Later that evening," continued Sir Julian, "the police raided Mr. Faulkner's home in the country and despite a desperate attempt to hide the evidence, thanks to an outstanding piece of police work by a young detective sergeant, the drugs were discovered inside a statue—" he paused—"a statue of Mr. Faulkner himself."

One or two members of the jury couldn't resist a smirk.

"The Crown," Sir Julian continued, "will not only produce the twelve grams of cocaine, and the eight hundred pounds Mr. Faulkner paid to the dealer, but Mr. Heath himself will confirm the role he played on this occasion. And as if that were not enough to condemn this man," he said, pointing to the defendant, "the Crown will also call two expert witnesses, namely Superintendent Lamont, the head of the elite drugs squad at Scotland Yard . . ."

Booth Watson made a second note, *Why not Warwick?*

". . . and Dr. Ruth Lewis, an eminent member of the government's Advisory Council on the Misuse of Drugs." Looking somber, Sir Julian turned to face the jury and said finally, "The Crown is confident, members of the jury, that after you have heard all the evidence in this case, you will find there is only one possible verdict, namely that the defendant, Miles Faulkner, is guilty on both counts."

Faulkner looked more closely at the jury as Sir Julian resumed his seat. They were all staring at the Crown's representative, and had they been asked to deliver a verdict there and then, the expression on their faces rather suggested Faulkner would have been hanged, drawn, and quartered before dawn. Booth Watson had warned him the worst moment of a trial for any defendant is immediately following the Crown's opening submission.

"Thank you, Sir Julian," said Mr. Justice Baverstock. "Perhaps this would be a suitable time to take a short break, after which you may call your first witness."

He then rose from his place, bowed, and left the court.

"Where's Heath?" demanded Sir Julian before he'd even sat back down.

"Under police protection in a cell on the ground floor," said Grace. "I'll pop down and warn him he'll be on shortly."

"And his girlfriend?"

"As soon as Heath is on the stand she'll be driven to the airport. A car is standing by to take Heath there to join her the moment he steps down."

"I think the case might well be over by stumps this evening," said Sir Julian. "Once Heath has spelled out the details of what took place in Faulkner's home that night, I suspect Booth Watson will do his damnedest to make a plea bargain on behalf of his client."

"And how will you respond?" asked Grace.

"My junior has already prepared a rather uncompromising statement that I shall deliver word for word."

◄○►

"Well, that was lethal," said Faulkner, leaning down from the dock to talk to his silk. "Sir Julian Warwick looked as if he couldn't wait to get Heath on the stand."

"Nor can I," said Booth Watson. "He's a flawed individual, and I intend to take him apart limb by limb. I remain confident of getting you off the more serious charge of supplying, although possession will still be a problem."

"The police planted the gear as revenge for their abject failure in the missing Rembrandt case," said Faulkner.

"I won't be mentioning the Rembrandt case," said Booth Watson. "It would only enable the Crown to inform the jury that you're serving a four-year suspended sentence for fraud. They're not allowed to mention any previous convictions unless we raise the subject first. However, three of your dinner guests are willing to swear under oath that no one was offered so much as a joint, and a fourth will testify that he's never known you to take a drug in your life."

"Then he can't have known me very long," said Faulkner.

◄○►

"You may call your first witness, Sir Julian," said Mr. Justice Baverstock, after he'd returned from the short recess.

"Thank you, m'lud. I call Mr. Adrian Heath."

Booth Watson studied the Crown's star witness with interest as he entered the court. He was smartly dressed, looking more like a City whiz kid than a reformed drug addict. Heath gave William a nervous smile as he made his way to the witness box, but he didn't even glance at Faulkner as he passed him in the dock. He delivered the oath with enough confidence for Booth Watson to be reminded that it wasn't the first time he'd been in a courtroom.

Sir Julian greeted him with a warm smile. "For the court's record, Mr. Heath, would you please state your full name and your current address?"

"Adrian Charles Heath, 23 Ladbroke Grove, London W10."

Booth Watson suspected that was his mother's address.

"Mr. Heath, can you confirm that in the past you were a drug addict?"

"In the past, yes I was, Sir Julian. But now, thanks to the support of a very special young woman who stood by me during my rehab, that's all behind me, and we plan on getting married in the near future."

"I'm sure we all wish you every happiness," said Sir Julian, turning to smile at Booth Watson, who showed no signs of joy. "Well, perhaps not all of us," he added, eliciting a smile from one or two members of the jury. Sir Julian accepted that he had to get his next question on the record, so that Booth Watson couldn't spring it as a surprise during his cross-examination.

"And you were, Mr. Heath, for a short period of time a drug dealer?"

"For a very short period. And then only when I was desperate for cash to pay for my addiction."

"And that is also now happily behind you."

"Yes, sir, I can assure you that I haven't had anything to do with drugs for over six months, and I'll never return to that way of life again."

"That does you great credit, Mr. Heath. And you now feel it is no more than your civic duty to give evidence concerning the last transaction you were involved in." Heath nodded and bowed his head while Booth Watson made another note. "Did you, on the evening of May the seventeenth this year, drive down to Limpton Hall in Hampshire to keep an appointment with the accused, Mr. Miles Faulkner?"

"Yes, sir, I did."

"Do you see him in the court today?"

"Yes, I do." Heath pointed to the man sitting in the dock, and then quickly turned away.

"What time was your appointment with the defendant?"

"Seven o'clock."

"And were you on time?"

"I may have been a few minutes late, but the butler took me straight through to Mr. Faulkner's study where he was waiting to see me."

"And he seemed keen to close the deal?"

"The door hadn't even closed before he asked me if I'd been able to get my hands on the merchandise he'd requested. I told him that I had, and handed a packet to him for inspection."

"Is that customary in such transactions?"

"Yes, sir. He wanted to be sure the gear was of the highest quality. So he insisted on trying a sample."

"And did he?"

"Yes, he tasted a small amount of the product and seemed well satisfied."

"Did he indeed? What happened next?"

"He paid me the eight hundred pounds in cash we'd agreed on, thanked me, and said he hoped we'd do business again."

"And after that?"

"He asked me to accompany the butler downstairs, where I handed the goods over to his chef."

Sir Julian paused for a moment. "To his chef?" he repeated.

"Yes. Mr. Faulkner told me he'd been instructed to set out ten portions on a silver platter for himself and his guests."

"Did the chef seem surprised?"

"No, sir, but then I assumed he'd dealt with Fortnum and Mason in the past."

Sir Julian looked down at his questions, but there was no mention of Fortnum and Mason in his notes. He glanced at Grace, who looked as surprised as he did.

"Are you telling the court that you picked up a consignment of the purest cocaine from Fortnum and Mason?"

"No, sir. The goods I picked up from Fortnum's that morning at Mr. Faulkner's request were a dozen jars of the finest Royal Beluga caviar."

Some of those in the court began to laugh, while others simply looked bemused. The judge frowned as he glared down at the witness.

Sir Julian paused for some time before asking, "Are you telling the court that you did not supply any drugs to Mr. Faulkner on this occasion?"

"On this occasion, or any other occasion, for that matter," said Heath. "In fact, it was the first time I'd ever met him."

Grace passed her father a hastily written note.

"May I ask what you've been doing for the past six months, Mr. Heath?"

"I've been living in a safe house in Lincoln while assisting the police with their inquiries, for which I'm to be paid ten thousand pounds."

The journalists looked delighted with this new piece of information, and their pens scratched away even more enthusiastically. The cacophony of murmured conversations that broke out in the court gave Sir Julian a little time to consider his next question.

"So, what did you have to offer the police that was worth ten thousand pounds?"

"I gave them the name of Tulip."

"Tulip?"

"Terry Holland. He's a big-time London drug dealer. Makes around a hundred grand a year. I also supplied them with the names of sixteen of his best customers, and in return I was promised ten grand and safe passage abroad for me and my girlfriend."

The journalists didn't stop scribbling.

"And was Mr. Faulkner one of those customers?" asked Sir Julian, trying to recover.

"No, he was not, sir," said Heath firmly.

Grace handed her father another note.

"You do realize that you're under oath, Mr. Heath?"

"I most certainly do, sir. Your daughter told me only this morning when she visited me in my cell how important it was that I told the truth, the whole truth, and nothing but the truth, otherwise I could go to jail for committing perjury. If you doubt my word, Sir Julian, I'm sure that Mr. Faulkner, his butler, and his chef will all confirm my testimony."

Faulkner nodded, and this time he noticed that several members of the jury were now looking in his direction. Sir Julian recalled his son's words when they had discussed Heath soon after he'd been expelled from school. *One of the brightest boys in his class, but not to be trusted.* He had to accept that Heath would have an answer to every one of his unprepared questions, as he'd obviously been rehearsing his responses for some time.

"No more questions, m'lud," Sir Julian managed, before slumping back down on the bench.

Mr. Justice Baverstock turned his attention to defending counsel. "Do you wish to cross-examine this witness, Mr. Booth Watson?"

"No, thank you, m'lud. I am quite satisfied with Mr. Heath's testimony."

"I'll bet you were," said William, a little too loudly from the back of the court, and although the Hawk frowned, he had to agree with him.

"Mr. Heath, you are free to leave the court," said the judge reluctantly.

"Thank you, m'lud," said Adrian, before stepping out of the witness box and heading straight for the nearest exit.

The judge rose and said, "The court is adjourned until two o'clock. However, I would like to see both counsel in my chambers."

The two advocates bowed, aware that this was not a request.

"Warwick," said Lamont, his eyes fixed on Faulkner, who was stepping down from the dock, "I need to know where Heath's going. And, Paul, you follow Faulkner. Don't let either of them out of your sight."

"I suspect they're both going in the same direction," suggested the Hawk.

William had to dodge in and out of the bustling crowd heading for the door, while at the same time trying to keep an eye on Heath. Once he was outside in the corridor, he dashed toward the wide sweeping staircase, and didn't stop running until he was out on the street, his eyes darting in every direction until he finally spotted a familiar figure climbing into the back of a Bentley.

"Damn," said William. He began looking around in vain for a taxi, and once again stared at the parked car that hadn't moved. To his surprise a motorbike screeched to a halt by his side.

"Jump on, sarge," said Paul, handing him a crash helmet.

◄O►

"Good to see you again," said Faulkner, when Heath joined him in the back of the car.

"Let's hope it's for the last time," said Heath, as the two men shook hands. "Because I don't want to be dragged back into the witness box and have to explain how the drugs ended up in your statue, if I didn't sell them to you."

"You won't be going back," said Faulkner. "That's the last thing I need." He handed Heath two first-class tickets to Rio de Janeiro, a new passport, and a small attaché case. "By this time tomorrow, you and your girlfriend will be on the other side of the world, leaving the Crown with no choice but to drop the case, and my wife will finally be left with no choice but to sign her divorce papers."

"Thanks to our mutual friend from Hampshire," said Heath, as he opened the briefcase and stared down at twenty thousand pounds stacked in neatly wrapped cellophane packets. "You've certainly kept your side of the bargain," he added. "Double what the fuzz were willing to pay me."

"Worth every penny," said Faulkner, "if it's going to keep me out of jail and Christina unable to cause any more trouble. I can't afford to hang about. I have to be back in my place by two o'clock, otherwise it will cost me a million pounds. Twenty thousand is one thing, a million is quite another."

"Understood," said Heath, as they shook hands a second time. "Good luck."

"Thanks to you I don't think I'll need it. Eddie, take my friend to Heathrow, because I wouldn't want him to miss his flight."

◄○►

"Can I offer you a stiff drink, Julian?"

"A bit early for me, m'lud, but yes, make it a double whiskey," he said, as Booth Watson entered the room.

"Same for you, BW?"

"No, thank you, m'lud," said Booth Watson, as he removed his wig. "I'm still trying to recover from what just happened out there."

"You're not going to pretend it came as a total surprise, are you?" said Julian, unable to hide the sarcasm in his voice.

"I was just as shocked as you," admitted Booth Watson. "Have you forgotten that I called your office only last week to ask if you would consider making a plea bargain, and you turned my request down, quite eloquently if I remember correctly?"

"Perhaps I might reconsider . . ." began Sir Julian.

"It's a bit late for that now," said Booth Watson. "I suspect you've no choice but to pack up your tent, climb back on your camel, and move your caravan on to a new watering hole."

"I shall take instruction from my masters at the CPS," said Sir Julian, playing for time. "But I fear they may well agree with you and recommend that all the charges be dropped."

"And you, BW?" asked the judge.

"Like Julian, I shall take instructions from my master."

18

The silver-gray Bentley Continental drew up outside terminal three.

Heath appeared relaxed as he got out of the car clutching firmly onto the briefcase, his only piece of luggage. He was heading toward the terminal entrance when a motorcycle skidded to a halt in the no-parking zone.

"You go after him," said Paul. "I'll catch up."

"I've seen that bike somewhere before," said William, as he took off his helmet and pointed to a black Yamaha that had been dumped in the disabled parking area. "But where?"

"It passed us on the motorway," said Paul. "The rider slowed down as he drew level with the Bentley, and looked in the back window before taking off again."

"No, I've seen it somewhere else," mumbled William, as he set off in pursuit of Heath. Once he was inside the terminal, he quickly checked the departures board. BRITISH AIRWAYS FLIGHT 012 TO RIO DE JANEIRO, 16:20. GATE 27 flicked up on the display. He passed quickly through the crowded concourse, avoiding suitcases and outstretched legs as he headed toward the check-in desks, his eyes continually searching for his quarry. And then he spotted Adrian, still dressed in his smart courtroom-appearance suit, embracing a young woman at the BA counter who he assumed must be Maria Ruiz. He slipped behind a pillar, and waited for Paul to join him.

William watched as they kissed and began chatting excitedly. He only wished he could overhear their conversation.

"How did it go?" asked Maria.

"Exactly as planned, except I ended up with twenty grand, not ten."

"Don't you feel a little guilty about what you've done to your old school friend?"

"Not if his father's half as bright as the press claim. By this time tomorrow, if not sooner, he'll have gone over the transcript of my testimony and seen that I've handed him a golden opportunity to trap Faulkner. So it's even more important we're well out of harm's way long before Faulkner finds out that I double-crossed him."

"Our flight leaves in forty minutes," said Maria, checking the departure board.

"Perfect. But it would be better if we split up, and meet again on board the plane. There might be someone looking out for us. You take this," he said, handing over the briefcase and her ticket.

Maria embraced him again, before reluctantly leaving to climb onto the escalator leading to departures. After waving to her, Adrian headed toward the men's room.

William watched as Maria disappeared from view. His instructions had made no mention of her. He was simply to arrest Heath and bring him back to the Old Bailey.

"On what charge?" he'd asked Lamont.

"My bet is he'll be traveling on a false passport, and there'll be enough evidence in that briefcase to prove his testimony was bought. Don't be surprised if you find it's a lot more than ten thousand."

A few moments later a voice said, "Do you want me to follow her, sarge?"

"No. We'll arrest Heath first and then go after her. She won't be going anywhere without him."

They both kept their eyes on the men's room, as they waited for Heath to reappear.

"He's taking his time," said Paul. "A change of clothes perhaps?"

"No, he didn't have anything with him when he went inside. My bet is they've agreed to meet up again on the plane."

"What makes you think that?"

"She's got the money."

"Should I go and check he's still in there?"

"Where else could he be?" said William, as a man they both recognized immediately came running out of the men's room.

"So now we know who was on the other bike," said Paul. "Which one do you want me to go after?"

"Tulip," said William, remembering where he'd last seen the black Yamaha. "And make sure you arrest him."

"On what charge?"

"I have a feeling I'm about to find out," said William, as he headed for the men's room. "Get going!"

Paul took off after Tulip, no longer caring about stray bags or stretched-out legs, and just as William had reached the entrance to the men's room another man came rushing out, shouting, "Help, somebody call the police, help!"

As William was about to go inside, a third man burst past him, struggling to do up his zip while on the move. William pushed open the door and tentatively entered the washroom. He came to a sudden halt, momentarily paralyzed by what he saw in front of him. During his time on the force, he had encountered several dead bodies: old people who'd died peacefully in their homes, drug addicts with needles sticking out of their arms, even a battered wife who'd hanged herself in front of her young children. But nothing could have prepared him for this.

Sprawled across the floor was the lifeless body of Adrian Heath, surrounded by a pool of blood. Only moments before he'd been looking forward to starting a new life with his girlfriend in Rio. Adrian's throat had been cut in one clean movement by someone who knew what he was doing, and his right eye had been gouged from its socket and left by the body as a warning to any other dealer who might even think about becoming an informer.

"Don't move!" shouted a voice from behind him.

William raised his arms and said firmly, "I'm a police officer. I'm going to show you my warrant card."

"Slowly," said the voice.

William extracted his card from an inside pocket and held it up for the officer to see.

He heard footsteps advancing toward him, followed by the words, "OK, sergeant, you can turn around."

William swung around to see an older police sergeant, trying to remain calm, accompanied by a young constable who couldn't stop shaking. Airport police usually deal with illegal immigrants, the occasional pickpocket, sometimes a passenger who has removed a bag from the carousel that isn't theirs. This certainly wasn't part of their job description. William accepted he would have to take charge.

"Listen carefully," he said. "The first thing I need you to do is cordon off the whole area. Make sure no members of the public are allowed anywhere near this washroom."

The young constable quickly left the room, a look of relief on his face suggesting he was glad to escape.

"Sergeant, I want you to phone Detective Superintendent

Lamont at Scotland Yard. Tell him Adrian Heath has been murdered, and DC Adaja is in pursuit of the suspect, known as Tulip." William made him repeat the message, as another officer appeared. He turned away the moment he saw the body.

"I need you to inform the airport's duty officer and take control of the crime scene," said William to the third officer. "The body is not to be moved until officers from the murder squad authorize it."

"Yes, sir," said another man who was only too happy to obey orders.

William squatted on one knee next to Heath's body and extracted a boarding card and passport from an inside pocket. The photograph was of Heath, although the name wasn't.

"Sorry, old friend," said William. "God knows, you didn't deserve this."

When William emerged from the men's room, he found two more policemen cordoning off the crime scene, while a group of exasperated passengers were demanding to know why they couldn't use the washroom. If he'd told them, they would have peed in their pants.

The older sergeant hurried back to join him.

"The forensic medical examiner should be with us fairly soon. I wasn't able to get through to Superintendent Lamont because he's been called to give evidence at the Old Bailey. A Commander Hawksby says you're to take over until a crime scene manager arrives."

"Understood. Make sure—"

"This is the last call for BA flight 012 to Rio de Janeiro. Will all remaining passengers please make their way to gate twenty-seven, as the plane is about to depart?"

"—that no one other than the lab liaison sergeant and the FME are allowed anywhere near the body. And one more thing—"

"You're leaving me in charge?" said the officer.

"Yes, but not for long," said William, as the sound of blaring sirens grew louder and louder. "There's someone I have to question before her plane takes off." Without another word he began running toward the escalator, taking the steps two at a time.

The officer at passport control looked up in alarm at the blood-stained, breathless man who'd jumped the queue. He was about to press the panic button below the counter when William produced his warrant card, shouting, "Rio?"

"The gate's about to close, sergeant," he said. "I'll call ahead and warn them you're on your way. I hope you catch the bastard."

William took off once again. Two ground staff were waiting for him by gate 27, and after a cursory check of his warrant card he was ushered down the walkway and onto the waiting aircraft, where he joined the last of the passengers looking for their seats. He checked the seat number on Adrian's boarding pass, before making his way down the aisle searching for a woman he'd never met. He came to a halt when he saw Maria Ruiz clutching on to a briefcase, anxiously searching for a different face.

William changed his mind. He turned around, walked back along the aisle to the exit, thanked the stewardess, and returned to the terminal.

BA flight 012 to Rio de Janeiro took off on time, although one of the passengers was a no-show.

◄o►

"That was the Director of Public Prosecutions," said Sir Julian, putting the phone down.

"It's not hard to guess what they'll be recommending," said Grace.

"Following Heath's evidence this morning, they're advising me to contact Booth Watson and try to make a deal."

"I know exactly what two words I'd say to that suggestion if I was BW," said Grace, "and one of them would have four letters. What sort of deal did the DPP have in mind?"

"We agree to drop the charge of intent to supply, in exchange for Faulkner pleading guilty to possession. He'll have to pay a heavy fine, but will only be given a two-year suspended sentence. However, typical of the DPP, they say they'll leave the final decision to us."

"That's why they're known as the Department of Pontius Pilate," remarked Grace. "So Faulkner will get away with it yet again. If he goes on like this, he'll be on suspended sentences for the rest of his life, and never see the inside of a prison cell."

"What would you do, Grace, if you were my leader on this case, and I were your junior?"

Grace was taken aback for a moment, as her father had never before sought her advice on such a major call. She thought about his question for some time, because although she was flattered, the look on his face left her in no doubt that he was waiting to hear her opinion before he came to a decision.

"I wouldn't let Faulkner off the hook quite that easily," she said. "He still has to explain away the twelve grams of cocaine that the police found in his home, and even if he could convince the jury that he didn't know how it got there, he won't find it easy to account for the twenty-pound note, which William's convinced is the one question he won't be able to answer."

"I agree with William. But we'll still need Faulkner to give evidence before we can raise the subject of the twenty-pound note. If I were representing him, I'd advise him strongly against going anywhere near the witness box. That will leave us with the task of having to prove him guilty beyond reasonable doubt, which will be nigh on impossible after Heath's evidence this morning."

"Then we'll have to try and appeal to Faulkner's vanity," said Grace, "and make it impossible for him to resist taking us on."

"And how do you propose to do that?" asked Sir Julian.

"By replacing the opening batsman," said Grace, as the phone on his desk began to ring.

He picked it up and listened to the caller for some time before he said, "Yes, I can see how that changes the situation, Desmond. Thank you for keeping me informed."

"What changes the situation?" asked Grace, after he'd put the phone down.

"Adrian Heath's dead."

◄○►

"The other side have made us an offer," said Booth Watson.

"After Heath's evidence this morning, that's hardly surprising," said Faulkner. "But you may as well tell me what it is before I dismiss the offer out of hand."

"They'll drop the charge of intent to supply, if you'll plead guilty to possession."

"What will the damage be?"

"A million-pound fine, and a two-year suspended sentence."

"That might be tempting if I didn't think the jury is going to find me not guilty on both charges."

"Possibly," said Booth Watson, "but why take the risk?"

"Because the odds are now heavily stacked in my favor, so you can tell Sir Julian Warwick QC to get lost."

"I'd advise against that, Miles, especially as I won't be putting you on the stand."

"Why not? I've got nothing to hide."

"Except twelve grams of cocaine."

"Which you can tell them Lamont planted."

"You know that's not going to wash, and the jury won't fall for it either. Lamont is a long-serving police officer with an unblemished record, and in my experience, juries tend to like the plain-speaking Scotsman, which is why I don't intend to cross-examine him."

"But you will after you've read this," said Faulkner, handing his silk a thick brown envelope.

Booth Watson took his time reading its contents before asking, "How did you get hold of this?"

"It's all a matter of public record," said Faulkner, "if you know where to look."

◄○►

"Am I to understand, Sir Julian, that you wish to make a statement on behalf of the Crown?" inquired Mr. Justice Baverstock.

"That is correct, m'lud. With your permission, the Crown will be dropping the first charge on the indictment, namely intent to supply. However, we still intend to proceed with the second charge, that of possession of a controlled substance, namely twelve grams of cocaine."

The judge raised an eyebrow, as he had been privy to the advice the DPP had given Sir Julian to drop both charges and beat an expeditious retreat. He was surprised that such a normally cautious man would ignore such sage opinion.

"So be it, Sir Julian. Then you may call your next witness."

"I call Detective Superintendent Lamont."

◄○►

The first thing William did on arriving back at the Yard later that evening, was to ask the commander if there was any news about Paul.

"It's not good, I'm afraid," said Hawksby. "He had a collision with another motorbike on his way back from the airport, and both of them ended up in hospital." William looked anxious. "But Paul got off pretty lightly, just a few cuts and bruises, and he should be discharged in a couple of days. Tulip unfortunately broke a leg, and won't be leaving the hospital for some time." The flicker of a smile appeared on the commander's face.

"Has he been arrested for Heath's murder?"

"Yes. The murder squad took care of that, and they'll post a guard outside his room night and day."

"Then I'll complete my report, and leave it on Superintendent Lamont's desk before I leave tonight."

"Good," said the Hawk. "Bruce was sorry that he couldn't help you out, but at short notice, he was asked to give evidence at Faulkner's trial."

"How did he get on?"

"Couldn't have done better. In fact, I'd be surprised if Booth Watson bothers to cross-examine him in the morning. It will only give him yet another chance to repeat the question, if Faulkner didn't put those drugs in the statue, who did?"

"Did the Crown raise the subject of the twenty-pound note?"

"No. I have a feeling they're saving that bombshell for when Sir Julian cross-examines Faulkner."

"That's assuming he gets the chance," said William. "If Faulkner doesn't go into the witness box, my father won't be allowed to present it as new evidence."

"Strange," said the Hawk. "It's so unlike Sir Julian to take such a risk."

"But it's not unlike his daughter," said William.

"Then let's hope they don't both live to regret it."

◄○►

William unlocked the door, hoping that a quiet evening at home with his wife would help put the image of Adrian Heath's dead body out of his mind. But when he stepped into the hall, he was greeted by a tearful, pregnant Beth, who threw her arms around him and clung on tightly.

"Now I know what Josephine Hawksby meant when she told me the thing she most dreaded was the day when her husband didn't come home."

"It wasn't that bad," said William, trying to reassure her.

"But to see your friend butchered in that way, and you helpless to do anything about it."

"How did you find out?" asked William.

"The story's been leading the news programs all evening, and Jackie rang to tell me you were the first officer on the scene."

"I was, but I'll be fine," he said, hoping he sounded convincing.

"You don't look fine," said Beth, as she started to remove his bloodstained shirt, only to be reminded of another scar from an earlier encounter in his career. But she feared this one would be mental, not physical. "I wish you'd called me."

"Not that easy when you're in the middle of a murder investigation. Lamont wasn't available, so I was left in charge."

"I know. Jackie filled me in on the gory details." *Only the details she wanted you to hear*, thought William. "How did Adrian's girlfriend react?" she asked.

William didn't reply.

"Is this one of those occasions when I shouldn't ask any more questions?" said Beth.

"Yes," said William quietly. "Not least because I'm not sure I made the right decision."

19

"Do you wish to cross-examine this witness, Mr. Booth Watson?"

"Yes, m'lud, but I won't be taking up too much of the court's time."

He remained standing while Superintendent Lamont made his way back to the witness box.

"Superintendent, I'm sure I don't have to remind you that you're still under oath." Lamont didn't respond, but stood glowering at his adversary like a boxer waiting for the bell so the first round could begin.

"For the record, superintendent, can I assume that's a yes?"

Lamont reluctantly nodded. First round to Booth Watson.

"During your evidence yesterday afternoon, in answer to my learned friend, you repeated ad nauseam that if my client did not conceal the drugs found in the statue at his house, then who did?"

"And I will be happy to repeat it again, Mr. Booth Watson, if you feel it might speed up proceedings."

No doubt who'd won the second round, thought William.

"I don't think that will be necessary, superintendent. However, what I would like to know is how many police officers invaded Mr. Faulkner's home in the middle of the night?"

"I couldn't be sure of the exact number."

"Despite the fact that you were in charge of the operation?"

174

"Fifteen, possibly twenty."

"In fact, the number was twenty-three, if you include all the officers from the drugs squad, the laboratory analysts, the drivers, and even a photographer, not to mention a couple of sniffer dogs. One might have been forgiven, superintendent, for thinking my client had stolen the Crown Jewels."

Lamont didn't respond, but the jury weren't in any doubt who had won the third round.

"Is it possible that one of those officers could have concealed the drugs in the statue without your knowledge?"

"Impossible," said Lamont, fighting back.

"By that, do you mean you can personally vouch for every last one of them, even the ones you didn't realize were there?"

"Of course I can't," snapped Lamont. "However, I can assure the court they were all, without exception, first-class profession-als, carrying out the job they were trained to do."

"Would you describe Detective Superintendent Jeremy Mead-ows as a first-class professional, who carried out the job he was trained to do?"

Lamont hesitated, clearly caught off guard, as another of Booth Watson's punches landed, this one below the belt.

"Take your time, superintendent, and please don't be offended if I remind you that you are still under oath."

Sir Julian rose to his feet. "M'lud," he said acidly, "I'm strug-gling to grasp the relevance of these questions, and where they are leading."

"Be assured, m'lud," said Booth Watson, clearly unmoved, "that will soon become crystal clear."

"I hope so, Mr. Booth Watson," interjected the referee, "as I have some sympathy with Sir Julian's view. Would you kindly come to the point?"

"I shall do everything in my power to oblige, Your Lordship." Booth Watson turned his focus back on Lamont, who still hadn't replied. "Do you need to be reminded of the question, superintendent?"

"No, I do not."

"Then I await your answer with interest."

"Yes, I would describe Detective Superintendent Meadows as a consummate professional, and I was proud to be a member of his team."

"A consummate professional? May I ask what rank you held when you were so proud to be a member of his team?"

"I was a detective sergeant in the murder squad, carrying out an investigation into the death of a notorious East End crime boss."

"Did that case come to court?"

Lamont nodded.

"Once again, superintendent, the court will need to know for the record if that was a yes."

"Yes," replied Lamont curtly.

"And what verdict did the jury come to on that occasion?"

"Not guilty," said Lamont.

"And can you recall, superintendent, the vital piece of evidence that caused the jury to reach that verdict?"

Booth Watson continued to stare at the witness.

"If you can't, I'd be happy to jog your memory." He waited for some time before saying, "Defense counsel, in that case, was able to prove that a gun had been planted on the suspect. Perhaps you could tell the court who planted that weapon on an innocent victim, superintendent?"

"Detective Superintendent Jeremy Meadows," said Lamont in a voice that did not reach the back of the court.

"And what became of Detective Superintendent Meadows following that incident?"

"He resigned from the force and was later sent to prison."

"Where is all this leading, Mr. Booth Watson?" asked the judge, as Sir Julian rose to his feet.

"I suspect we're about to find out, m'lud," said Booth Watson, ignoring Sir Julian.

"And as you have told us, superintendent, you were one of the officers serving on that case."

"I had that honor."

"Honor? But this was a case in which a senior police officer planted a gun on an innocent man in order to dishonestly secure a conviction."

"And less than a month after that man was found not guilty, he murdered another innocent victim."

"So you approved of your boss's action?" said Booth Watson.

"I didn't say that."

"You didn't need to. Tell me, superintendent, are you an advocate of 'noble cause corruption'?" Booth Watson waited for a response, but none was forthcoming. "Perhaps the time has come for you to satisfy the court's curiosity as to the role you played on that occasion. Following the conviction of your boss, the honorable Detective Superintendent Meadows, a tribunal was set up to investigate whether anyone else on the team was implicated in the crime. Under oath you admitted that as an impressionable young detective sergeant, it was possible you might have turned a blind eye. Could you tell the court what the tribunal decided was the appropriate punishment in your case?"

"I was demoted from detective sergeant to constable, and spent two years back on the beat, before I was reinstated to my former rank."

"So, after an independent tribunal had assessed your honesty and integrity, it recommended that you be demoted."

"After which I was reinstated."

"And you're now asking the jury to believe you're a reformed character?"

"We all make mistakes," said Lamont. "Some of us learn from them."

"Indeed we do," said Booth Watson. "But the jury will want to know if you've learned not to turn a blind eye when you can't secure a conviction by honest police work."

Lamont stared defiantly at the defense counsel, but Booth Watson didn't flinch.

"Were you the officer in charge of the case when my client was falsely accused of stealing a Rembrandt, which he had in fact recovered for the Fitzmolean Museum at great personal expense?"

"The jury decided he'd illegally held on to the painting for seven years," said Lamont, getting back up off the canvas, "and the judge gave him a four-year suspended sentence for fraud, and fined him ten thousand pounds."

"Well done," whispered Sir Julian. "Now it's on the record."

Booth Watson dodged the onslaught. "Just answer the question, superintendent. Were you in charge of the case?"

"Yes, I was."

"And was that yet another example of noble cause corruption?"

Sir Julian was quickly on his feet. "I must object, m'lud. The superintendent is not on trial in this case."

"I agree, Sir Julian. Move on, Mr. Booth Watson."

Booth Watson turned a page of his notes. "Finally, superintendent, may I ask how long it took you on the night of May the seventeenth, to drive from the entrance gates of my client's property to the front door of his home?"

"About a minute, a minute and a half."

"How interesting. Because when I carried out the same exercise a week ago, it only took me forty-two seconds. But then it's possible you weren't in a hurry."

Lamont reeled back.

"And how long did it take for the butler—who will give evidence if required, m'lud—to open the front door and let you in, after you'd kept your finger pressing the bell?"

"A minute, possibly two."

"So, no more than three, possibly four, minutes in all before you and twenty-two highly trained officers burst into my client's home looking for drugs. And after searching for more than two hours, all they could come up with was one Ecstasy tablet and a couple of marijuana cigarettes."

"But later we found—"

"'Later' being the key word. But how much later, I'm bound to ask. Were you the first officer to enter Limpton Hall, superintendent?" said Booth Watson, changing tack.

"Yes," said Lamont, sounding puzzled.

"And where was my client at the time?"

"Standing at the top of the stairs."

"And how was he dressed?"

"He was wearing a red silk dressing gown."

"So after you'd rung the front doorbell, he somehow managed to get twelve wraps of cocaine into a statue inconveniently placed near the front door, rush back upstairs, change out of his dinner jacket, put on his pajamas and a red silk dressing gown—thank you for that fascinating detail, superintendent—and still found time to be standing at the top of the stairs waiting for you when you charged in, all in under three minutes?"

Lamont didn't respond.

"The Keystone Cops couldn't have come up with a better story," said Booth Watson, looking directly at the jury.

"It's my belief that the defendant had concealed the twelve wraps of cocaine in the statue before our arrival, with the intention of distributing them among his guests later that evening. We just got our timing wrong."

"It's my belief that you got your timing right, and having failed to come up with anything incriminating after searching my client's home for more than two hours, someone carried out your orders and conveniently planted the drugs in the statue."

"That's a ridiculous suggestion," said Lamont, trying to control his temper.

"Would it also be ridiculous to suggest that, not for the first time in your career, you chose to turn a blind eye when false evidence was planted by one of your colleagues in an attempt to secure a conviction?"

"Quite ridiculous," came back Lamont, almost shouting.

"Possibly a young, impressionable detective sergeant who wanted to please the officer in charge of the investigation?"

"Even more ridiculous," said Lamont, his voice rising with every word.

"A detective sergeant who just happened to know exactly where the drugs were, because that's where he'd planted them?"

"That's a scurrilous accusation, My Lord," said Sir Julian, leaping to his feet.

"Especially when the detective sergeant in question just happens to be the son of the Crown's leading counsel."

Sir Julian would have responded, but he wouldn't have been heard above the outburst that followed, when several people turned around to look at William, who was unable to hide his anger.

The judge waited for the clamor to die down before he frowned at the defense counsel, and said, "I do hope, Mr. Booth Watson, that you have some proof of these random accusations, otherwise I shall have no choice but to advise the jury to ignore your words and ask you to be more circumspect in future."

"Perhaps they wouldn't have been random accusations, My Lord, had Sir Julian allowed Detective Sergeant Warwick to give evidence from the witness box under oath rather than his boss."

This time the outcry lasted for some time before the judge was able to regain order when he pronounced, "Do not try my patience any further, Mr. Booth Watson, or I may have to order a retrial, and consider you in contempt of court."

"And we wouldn't want that, would we, My Lord," said Booth Watson, the only person who'd remained calm during this exchange. He turned his attention back to the witness before the judge could respond and said, "Superintendent, would I be right in thinking that you regard Mr. Faulkner as a dangerous criminal, who should be locked up for the rest of his life because the jury got it wrong?"

"At last we've found something we can agree on," shouted Lamont, jabbing a finger at Booth Watson.

"A little louder please," said Booth Watson, "just in case the jury didn't hear you the first time—and might also get it wrong." He looked up at the bench and said, "No more questions, m'lud."

Everyone remained on the edge of their seats, waiting for Sir Julian to come out fighting, but were once again taken by surprise when the Crown's leading advocate rose from his place and said with an exaggerated sigh, "That completes the case for the Crown, m'lud. However, I wonder if I might be allowed to make a personal statement?"

Mr. Justice Baverstock nodded, and Booth Watson settled back, closed his eyes, and crossed his arms, giving the impression of a victorious general awaiting triumphant news from the battlefield.

But to his surprise Sir Julian wasn't yet ready to agree the terms of surrender.

"It is, as you know, m'lud, an established practice at the criminal bar for a leader to allow his junior to cross-examine a defense witness. So, if Mr. Booth Watson plans to call the defendant to give evidence, I shall step aside and leave that responsibility to my junior, Ms. Grace Warwick, if it so pleases Your Lordship."

Booth Watson opened his eyes, unfolded his arms, and said in a voice loud enough for those around him to hear, "What's he up to?"

William smiled, but then he knew exactly what his father was up to.

"I shall look forward to that with pleasure, Sir Julian," said the judge, before he added, "we will reconvene at ten o'clock tomorrow morning."

◄○►

"I would strongly advise against it," said Booth Watson.

"Why?" demanded Faulkner.

"Because you have nothing to gain from it, while she has nothing to lose."

"But don't forget, it's the pupil I'll be up against, not the master."

"Who has been well tutored by the master over many years."

"Then perhaps it's time to remind the Warwicks exactly who they're up against. In any case, what have I got to lose?"

"Your freedom."

"But I might never get another opportunity like this to publicly humiliate Sir Julian Warwick and destroy his daughter at the same time, with Hawksby, Lamont, and the choirboy all having to watch from the sidelines."

"I've given you my opinion, Miles. Avoid appearing in the

witness box at all costs, because I think you'll find the curtain has already come down."

"Not on my performance it hasn't," said Miles.

"Which will be unscripted, don't forget."

"Let's face it," said Miles. "You were nothing more than the gravedigger. They're now waiting for Hamlet to make his entrance."

"And we all know how that ended."

20

When Grace awoke, she wasn't sure if she'd slept at all, as her mind was buzzing with fear and anticipation.

She lay still for a few moments, not wanting to wake Clare, before slipping quietly out of bed and padding barefoot across the carpet to the bathroom. She closed the door quietly and turned on the light.

She looked at herself in the mirror. A lot of work to be done, but not now. She needed her brain to be at its sharpest if she were to have any hope of ambushing Faulkner. After dousing her face with cold water and brushing her teeth, she put on her dressing gown, turned off the bathroom light, tiptoed back across the room and out into the corridor, pleased that she hadn't woken Clare.

As she walked downstairs, Grace realized she must have left the kitchen light on before going to bed, and cursed under her breath. Her dear mother would have chastised her for being "fuelish." But when she opened the kitchen door, she found Clare sitting at the table, pen in hand, surrounded by legal papers.

"Good morning, Grace," she said as if she was sitting in her office at work. "I've just been going over your questions in preparation for this morning's cross-examination. I've rearranged the order slightly, to make it more difficult for Faulkner to work out where you're coming from. But you can't relax for one moment because that man's extremely sharp and fast on his feet, so you'll always have to try and remain one step ahead of him. He mustn't see the sucker punch coming, so when you land the second blow in his solar plexus, he won't have time to recover, because the third one has to knock him out. And by the way, I've gone over Adrian Heath's testimony again, and your father was right—he did send us a coded message on how to trap Faulkner. Let's hope he and Booth Watson haven't spotted it. Now, you sit down and go through what I've done, while I boil you an egg, because you must have a hearty breakfast."

"Before I'm hanged," said Grace. They both laughed nervously. Grace sat down and began to consider the new order of questions. Clare was right, switching a couple of them around would give Faulkner less chance of anticipating "Can I return to the eight hundred pounds?"

"Right," said Clare, placing a cup of tea in front of Grace. "Now let's do it for real. I'll be Faulkner, while you play the leading advocate in the land. Go for it."

Grace rose from her chair. "Mr. Faulkner, do you believe Mr. Heath was telling the truth when he stated under oath . . ."

For the next hour, they exchanged barbed remarks and sharp rejoinders, jousting with each other as if they were deadly rivals, often stopping to deliver a sentence in a different way, or emphasize a word to give it more impact. After the third cup of tea, Clare threw her arms in the air and exclaimed, "'She's got it, I think she's got it!' Now, go and get ready. You also have to look your best if you're going to disarm the jury."

Grace gave her partner a kiss before going back upstairs to take a shower. How had she got so lucky, she wondered, not for the first time. She and Clare had met at a Law Society symposium on the role of foster parents in the modern world, and they'd hardly spent a day apart since. They liked to hold hands and giggle about men they'd met, who imagined they were so irresistible. But only in the privacy of their own home. Once, when they were walking through the park hand in hand, a teenage boy had brushed past them on his bike shouting, "Lesbos, lesbos, lesbos," before pedaling off. Clare had raised a finger, which she later regretted.

"I shouldn't have lowered myself to his level," she told Grace, clearly angry with herself.

How could a moron like that begin to understand that love took many forms? Clare was kind, generous, warm, witty, and as smart as two whiplashes. And as she was a solicitor and Grace a barrister, it made for an ideal partnership. In fact, one of her male colleagues had been overheard in chambers saying, "If you're up against those two, don't think of them as partners, more like an advancing army."

Grace checked herself in the mirror. A neatly tailored navy-blue suit and sensible black shoes. Never, ever wear high heels in the courtroom, a woman judge had once advised her. You can be on your feet for hours, and comfort is much more important than gaining a couple of inches in height. Grace continued to rehearse her questions and even the pauses, as she brushed her hair and stared at the defendant in the mirror.

Clare's sharp reminder—"It's time to get going, Grace, or he'll be found not guilty before you turn up!"—brought her quickly back to earth.

◄○►

"I called this morning's meeting a little earlier than usual," said Hawksby, "as Superintendent Lamont has to be back at the Old Bailey by ten o'clock." Lamont made no comment. "Don't worry,

Bruce. If Faulkner is foolish enough to take the stand, Sir Julian will tear him apart limb from limb."

"He won't be up against Sir Julian," said Lamont. "His daughter will be conducting the cross-examination."

"Then God help the poor man," said William, although neither of the two senior police officers looked convinced.

"While we've been concentrating on Faulkner," continued Hawksby, "DC Adaja and the rest of the team have been keeping a close eye on Rashidi. Are you any nearer to finding out the location of his drugs factory, Paul?"

"Possibly a step nearer, sir," said Adaja, "but I can't claim much more. We've been checking every tower block in Brixton, as I'm sure the slaughter has to be on the top floors of one of them, but I still don't know which one."

"What makes it more difficult," said William, "is that we can't risk the same officers following Rashidi for more than two days in a row. So locating the slaughter could take weeks, even months."

"As I blend into the Brixton scene a bit more convincingly than you lot," said Paul, "perhaps I could manage three days?" Which elicited the first laugh of the morning.

"I was wondering if your UCO had been in touch, sir," said William. "He might even have found out where the slaughter is by now."

"No, he hasn't," said the Hawk sharply, recalling the last occasion DS Warwick had questioned him about MM. "Never forget, DS Warwick, he risks his life every day. If the other side were to suspect even for a moment that he was a member of our team, we'd find his body floating down the river the next morning."

Jackie could well remember where she'd heard almost those exact words when her lover was talking about himself.

"And frankly, I wouldn't want that on my conscience," added the Hawk, immediately regretting his words.

William was tempted to remind the commander that if they'd arrested Tulip in Felixstowe, Adrian would still be alive, but he resisted the temptation.

"If Rashidi's slaughter's on the top floor of one of those tower blocks," said Paul, coming to William's rescue, "it will be difficult, if not impossible, for us to enter the front door before a lookout's warned them we're on the way. They could shut up shop and have disappeared long before we reach them, and all we would have achieved would be to mildly inconvenience the bastards."

Commander Hawksby looked out of the window. "Then we'll just have to wait until it snows."

Court number one at the Old Bailey is known in the trade as the show court, and usually plays to full houses. But the idea of Sir Julian Warwick QC's understudy taking the lead on the press night guaranteed that it was packed long before Ms. Grace Warwick walked onto the stage.

Clare was just a pace behind, but as she wasn't an official member of the Crown's team, she slipped into a spare seat next to William near the back of the courtroom.

"Revenge in the name of your brother," had been her final instruction before Grace made her way to the front bench to join her father.

"Good morning, Grace," he said. "Do you have enough stones in your pouch to slay Goliath?"

"You seem to forget, Father," she replied, "that David only needed one stone."

"Then you'll have to make sure it strikes him squarely on the forehead and doesn't fly harmlessly over his shoulder, because I can tell you Faulkner will duck and dive in every direction as you hurl each new stone at him."

Booth Watson took his place at the other end of the bench, and the two QCs exchanged cursory nods, more out of convention than conviction. Grace glanced across at the dock to see her adversary glaring down at her. A shudder ran down her spine as their eyes locked and he licked his lips. She turned her attention to Clare, who gave her a thumbs-up sign.

"If that's Clare sitting next to William," said her father, "why don't you ask her to join us? After all, she probably knows as much about the case as we do."

"Thank you," said Grace, who turned and beckoned to her partner.

Clare, unable to hide how nervous she felt, moved cautiously to the front of the courtroom, and took a seat directly behind Sir Julian and Grace.

"Good morning, Clare," said Sir Julian. "Welcome to the home team. Don't hesitate to pass a note to Grace or me if you think we've missed something, because you can be sure we might well have."

"Thank you, Sir Julian," said Clare, taking a yellow pad and two pens out of her briefcase.

"All rise."

Mr. Justice Baverstock shuffled in, pleased to see his court so packed. The gallery above him was overflowing with eager onlookers, some leaning over the railing to get a better view of proceedings. His Lordship bowed, took his place in the high-backed chair, and waited for the jury to file into their places. He finally checked that all the actors were standing in the wings awaiting their entrances before he allowed the curtain to rise.

Faulkner was in the dock, the prosecution and defense teams were seated on the front bench—although he thought Ms. Warwick looked more nervous than the defendant—while the members of the press, pencils poised, were waiting impatiently for proceedings to begin. Once the jury had settled, the judge turned his attention to defense counsel, who was rearranging some papers.

"Good morning, Mr. Booth Watson. Are you ready to call your first witness?"

"I am indeed, m'lud. I call Mr. Miles Faulkner."

The judge looked surprised, and the press looked delighted, which only made Grace feel even more nervous. She had been prepared to declare war on Faulkner, but could she now defeat him in battle?

Faulkner stepped down from the dock and walked, almost swaggered, across the court before taking his place in the witness box. He placed his right hand on the Bible and read out the oath as if he had written it.

Mr. Booth Watson looked across at his client and smiled. "Can I ask you to state your full name and occupation for the record?"

"Miles Adam Faulkner, and I'm a farmer."

"May I begin, Mr. Faulkner, by asking you about the evening of May the seventeenth, 1986, when you held a dinner party for some friends at your country home, Limpton Hall, in Hampshire."

"Business colleagues as well as friends," said Faulkner, "some of whom I've known for over twenty years."

"And the purpose of the dinner party was purely social?"

"No, sir. We are a group of like-minded people who have been successful in our professional lives, and now feel the time has come to give something back to society."

"Highly commendable," said Booth Watson. The judge frowned. "Do you have any particular good causes in mind?"

"We are all lovers of the arts, in its many different forms, and feel strongly that culture can play a positive role in the education of young people."

"Particularly acting," murmured Sir Julian, "and being able to remember your lines when working from a prepared script."

"Most commendable," purred Booth Watson.

"Tread carefully, Mr. Booth Watson," said the judge wearily.

"At least the judge can see what they're up to," whispered Grace.

"Yes, but will the jury?" retorted her father.

"I do apologize, m'lud," said Booth Watson, not looking at all apologetic. "However, Mr. Faulkner, are you able to confirm that you recently donated two major works of art from your collection, worth several million pounds, to one of our national museums?"

"Yes, I sadly parted with a Rembrandt and a Rubens, but I've had so much pleasure from them in my lifetime, that it will give me even greater pleasure to know how many young people," he paused, "and not so young, are now able to enjoy them." He turned and smiled at the jury, just as Booth Watson had instructed him to do at that point, and was rewarded by one or two of them returning his salutation.

"Now, I'd like to turn to the one charge being made against you, namely that on the night of May the seventeenth, you were found to be in possession of twelve grams of cocaine for your personal use."

"Well, if I had been, it would have been enough to last for a year."

Clare wrote, *How does he know twelve grams would be enough to last for a year?* and passed the note to Grace.

"Remembering that you are under oath, Mr. Faulkner, could you tell the court if you have ever taken a controlled substance in your life?"

"Yes, sir. I once smoked a joint when I was at art school, but it made me feel sick, so I didn't bother to try another one."

"So, you deny that Mr. Adrian Heath went to your home on May the seventeenth and offered to sell you twelve grams of cocaine for eight hundred pounds?"

"I don't recall the exact sum, Mr. Booth Watson, but as Mr. Heath testified, it was for the finest Royal Beluga caviar, supplied by Fortnum and Mason."

Clare wrote down £20, underlined it, and passed it to Sir Julian, who smiled and nodded.

"And you'd never met Mr. Heath before that night?"

"No, never. I was horrified when I learned of his tragic death, and at the same time somewhat mystified."

"What are you getting at, Mr. Faulkner?" asked BW innocently.

"I was mystified as to how two Scotland Yard detectives just happened to arrive on the scene of the crime moments before the murder took place."

"Stop there, Mr. Faulkner," interrupted the judge. Looking across at the jury, he said, "You must dismiss those words from your minds."

"But they won't," whispered Sir Julian, "as Faulkner knows only too well."

"Move on, Mr. Booth Watson," said the judge firmly.

"Mr. Faulkner, do you have any explanation as to how twelve grams of cocaine ended up in a statue at your home?"

"None whatsoever. I refuse to believe that Superintendent Lamont or one of his men could have been involved in something as corrupt as planting drugs in the home of an innocent person, with the intention of securing a false conviction." He paused. "For a second time."

The judge was just about to intervene again when Faulkner added, "Mind you . . ." and paused again.

"Mind you?" said Booth Watson.

"I was shocked that when Superintendent Lamont arrested me, he said, 'I've been looking forward to this for a long time.'"

The judge waited for the uproar to die down, before he said, "Do you have any proof, Mr. Faulkner, that Superintendent Lamont said those words? Or are you just relying on your memory?"

"M'lud, I made a written note at the time of the arrest," interjected Booth Watson. "Ah, yes, here it is. 'I've been looking forward to this for some time.' Mr. Faulkner did get one word wrong."

The judge wrote the words down before saying, "Carry on, Mr. Booth Watson."

"Thank you, m'lud. Mr. Faulkner, you do not dispute that the police found two marijuana cigarettes and an Ecstasy tablet during the two hours they spent ransacking your home."

"That's correct. They found the Ecstasy tablet in the kitchen and the joints in the stables. Two members of staff admitted that they were theirs, and I had no choice but to let them go."

"Finally, Mr. Faulkner, can I ask what your attitude is to people who indulge in the use of illegal drugs?"

"I feel sorry for them. They're often sad, helpless individuals who are in desperate need of medical help. But when it comes to the dealers, I consider them vile, despicable people, and a stain on our society. They deserve to rot in hell."

"No more questions, m'lud."

"Thank you, Mr. Booth Watson. I think this would be an ideal time to take a break. Let's resume at two o'clock, when I shall call on Ms. Warwick to conduct her cross-examination of this witness. All rise."

21

"Do you think I could ask Dad to take my place?" said Grace, as she collapsed onto the nearest seat.

"Don't even think about it," said Clare. "Not least because he'd refuse, and would never take you seriously again."

"But you saw how Faulkner handled Booth Watson from the witness box. He was so assured and self-confident, and he had an answer to every one of his questions."

"Of course he did. He knew every question that was coming, even before Booth Watson had opened his mouth, so it wasn't difficult for him to have a well-rehearsed, apparently off-the-cuff, remark ready to impress the jury."

"But if he already knows about the smoking gun . . ."

"If he did, Booth Watson would have pulled the trigger this morning and blown a hole right through your cross-examination."

Grace was about to respond when her father walked into the corridor, clearly looking for his junior.

"I'm going to ask him to take my place," she whispered.

"We should be heading back in to court," said Sir Julian. "Everyone's waiting for you. Even your mother's sitting in the gallery."

"Grace has just been telling me how much she's looking forward to the challenge," said Clare.

"I'm glad to hear it," said Sir Julian, "although one shouldn't be overconfident on these occasions. First time at the Bailey is always a bit of an ordeal, but once you're on your feet . . ." Grace didn't move. "Still, we'd better get going. Can't afford to keep the judge waiting."

When Grace stood up, her legs almost gave way. Clare quickly took her arm and led her slowly but firmly back into the arena.

"Do you think Faulkner's as nervous as I am?" she asked, as Mr. Justice Baverstock entered the court and took his place.

"No," said Clare. "Which is why you'll kill him."

Once the court had settled, the judge looked expectantly down at the Crown's bench. Grace glanced at her father, but he didn't move. Booth Watson looked puzzled, while Faulkner glowered at her from the witness box.

"Stand up!" whispered Clare sharply.

Grace rose unsteadily to her feet. It didn't help that everyone in the courtroom was staring at her. She looked down at her carefully prepared list of questions, opened her mouth, but no words came out.

"When you're ready, Ms. Warwick," said the judge, giving her an encouraging smile. But still nothing.

"Get on with it!" Clare whispered from behind.

"Mr. Faulkner," she managed. "I won't be keeping you for too long—" a leaf she'd taken out of Booth Watson's book—"but I would like to go into a little more detail about your meeting with Mr. Heath on May the seventeenth, when, at your request, he went to your home to deliver a box of the finest Royal Beluga caviar."

Booth Watson clung on to the lapels of his gown, a prearranged signal that his client should remain silent.

"For which you paid him eight hundred pounds."

"That is correct," said Faulkner, feeling on safe ground.

"And indeed, Mr. Heath confirmed that amount when he testi-fied on the first day of this trial."

"He did indeed," said Faulkner, defiantly. "So, are you now finally going to admit that he was telling the truth?"

"When it comes to the eight hundred pounds, I accept that you were both telling the truth, but before I return to Mr. Heath's testimony, may I take you back to another witness, Dr. Ruth Lewis, who gave evidence yesterday."

"The government's lickspittle who was speaking on behalf of the Crown?" said Faulkner, ignoring Booth Watson, who had warned him to keep his answers to the barest statements of fact and make sure not to insult anyone.

"Dr. Lewis told the court that the street price of twelve grams of ninety-two percent pure cocaine would also be around eight hundred pounds. Didn't you find that a bit of a coincidence?"

"No, I did not. Once she knew the amount I'd paid Heath, she conveniently used it to bolster her case. Now that's what I would call a coincidence, if it wasn't for the fact that she's working for you."

That stone having flown harmlessly over Faulkner's shoulder, Grace selected another one from her heavy pouch.

"Are you suggesting, Mr. Faulkner, that Dr. Lewis made up the figure of eight hundred pounds in order to mislead the court?"

"Your words, not mine," said Faulkner, looking rather pleased with himself.

"Then I'm bound to ask, if you doubted her veracity at the time, why your distinguished counsel didn't dispute her findings? In fact, as I'm sure you will recall, Mr. Booth Watson chose not to cross-examine Dr. Lewis, which would rather suggest that he accepted her evidence without question."

Booth Watson was now tugging his lapels furiously, causing Clare to scribble another note, which she quickly passed to Sir Julian. He hadn't noticed what Booth Watson had been up to until then, but immediately turned to stare pointedly at defense counsel, who reluctantly folded his arms.

"Is it also another coincidence that twelve grams was the amount of pure cocaine the police found inside the statue at your home?"

"He knew the exact amount to plant that could be bought for eight hundred pounds," said Faulkner, pointing at Lamont.

"I don't think so, Mr. Faulkner. Mr. Heath left your home with the money before anyone else knew how much was involved—except you."

"As I said earlier, Ms. Warwick, I can't be sure of the exact sum I paid Mr. Heath."

This time Faulkner hadn't ducked in time, but he stared defiantly at junior counsel, as if the blow hadn't landed.

"Mr. Faulkner, a twenty-pound note was found on the desk in your study."

"Which Dr. Lewis confirmed had no traces of cocaine on it, if I remember correctly."

"I wasn't going to suggest otherwise, Mr. Faulkner," said Grace. "However, I'm glad you agree that it is part of the evidence already accepted by both sides, and, indeed, your signature is on the list of items taken from your home by the police on the night of your arrest. But let's be sure, shall we? M'lud, may I ask the defendant to study the note in question and confirm that it was the one found on his desk?"

The judge nodded and the clerk extracted a small cellophane bag from the bundle of evidence, walked across to the box and handed it to the defendant.

"So it's the note you found on my desk. Big deal," said Faulkner after glancing at it briefly. "What does that prove?"

"Would you read out the serial number of the note to the court?"

Booth Watson was on his feet unusually quickly. "M'lud, is my client to be subjected to the latest parlor game?"

"I suspect we are about to find out, Mr. Booth Watson," said Mr. Justice Baverstock, before turning to the defendant and saying, "Please read out the note's serial number."

Faulkner hesitated for some time before saying, "KA73863743."

"Thank you," said Grace. "I will now ask the clerk of the court to show you the packet of twenty-pound notes that the police found on Mr. Heath when they apprehended him soon after he left your house."

Once again Booth Watson was on his feet. "We only have the police's word that these are the notes in question."

"I agree with you," said Grace, giving Booth Watson a warm smile. "But if Mr. Faulkner would be kind enough to read out the serial numbers of the notes in question, we can then be certain this was the money he handed over to Mr. Heath."

Faulkner looked imploringly at his counsel, but Booth Watson's arms were folded.

"We are all waiting, Mr. Faulkner," said the judge.

Faulkner began reading out the serial numbers. "KA73863744, KA73863745, KA73863746 . . ."

"If you look at the note found on your desk," said Grace, "you'll find it is KA73864543. Making eight hundred pounds in total."

William couldn't help feeling rather pleased with himself.

"What does that prove? I've already told you I gave Heath eight hundred pounds for twelve jars of caviar."

"I'm so glad you've raised the subject of the caviar, Mr. Faulkner. Last Saturday, I visited Fortnum and Mason in Piccadilly, and purchased a small jar of caviar." She produced it with a flourish from below the bench, and held it up for all to see, then paused for a moment before saying, "Allow me to read the description on the label. 'Finest Beluga caviar. Will complement any meal. Contains two portions.' I confess, Mr. Faulkner, that I considered the price a little extravagant, but the manager assured me that it is a top-of-the-range product and is enjoyed by Fortnum and Mason's most discerning customers. And as Mr. Heath told us, you're only interested in top of the range, even if you're not one of Fortnum and Mason's most discerning customers."

"M'lud," said Booth Watson, once again rising to his feet, "I am sure we are all enjoying this little conjuring trick performed by junior counsel. However, as her recent purchase was not offered in the bundle of evidence, can I presume that you will rule it as inadmissible?"

"He's worked it out," Sir Julian whispered to Grace. "Let's hope Faulkner hasn't."

Faulkner kept staring at him, a puzzled look on his face.

"And if not, may I request a short break in proceedings, so I can consult my client?" added Booth Watson.

"I had a feeling he'd be consulting you," said the judge. "Ms. Warwick, may I see the evidence before I make my decision?"

"Most certainly, My Lord," said Grace, producing three more jars of caviar from below the bench and handing them to the clerk of the court, who in turn gave one to the judge, one to Booth Watson, and the third to the defendant.

After the judge had read the label and studied the jar, he said, "The jury should be allowed to examine the evidence before we continue."

"As Your Lordship pleases," said Grace, producing two more jars and feeling relieved that she'd taken Clare's advice and bought a box of six. She handed them to the clerk, who passed them to the foreman of the jury.

"Please continue, Ms. Warwick," said Mr. Justice Baverstock once the jury had considered the new evidence.

"Mr. Faulkner, can I ask you how many people sat down for dinner at your home on the night of May the seventeenth?"

"Ten, including me, as has already been stated several times."

"And they all enjoyed a portion of caviar, before moving on to the main course?"

"Without exception. In fact, one or two of them had a second helping."

"Did they indeed?"

Booth Watson once again began tugging repeatedly at the lapels of his gown, despite the fact that Sir Julian was staring at him.

"I only ask, Mr. Faulkner, because a single jar of Royal Beluga caviar, like the one you have in your hands, enough for two portions, is on sale at Fortnum and Mason for three hundred forty pounds. But to be sure, I asked Fortnum's manager, a Mr. Nightingale, how much I would need if I were holding a dinner party for ten. He recommended seven hundred and fifty grams." She looked directly at the jury as she said, "Not twelve grams, which would just about fill a teaspoon."

The trap had been set, and Grace waited for Faulkner to step into it. But at last Booth Watson had caught his client's attention, and he remained silent.

"You won't be surprised to learn, Mr. Faulkner, that I then asked Mr. Nightingale how much seven hundred and fifty grams of caviar would cost—enough for ten people. He told me seventeen hundred pounds, but said he would throw in the biscuits for free."

A little laughter broke out in the gallery, but the judge's frown ensured that no one in the body of the court joined in.

"M'lud," said Grace, "Mr. Nightingale will be happy to appear before the court to confirm these figures, but you may feel that won't be necessary, as Mr. Faulkner has already sworn under oath that his chef served ten portions of caviar for himself and his guests that night, on silver platters, and that one or two of them enjoyed a second helping."

An outbreak of chattering broke out in the courtroom. Grace took a deep breath and waited until she once again had everyone's attention.

"I accept, Mr. Faulkner, that when it comes to the price of cocaine, you are clearly well informed, as you made clear when you said under oath that if the twelve grams found in your home had been for your personal use, it would have been enough for a year. I also acknowledge that you enjoy a reputation as a brilliant dealmaker. But I doubt if even you could have talked Fortnum and Mason into selling seventeen hundred pounds' worth of their finest Beluga caviar for eight hundred pounds." Grace smiled at Faulkner. The trap had been sprung, and she now felt confident he could not escape. However, she still had one final question.

"Do you think Mr. Heath was telling the truth when he said, 'The goods I picked up from Fortnum's that morning at Mr. Faulkner's request were a dozen jars of the finest Royal Beluga caviar'?"

Faulkner looked as if he wanted to answer back, but no words came out of his mouth.

"Mr. Nightingale will also confirm that he was on duty at the store that morning, and the only dozen jars of caviar that were purchased were from a representative of the Queen Mother."

Faulkner's lips were now pursed, his cheeks flushed, and he had to grip the edge of the witness box to stop himself shaking.

"Dare I ask, Mr. Faulkner, if the Queen Mother was one of your dinner guests at Limpton Hall that night?"

This time the judge made no attempt to quell the laughter that followed, and even allowed himself a smile.

Grace waited for complete silence before she turned to face the jury and said, "No more questions, m'lud."

She collapsed on the bench, exhausted, as the rest of the home team gathered around to congratulate her.

When they returned home that night, Grace told Clare that of the many plaudits heaped on her following her cross-examination, none could compare with overhearing her father telling an elderly colleague, "She's my daughter, you know."

◄○►

After the judge had called on leading counsel to make their closing remarks, a suddenly revived and reinvigorated Sir Julian rose from his place and delivered a damning indictment of the accused to a spellbound jury.

The price of caviar was mentioned on more than one occasion, and he ended by reminding them that the accused seemed to be well aware of the cost of twelve grams of pure cocaine, even if he had no idea of the price of the finest caviar. He threw in for good measure Mr. Nightingale's evidence concerning the Queen Mother, which Booth Watson didn't dispute. By the time he sat down, Sir Julian was in no doubt that the jury was well capable of working out who had been responsible for hiding the drugs in Faulkner's statue on the night in question, and it certainly wasn't his son.

Booth Watson didn't cut quite such a convincing figure, as he tried gallantly to defend his client's credibility. Rembrandt and Rubens received several honorable mentions, whereas Fortnum and Mason and Mr. Nightingale were not referred to. He described Miles Faulkner as a good and honorable man, who had served both the nation and his local community with distinction. He suggested that the tragic death of Adrian Heath had robbed his client of the opportunity of a fair trial, and told the jury they should keep that in mind when considering their verdict, because if they were not convinced of Mr. Faulkner's guilt beyond reasonable doubt, they must release him from the dreadful prospect of prison so that he could continue his charitable works on behalf of his fellow men.

Mr. Justice Baverstock's summing up was both thorough and impartial, although he did point out that if the jury came to the conclusion that it was Faulkner who had hidden the cocaine in the statue, it could clearly not be regarded as being for his own "recreational" use in the privacy of his home, as he himself had confirmed it would be enough to last him a year. However, he added, the Crown had failed to provide any evidence to show that Mr. Faulkner had taken an illegal substance in the past, and the presence of the twenty-pound note found in his study did not prove that it had been used for snorting cocaine. If, after considering all the evidence, they were not convinced of Mr. Faulkner's guilt beyond reasonable doubt, they should return a verdict of not guilty. On the other hand, if they were not persuaded by Mr. Faulkner's explanation as to how the twelve grams of cocaine ended up in his statue, it was their duty to deliver a guilty verdict.

"Your final decision should be based only on the evidence you have heard in this courtroom, and should not be influenced by the opinions of others, however close they may be to you, because they have not had the benefit of considering all the evidence presented in this court. Remember, you are the sole arbiters of justice in this case. Please take your time before reaching a verdict."

He then invited the seven men and five women to retire to the jury room to consider their verdict. The court fell silent as the bailiff led them out.

"Now we must all endure the worst part of any trial," said Sir

Julian. "The interminable wait before we learn the jury's verdict. My father always spent the time playing chess with his opponent." He glanced across at Booth Watson, and said, "Fortunately, he doesn't play the game."

"What do you think the odds are of the jury coming down in our favor?" asked Clare.

"Trying to second-guess a jury is a fool's game," said Sir Julian. "Let's just hope they're all enjoying the caviar while they consider their verdict, because they'll soon discover that a couple of jars wouldn't be enough for ten people, let alone twelve."

"What do you think of our chances, BW?" asked Faulkner as he stepped out of the dock and joined his counsel.

"No idea. One jury will go one way, one another. But they're certain to take their time before they reach a verdict, so you'll have to be patient for a change."

"Then why don't you join me for dinner at the Savoy? I've already booked a table."

"Thank you, Miles," said Booth Watson, but he didn't add, *Don't bother to book a table for tomorrow night.*

◄○►

"How much do you think they're worth, Mr. Davage?" asked Christina, as they made their way back into the drawing room.

"It's difficult to put an accurate figure on such an important collection," said the managing director of Christie's, "but I'm confident they would fetch at least thirty million, possibly more. Not least because your husband has been in touch with all the leading auction houses to let them know that if any of his pictures should come under the hammer, he's to be informed immediately."

"That's good news," said Christina, as she poured him another coffee.

"If you are considering putting the collection up for auction, Mrs. Faulkner, Christie's would of course be honored to conduct the sale."

"Thank you. But I won't be able to make a final decision until I know the outcome of my husband's trial."

"Of course," said Mr. Davage. "We all hope and expect your husband will be found not guilty, and be able to return home with his reputation restored."

"Not all of us," said Christina, as the front doorbell rang. "Good timing," she said, rising from her place. "That must be Mr. Nealon, who's come to value the house."

22

"Will all those involved in the case of the Crown versus Faulkner please return to court number one, as the jury is about to return?"

Sir Julian was doing up his fly buttons. Grace and Clare were having a coffee in the barristers' room. Mr. Booth Watson was writing an opinion on insider trading for a client in Guernsey, while Miles Faulkner was exchanging phone numbers with a woman he'd just met in the corridor.

They all began to make their separate ways back to court number one to hear the jury's verdict. The journalists didn't care which way the decision went. *The Evening Standard* already had two headlines set in store: BANGED UP, and ESCAPED AGAIN, and two articles to go with them, both written by the same journalist.

Faulkner returned to the dock, while everyone else took their places and waited for the judge to reappear. An anticipatory silence fell over the court as Mr. Justice Baverstock made his entrance. Once he was seated, he nodded to the bailiff to indicate that the jury could return.

All eyes were fixed on the seven men and five women as they filed back into the jury box for the last time. They had chosen a matronly looking middle-aged woman as their foreman. She'd squeezed into a tightly fitted suit, wore no jewelry, and little makeup. Sir Julian studied her closely, but could deduce little from her calm and professional demeanor. A headmistress or a hospital matron, certainly someone used to making decisions.

Once they had settled, the judge nodded to the clerk of the court. He rose from his place, took a pace forward, and faced the jury.

"Will the foreman please rise?" The middle-aged lady stood up, and if she was at all nervous, there was no sign of it. "Have you reached a verdict on which you are all agreed?" the clerk inquired.

"We have, My Lord," she said, looking up at the judge.

"Do you find the defendant guilty, or not guilty, of being in possession of an illegal substance, namely twelve grams of cocaine?"

Faulkner held his breath. Grace closed her eyes, while William stared directly at the accused.

"Guilty."

Hawksby and Lamont shook hands while several journalists sprang from their places and quickly left the court in search of the nearest phone. Clare hugged Grace as William made his way toward the Crown bench to join them. But the majority of those in court remained in their places, impatiently awaiting the judge's final pronouncement.

"Will the prisoner please stand?" said the clerk once a semblance of order had been restored.

Faulkner rose unsteadily to his feet and gripped the sides of the dock, as he waited to learn his fate.

"This has been a most unusual case, for several reasons," Mr. Justice Baverstock began, "and I will require a little time to consider its full implications before I pass sentence. I would therefore ask all interested parties to return to this court at ten o'clock tomorrow morning, when I will pass sentence."

"My Lord," said Booth Watson, rising from his place. "Can I assume that my client will remain on bail overnight?"

Grace was about to leap up and object, when His Lordship said, "No, you cannot, Mr. Booth Watson. He will be remanded in custody pending sentencing, because if I were to grant your request, I am not convinced your client would reappear in court tomorrow morning to hear my judgment."

Booth Watson sank back in his place without further comment.

"Take him down," said the clerk of the court.

Two policemen stepped forward, gripped Faulkner firmly by the arms, and led him downstairs to the cells.

"All rise."

William watched as Faulkner disappeared out of sight and could only wonder what must be going through his mind.

"Congratulations, Grace," said Sir Julian. "I couldn't have done it without you."

"Thank you, Father. And there are several reasons why I couldn't have done it without you."

They both smiled.

"I fear, young lady, that it will not be long before you take silk, and I will no longer be able to call upon your services as my junior. And thank you, too, Clare, even if I suspect that in future you'll be known as Caviar Clare. But congratulations to both of you on a famous victory."

"How long do you think the sentence will be?" asked Clare, as they made their way out of court.

"Pick a number," said Sir Julian, "and you'll get it wrong."

◄○►

"I don't suppose there's the slightest chance you could influence the judge, BW?" said Faulkner, as he sat down on the thin, hard mattress. "You managed it last time."

"No, I didn't. It was the judge who influenced you," Booth

Watson reminded him as he pulled up a chair. "I have hinted to the Criminal Appeal Office that as our prisons are so overcrowded they might consider a heavy fine more appropriate than a custodial sentence in this case, but so far the idea has fallen on deaf ears."

"If only I'd taken your advice, BW, and refused to be cross-examined, we'd be having dinner at the Savoy this evening."

This was one of those rare occasions when Booth Watson didn't offer an opinion, personal or professional.

◄○►

"Four million?" repeated Christina.

"Possibly more," said Mr. Nealon. "I have two or three clients on my books who've been looking for a property like this for some time, and once it's been advertised in all the glossy magazines and journals, who knows how much it might fetch?"

"That sounds promising," said Christina.

"So, would you like me to put it on the market, Mrs. Faulkner?"

"Yes, but not until I'm no longer Mrs. Faulkner, which shouldn't be too long now."

◄○►

"All rise."

Mr. Justice Baverstock entered his fiefdom for the last time in the case of the *Crown v. Faulkner.* He placed a thick red-leather folder marked EIIR on the bench in front of him, sat down, and adjusted his red robes before looking down on the court and waiting for everyone to settle. He placed a pair of half-moon spectacles on the end of his nose and nodded to the clerk.

"Will the prisoner please rise?"

Faulkner stood up and faced His Lordship. It was clear for all to see that he hadn't slept the previous night.

The judge opened the red folder, looked down at his handwritten words, and began to deliver his judgment.

"There is no doubt in my mind, Mr. Faulkner, that you are a ruthless, unprincipled, and amoral man, who lacks any sense of decency or decorum, and who, because of your wealth and status, feels you are above the law. With this in mind, and remembering the seriousness of the offense, you are sentenced to serve six years in prison."

Grace wanted to leap in the air, but somehow managed to control herself, while several of those around her could not. From the look on Sir Julian's face it was clear that he did consider his daughter's behavior appropriate, but didn't comment.

"But, given the circumstances," continued the judge once he'd regained everyone's attention, "I have decided to suspend the sentence and fine you one million pounds, over and above any legal costs involved in this trial, which you will also bear."

Faulkner wanted to leap in the air and cry hallelujah, although he was surprised to see his advocate didn't appear to share his relief but continued to sit there, looking po-faced.

"However," the judge continued, as he turned a page, "I have been reminded you are currently serving a four-year suspended sentence for a previous offense of fraud. Mr. Justice Nourse, who presided over the trial, made it clear that should you commit another crime during your probationary period, however minor, you would automatically be sentenced to serve four years in a maximum-security prison with no remission, and as I have no authority to override that decision, you will now carry out that sentence."

Faulkner collapsed back into his chair, and placed his head in his hands.

"And because of that previous judgment, I am advised by the

Crown Prosecution Service I have been left with no choice but to add the six years I have proscribed to the original four, so that your sentence will now be for ten years."

Mr. Justice Baverstock closed his red folder and once again nodded to the clerk of the court. The uproar was such that few people heard the clerk say, "Take the prisoner down."

—◦—

Sir Julian uncorked a bottle of champagne and began to pour glasses for his victorious team.

"How many jars of caviar did you manage to retrieve?" asked Clare.

"The jury polished off both of theirs," said Grace. "Claimed they needed to sample the evidence. Booth Watson's has gone missing, and I don't expect to see Faulkner's again. But the judge kindly returned his."

"That's going to cost you more than you've earned as my junior on this case," said Julian, handing her a glass of champagne.

"Won't the DPP cover the cost?" said Clare. "After all, we did win the case, despite their learned advice."

"Not a hope. But the good news is that Faulkner will have to stump up the Crown's costs, as the judge ruled that all the legal expenses were to be paid by him."

Glasses were immediately raised in an unlikely toast to "Miles Faulkner."

"And a toast to Grace, who secured the verdict," said Sir Julian, raising his glass a second time.

"To Grace!" they all cried, following suit.

"Coupled with the name of Adrian Heath," said William, "who supplied us with the vital clue that brought the bastard down."

"Adrian Heath," they all repeated, as they raised their glasses a third time.

◄○►

"Good news," said Barry Nealon. "We've had an offer of five million for Limpton Hall."

"Five million?" repeated Christina in disbelief. "But that's way above the asking price."

"It most certainly is," said Nealon, "and the buyer's solicitors have offered to pay a deposit of half a million if you'd be willing to take the property off the market immediately."

"What do you recommend?"

"I would advise you to accept the offer. Not least because the buyer has agreed that if he doesn't complete the purchase within thirty days, he will forfeit his deposit, so I can't see a downside."

"Who's the 'he'?"

"I have no idea," said Nealon. "The transaction has been conducted by his solicitor."

◄○►

Within a week of his arrival at Pentonville, prisoner number 4307 had been moved into a single cell. After a fortnight, he had his own table in the canteen, and no one else was allowed to join him unless they were invited. After three weeks, he was taken off latrine-cleaning duties and appointed an orderly in the library, where he wasn't troubled too much by the other inmates. By the end of the month, he had his own time slot in the gym, with a personal trainer who charged by the hour. By the time another month had passed, he'd read *War and Peace, A Tale of Two Cities, The Count of Monte Cristo,* and lost a stone. He'd never been fitter, or better read.

During the third month, the *Financial Times* was delivered to his cell just after eight every morning, along with a cup of tea, not a mug. But his biggest coup took a little longer to achieve: access to his own phone for fifteen minutes a day, thirty on Sundays.

His weekend visitors—he was only allowed two, like every other inmate—were not friends or relatives but business associates, as he had no time to waste on frivolous matters. Once a fortnight he was entitled to spend an hour with his legal adviser. He was the only one who could afford such a luxury on a regular basis. He instructed Booth Watson to put in an appeal for a retrial on the grounds that the original trial should have been thrown out as Adrian Heath was unable to give further evidence. Appeal rejected. His second appeal was against the length of his sentence, on the grounds that it was excessive for such a minor offense. He hadn't yet heard back from the CPS. He then applied to be moved to an open prison, on the grounds that he had no history of violence. This, too, was rejected. He finally wrote to the Home Secretary, demanding that his sentence be halved for good behavior. He didn't even receive an acknowledgment of his letter.

He had surprised Booth Watson at their first meeting, a rare feat, when he instructed him to put in an offer for Limpton Hall, with a solicitor he'd never used before.

"I didn't realize it was on the market," admitted Booth Watson.

"It isn't," Faulkner had replied. "And it will be off the market by next week. I also want you to get in touch with Mr. Davage at Christie's, and make it clear you will be bidding for any of my pictures should they come up for auction."

"What makes you think she'll put them up for sale?"

"Christina won't have any choice in the matter," said Faulkner. "If she carries out her plan to buy the dream property in Florida, she's bound to put her account in the red."

"And the pictures?"

"The walls of Limpton Hall will be empty long before then, along with her bank account."

Booth Watson was a man who knew when to stop asking questions he didn't want to know the answer to. He was relieved when SO Rose returned to tell him their hour was up.

If the prison authorities had been more diligent, they would have taken a greater interest in 4307's reading matter, and in one particular prisoner who regularly walked around the yard with him—and the offense he'd been convicted for.

—◦—

"Sign here, here, and here," said Sir Julian, as he handed Mrs. Faulkner his pen.

"So, it's finally all over," said Christina once the ink had dried. "Frankly I'm surprised Miles agreed to part with his precious paintings, considering he's always loved them more than me. Still, he'll be able to buy them all back when they come up for auction, although I'll make sure they don't come cheap."

Sir Julian raised an eyebrow.

"I'll have a bidder in the room making sure they all go way above the auctioneer's estimate," explained Christina.

"In which case you will be breaking the law, Mrs. Faulkner, which I would strongly advise against."

"How come?"

"You would have formed a cartel with no other purpose than to force up the price for your own advantage, and, be assured, your husband will have already worked that one out."

"Ex-husband," she said, looking at the recently signed papers.

"Not until he's also signed the annulment," said Sir Julian.

"What choice has he been left with, now he's locked up in prison?"

"With hours to think about little else except what you're up to. And nothing would please him more than for you to end up in jail for breaking a law you didn't even know existed. In fact, I suspect this would be one of those rare occasions when Booth Watson would be happy to appear on behalf of the Crown."

"Then I'll have to be satisfied with what they raise at auction."

"I think that might be advisable, Mrs. Faulkner, and don't forget you have already had an offer of five million for Limpton Hall, and I've had it confirmed that the five hundred thousand pounds has been deposited with the other side's solicitors."

"Which will make it possible for me to put down a deposit on my dream house in Florida on the same terms."

"When are you thinking of moving to the States?"

"As soon as the paintings have been sold. Christie's have valued the collection at around thirty million, and will be picking them up next week, ready for their spring sale. The timing couldn't be better."

"Are you confident that they're all originals, and not copies?" asked Sir Julian. "Something your ex is well capable of arranging."

"I'm certain. They've all been authenticated by the relevant experts at Christie's. Otherwise I would never have signed the divorce papers."

"And where will you live once Limpton Hall is sold?"

"In our apartment in Eaton Square. It's only got a few months left on the lease, but that should be more than enough to see me through before I take up residence in Florida."

"Then everything is settled, unless there is anything else you need to seek my advice on?"

"Yes. I have a gift for your daughter-in-law, or to be more accurate, the Fitzmolean. It's my way of saying thank you for all your family has done for me."

She picked up a Sainsbury's carrier bag by her side, took out a small painting, and held it up for Sir Julian to admire. He stared in awe at *The White Lace Collar* by Vermeer, the masterpiece Beth had raved about after having tea with Christina at Limpton Hall.

"That's extremely generous of you," he said. "But are you sure you're willing to part with such a valuable painting?"

"Quite sure," said Christina. "After all, there are seventy-two more where that came from."

◄○►

The phone was ringing on his side of the bed, but he didn't manage to grab it before a heavily pregnant Beth had turned over and groaned.

"Sorry," he whispered, as he picked it up. "Who's this?"

"Hawksby."

"Good morning, sir."

"Get yourself to Battersea heliport as quickly as possible, DS Warwick. A car will be with you in a few minutes' time. Don't keep me waiting."

"Anything I ought to know, sir?"

"It's snowing," said the Hawk before the line went dead.

William put the phone down and quickly threw on yesterday's clothes, before kissing Beth, which elicited a second groan, as he headed for the door.

"Where are you off to at this time in the morning, Caveman?"

"I wish I knew," he said, and had closed the bedroom door before she could ask any more questions he couldn't answer. As he opened the front door a squad car was pulling up outside.

"Morning, sarge," said a familiar voice as the car drove off through the falling snow.

"Morning, Danny. Any idea what's going on?"

"Above my pay grade. All I know is that I've got to get you to Battersea heliport sharpish, where you'll meet up with Commander Hawksby."

Danny sped off down Royal Hospital Road, blue light flashing, but no siren. "Wouldn't want to wake the neighbors, would we?"

"Or Beth," said William, as he thought about his pregnant wife. Not long now.

There wasn't much traffic on the road at that time in the morning, so Danny didn't need to perform his usual box of tricks, though William still had to cling on to the dashboard whenever he took a corner, as if they were on a vast skid pad.

"I bet the Hawk's already standing there waiting for us," said William, as they shot across Battersea Bridge and took a sharp left.

"Sitting, actually, sarge, in the back of the helicopter."

"Of course he is," said William, as they passed through the front gate of the heliport. He jumped out of the car as it skidded to a halt, nearly losing his balance as he sloshed through the snow to the waiting helicopter. He dived into the back.

"Good morning, sir," William said, as he strapped himself in.

"A perfect morning for what I have in mind, DS Warwick," responded the commander as the rotor blades began to spin. "As you're about to find out."

"Where are we going?"

"Wrong question. It's not where we're going that's important, but what we're looking for. So keep your eyes peeled."

"Any clues?" asked William, as the helicopter rose into the sky, and he looked back over his shoulder to see the House of Commons covered in snow, looking like a Christmas card.

"Not if you're hoping for your next promotion."

The helicopter banked left and headed southeast, leaving Westminster behind them.

"Any observations you want to share with me?" asked the Hawk after a few minutes.

"We're flying over Wandsworth, Southwark, and Brixton," said William. "So we must be looking for tower blocks, and one in particular?"

"You're halfway there," said the commander, as the pilot made a smooth 180-degree turn, before heading back toward Brixton. "So, what's unusual about this morning?"

"It's snowing heavily," said William, but didn't add, *so what?*

"You're so sharp, DS Warwick, you could peel an apple."

They flew over Battersea Bridge for a second time, but William was still none the wiser, although the commander clearly knew exactly what he was looking for, as his eyes remained focused on the buildings below.

After the pilot had turned back for a third time and took a slightly different route, the Hawk suddenly declared, "There it is, staring us both in the face."

"There's what?" said William, as the helicopter swooped down to hover for a moment above one particular tower block.

"Take a closer look, DS Warwick, and tell me what you see. Or more important, what you don't see."

William stared through the falling snow and then suddenly let out a yelp of triumph. "Got it!"

"What have you got, DS Warwick?"

"The roof that isn't covered in snow."

"And what does that tell you?"

"Has to be above a drugs factory where they're growing cannabis."

"Why?"

"Because the rising heat from the massive arc lights inside is melting the snow the moment it settles."

"In one. So now we've discovered where Rashidi's slaughter is, we can move on to the more difficult challenge of how we get inside without him realizing we know his most closely guarded secret."

A job for your UCO, thought William, but didn't offer his opinion as the helicopter headed back to Battersea. If he had mentioned it, the commander would have agreed with him, although he wouldn't have told him he had an appointment with Marlboro Man later that morning.

◄○►

"What's it going to cost me?"

"In and out, clean job, five grand cash should do it," his fellow prisoner said, as they continued their slow perambulation around the yard. "But it won't be possible if anyone else is on the premises."

"Then it will have to be on a Friday," said Faulkner. "That's the housekeeper's day off when she visits her mother in Sevenoaks. They have lunch together and go to the local cinema, before she spends the evening at her mother's house. She's rarely back at the Hall much before eleven."

"You seem remarkably clued-in about her movements, remembering we're banged up in here."

"Although my ex-wife has sacked most of the staff, she's kept my chauffeur on. He's currently receiving two pay packets a week, and I pay both of them."

"How do I get paid?"

"Makins, who used to be my butler, will be waiting at the Hall next Saturday evening. He has another job to do for me during the day, so if your man turns up at around seven, he'll receive the first thousand."

"And the rest?"

"You'll get that when it's clear for all to see that the job's been done."

They shook hands. The only way a contract can be closed in prison. A long buzzer sounded, and the prisoners began to drift out of the yard and make their way slowly back to their cells.

"And the young man?" said Faulkner before they went their separate ways. "Don't forget we'll need his services the night before."

"Got the ideal person for the assignment. But that will cost you another grand."

"I'll need to make a phone call this evening," Faulkner murmured as he passed the duty officer.

"No problem, Mr. Faulkner. I'll come and get you around seven o'clock."

23

Christina picked him up in Tramp, fed him, plied him with champagne, and then took him back to her flat in Eaton Square. She knew it ought to be the other way around, but she was no longer twenty-two or thirty-two, and it wouldn't be long before she was forty-two. When she woke the following morning, she was surprised to find Justin was still there, looking just as appetizing as he had the night before. Bless him.

She slipped out from under the covers and made her way into the bathroom, where she tried to remove a few years with the help of a little makeup and a dab of perfume, before returning to bed to pretend she'd just woken. She began to stroke the inside of his leg, slowly arousing him, until he could no longer control himself. After they'd made love for the third time—or was it the fourth?—they enjoyed a long bath and an even longer breakfast, over which she discovered Justin didn't have a job. But then why would one bother when you were that good looking?

Christina began to wonder if she could hold on to him until she moved to Florida. As he was leaving he asked if she could lend him a fiver for a taxi. She gave him ten, and they agreed to meet for dinner that night. She checked her watch, aware she'd have to get moving if she was going to make it to Limpton Hall by eleven, when she would be overseeing the loading of the paintings by Christie's.

As she left the flat, the chauffeur saluted and opened the back door of the Bentley so she could get in. Eddie climbed behind the wheel and they set off for Hampshire.

Once the pictures had been collected by Christie's, Christina intended to ask Partridge's in Bond Street to value the furniture, as she had no intention of taking anything to Florida that would remind her of Miles. For a moment she almost felt sorry for him. But only for a moment. Ten years was more than she'd expected, but no more than she'd prayed for.

An hour later, as they were passing through the village of Limpton, her mind drifted back to Justin, and where she would take him to dinner, when a police car overtook them. Annabel's was the obvious choice. Not much chance of him picking up another woman there. They would either be accounted for or out of his financial league. And then she realized he hadn't given her his phone number, and she didn't know his surname.

Eddie turned left off the main road and down a lane that led to only one house, Limpton Hall. That was when she first saw the smoke. There was no one on duty as they drove past the gatehouse. She'd sacked the guard, the butler, the cook, and the gardener some time ago, retaining only a housekeeper and the chauffeur to look after her on the few occasions she needed to visit her country home.

Long before they'd reached the end of the drive Christina began screaming hysterically. Deep orange flames were leaping into the air and spitting their way through thick black clouds of smoke. It was clear that the three fire engines in attendance were fighting a hopeless battle.

Four hours later, despite the firefighters' gallant efforts, all that was left of Limpton Hall was a large pile of rubble and smoldering ash, while a vast black cloud obscured the morning sun. Christina hadn't noticed that Eddie didn't seem surprised.

◄○►

"Are you growing a beard, Caveman?" asked Beth after supper that evening. She leaned across the kitchen table and stroked the stubble on his chin.

"Depends how long my present assignment lasts."

"Not for too much longer, I hope," she said, getting up to stack the dishwasher, while he cleared the table. "What have we got planned for this evening? Assuming you aren't called out at a moment's notice to save the world?"

"I was hoping a beautiful damsel would gently stroke my forehead while I watched *Match of the Day*."

"Think again, Caveman. I've already chosen a film that I'm sure will suit your lowbrow tastes."

"Lots of sexy women?"

"No, but the men are dishy," she said, as she closed the dishwasher and began to lay the table for breakfast.

"Dare I ask?"

"*The Guns of Navarone*, starring David Niven and Gregory Peck," said Beth, as they strolled through to the living room.

"I would have preferred Kerry Dixon scoring the winning goal against Arsenal."

"Well then, you're out of luck. But before David Niven strokes my forehead, there's something a little more serious I have to discuss with you."

"That sounds ominous."

"There's a major appointment coming up at the Fitzmolean."

"Will you be applying?"

"No, I'm not qualified for the job. But you are," Beth said as she lowered herself gently onto the sofa and took his hand.

"Enlighten me, as the Hawk would say."

"The Fitz is looking for a new head of security."

"Sounds exciting," said William, stifling a yawn.

"What's exciting about it is that the hours are nine to five, five days a week, with three weeks' holiday a year. And the clincher is that the pay's better than you're getting as a detective sergeant with the Met."

"Sounds to me like a job for a retired officer who wants to supplement his pension."

"I knew you'd say that. But at least promise me you'll think about it."

"I already have. Now can we watch the film?"

"Not yet, because I have another piece of news that's not quite so pleasing."

"You'd be my boss?"

"I already am. Be serious for a moment," she said, not letting go of his hand. "Christina called just before you got back this evening. She sounded in a dreadful state. Said she needed to see me urgently. My first thought was she must have changed her mind about giving us the Vermeer."

"It wouldn't have been mine," said William. "But then you've always been a glass half-empty person."

"But it's the official unveiling next week, just in case you've forgotten."

"I expect she's just overreacting to something her ex-husband has done," he said, as he switched on the TV. "But what exactly can he get up to while he's in jail?"

"I don't know, but she did sound desperate," Beth said, as the opening titles began to roll. "And I wouldn't know what to do if she—"

"Shh," said William, as she settled in his arms. "This looks quite promising."

Beth was beginning to enjoy the company of David Niven and Gregory Peck, even if William had fallen asleep, when, to her surprise, he suddenly sat bolt upright and said, "Why didn't I think of that?"

"Think of what?" said Beth.

"How to get into a building without being seen."

◄○►

They'd agreed to meet at the Fitzmolean at nine the following morning, which only made Beth more apprehensive. Nine o'clock was not an hour she normally associated with Christina. It didn't help that Christina burst into tears the moment she saw a picture draped in a velvet cloth hanging in the entrance hall. She began to tell Beth in fits and starts why she needed to see her so urgently. Beth began to wonder if she'd seen *The White Lace Collar* for the last time.

"He's done what?" she said, unable to believe what Christina was telling her.

"Miles has burned down the house and stolen my pictures."

"But he's in jail."

"Surrounded by some of the country's leading criminals, who would have been only too happy to oblige, as long as the price was right."

"Well, at least you have one consolation," said Beth. "The insurance will cover your loss."

"No, it won't."

"How come?"

"Because Miles deliberately let the insurance lapse."

"But didn't the insurance company warn you that the policy was about to expire?"

"Yes, they did. But because I already had an offer on the table of five million for Limpton Hall, and the buyer had put down a deposit of half a million, I assumed the sale would be completed quickly. But of course, the buyer has now withdrawn his offer, and wants his deposit back."

"Understandably," said Beth, while she tried to think about the consequences. "But why didn't you at least reinsure the paintings?"

"Because once they were in Christie's possession, they'd be covered by their overall company policy. I'd already signed a contract with them, and the pictures were due to be collected on Monday, so I didn't give it a thought. Although Miles clearly had."

"But if he did get someone to burn the house down, there's certain to be a police investigation, bearing in mind who's involved."

"Unlikely," said Christina. "No insurance company had to pay up, and the chief fire examiner's report states that he found no reason to suspect arson. An old house with faulty wiring, and no one on the premises at the time."

"What a nightmare," said Beth.

"All dreamed up by Miles. And it gets worse. I've put down a deposit on my dream home in Florida, and if I don't complete in less than three weeks . . ." Christina burst into tears. "And it doesn't help that I know he's stolen the pictures and got away with it."

"But you told me Miles had informed Christie's that if they came up for auction, he would be bidding for them."

"Only because he was well aware that he'd never have to. Like the deposit on the house, it was all part of an elaborate ploy. And I fell for it."

"Then we've got to find the pictures and make sure he doesn't get away with it."

"It's far too late for that. They'll be halfway around the world by now."

"Forgive me for asking," said Beth, "but does that mean the gallery will have to return the Vermeer?"

"I don't have any choice," said Christina. "Otherwise I'll lose my deposit on the house in Florida and be completely wiped out." She paused. "Which is clearly what Miles had always planned."

Beth didn't speak for some time, until she eventually said, "Unless of course William was able to prove that Miles had removed the pictures before he burned the house down."

<o>

"Do you by any chance have any contacts in the SAS, sir?"

"Thinking of joining up, William?" asked Hawksby, looking up from behind his desk.

"Not at the moment, sir."

"Then why do you need to know?"

"I think I may have come up with a way to get into Rashidi's slaughter without having to take the stairs or the lift."

"When I did my national service," said the Hawk, "my commanding officer was a Major Jock Stewart, who'd played scrum half for the army and boxed for the regiment. But his exploits as a young lieutenant with the SAS during the Second World War are the stuff of fiction. A cross between Biggles and Richard Hannay."

"Sounds like the ideal man," said William. "How do I get in touch with him?"

"You don't get in touch with the SAS. They get in touch with you, and then only when they plan to kill you."

"Very droll, sir. And if I don't want to be killed?"

"Stewart ended up as a colonel in the Coldstream Guards, so their regimental adjutant will probably know how to contact him. But be warned. If he growls, start looking for some undergrowth."

24

They had chosen the hour carefully.

He walked along the south wall of the cathedral until he reached the sacristy door. The choir had just sung Matins, and wouldn't be back until the next service, a christening at two o'clock.

He turned the handle, pushed the heavy door open, and entered the cathedral. He knew exactly where he was going, but then he'd carried out this exercise several times before, and for several different supplicants.

"Good morning, my child," he said, as he passed a cleaner in the corridor on his way to the vestry.

"Good morning, Father," she replied, giving him a slight bow. He had learned over the years that if you look and sound as if you're in your natural habitat, no one questions your presence.

He disappeared into the vestry, relieved to find the last chorister had left. He went straight to a cubicle that bore the name FATHER MICHAEL SEED, his confessor, and an old friend he had little in common with except that they were roughly the same size.

He removed his jacket and tie and replaced them with a long black cassock, a surplice, holy bands, and a dog collar that would transform him from a layman to a priest for the next hour. He felt a bit of a fraud, but he hoped the Almighty would forgive his transgression, and accept that it was for the greater good.

Glancing in the long mirror on the wall only made him feel even more guilty. He slipped back into the corridor, and made his way through the outer sacristy and into the nave. He kept a steady pace as he passed the Chapel of the Blessed Sacrament, having no desire to stop and talk to any of the parishioners, although he was well practiced at playing the part of a priest going about his pastoral duties should any of them question him.

When he reached a secluded corner below a bronze relief of St. Benedict, he stepped into the dark, cramped space, and settled down to wait to hear the confession of the only sinner he had an appointment with.

After a few moments the door to the confessional opened, and someone entered and sat down. He drew the red curtain.

"Good morning, Father," said a voice he immediately recognized.

"Good morning, my son."

"I'm sorry it's been so long since my last confession, but my life has been in turmoil."

"Is there any way I can help?" asked the commander, replying to the coded message.

"As you know, when I last attended confession, Father, Tulip was in hospital after swallowing a wrap of cocaine in an attempt to avoid arrest. I confess that I hoped he would die."

"That is indeed a mortal sin, my son, but one with which, given the circumstances, I feel our Lord might have some sympathy."

"In his absence I became a runner for several dealers, whose names I feel I must share with you, to atone for my transgressions."

"May the Lord bless you and keep you."

A slip of paper was pushed through the latticed screen. The commander took a quick look, and was delighted to find the names of several new sinners he hadn't come across before.

"May the Lord have mercy on their souls," he said, as he put the slip of paper into an inside pocket. "But have you located the Viper's nest?"

"Tulip's arrest for the murder of Adrian Heath created a vacancy in the hierarchy, Father, and I was promoted, which happens fairly regularly when you're on a battlefield."

"And?"

"Block A, Mansfield Towers, Lavenham Road, Brixton," came back the immediate reply.

"That confirms our own intel. Am I also right in thinking that Rashidi's headquarters are at the top of the building?"

"The top three floors. The twenty-fifth floor is where they grow the cannabis. The twenty-fourth is where the drugs are prepared for the street dealers. Heroin, cocaine, Ecstasy tablets, and cannabis."

"And the twenty-third?"

"The distribution center. Where the dealers pick up their supplies and hand over their takings."

"Who's in charge?"

"Rashidi has four deputies. All of them are on the list I just gave you: a disbarred lawyer, a disqualified accountant, a doctor who's been struck off the medical register, and a former sales manager who was sacked by John Lewis for embezzlement. He makes so much money now he no longer needs to embezzle. Rashidi also has a second-in-command, but I haven't managed to find out his name or where he lives, but I'm fairly sure it's not in the building. The whole operation is as well run as any City institution."

"And the security?"

"He has four lookouts watching the building at all times. There are two entrances to the slaughter on the twenty-third floor; the front door, which is made of reinforced steel, only opens from the inside, and has a grille so the gatekeeper can check on anyone who wants to come in. The doors are protected by a New York stop, a safety device invented by the Mafia to keep out any unwelcome visitors. However, that's not your biggest problem. Rashidi doesn't use that door. He has his own private entrance and exit."

The commander didn't interrupt the confession.

"Blocks A and B are joined by a walkway on the twenty-third floor. Rashidi has a large flat on the twenty-second floor of Block B, so at the slightest hint of trouble, he can be well out of harm's way before anyone can reach the front door of the slaughter."

"What about the lift?"

"Takes forty-two seconds to reach the twenty-third floor, and is permanently manned by a thug called Pete Donoghue, who'd be on his way up to the slaughter the moment any of the four lookouts spotted anything suspicious. Long before the firearms team had run up twenty-three flights of stairs, broken down the reinforced steel door, and forced their way into the slaughter in Block A, Rashidi would be watching television in his flat in Block B, and wouldn't come out again until the coast was clear."

"What about his workers?"

"Most of them are illegal immigrants and petty criminals, who Rashidi accommodates in squalid little flats in Block A. If there was any trouble, they'd have to leave by the front door, so you might catch a few of his minions on the way down, but not Rashidi or his right hand."

"How often does Rashidi visit the slaughter?"

"He goes there to collect the cash between eight and midnight every evening from Monday to Thursday. He's always accompanied by two armed ex-cons, who make sure no one gets introduced to their boss unless they have an appointment."

"I need to know who owns the two blocks," said the commander.

"I have no way of finding that out, sir, but I wouldn't be surprised if it's Rashidi himself. He's resourceful and well organized enough, and like all sociopaths, wouldn't care if you killed his best friend. Come to think of it, I'm not sure he has any friends." He paused for a moment before saying, "I have nothing more to confess, Father."

"Thank you, Ross," said the commander. "You've given me and the team more than enough ammunition to move on to the next phase of our plan."

"And there'll be more where that came from, sir, because I'm determined to be there on the night of the raid. Let me know when you've settled on a date."

"Will do. But don't take any unnecessary risks. You've done more than enough. The moment you want out, just say the word. An inspector's position has come vacant in Hackney, and I'd be happy to recommend you."

"I'm not sure I could handle being back in uniform, after all this time."

"That's understandable. But if you change your mind, let me know via the usual channels."

"Will do, sir," said Ross. "But I'm hoping you'll personally arrest me when the boys raid the slaughter."

"Nice idea, but I'll leave Choirboy to do that."

"Will I recognize him?"

"You won't be able to miss him," said the Hawk, with a grin Ross couldn't see from the other side of the screen. "You'd better leave now, and I'll hang around for a couple of minutes. And Ross, I know it's inadequate, but once again, thank you."

The Hawk heard the door swing open and close. He was think-ing about how he could get his men all the way up to the twenty-third floor before Rashidi had time to escape, when a voice said, "Father, I have sinned, and seek the Lord's forgiveness."

Help, the Hawk wanted to say, *you're not my type of sinner.* But he satisfied himself with, "How have you transgressed, my son?"

"I covet my neighbor's wife."

"And have you had carnal relations with her?"

"No, Father, but the Bible tells us the thought is as wicked as the deed."

Then I'm guilty of several murders, thought the Hawk, includ-ing Faulkner and Rashidi among my hypothetical victims. "In-deed, my son. You have committed a grievous sin, and you must reject the temptations of the devil and dismiss these unworthy thoughts from your mind."

"And if I can't, Father? Will I be cast into eternal darkness and everlasting damnation?"

"No, my son. Not if you repent your sins and return to the path of righteousness. Hail Mary, Mother of God . . ."

"Thank you, Father," said a relieved voice, before the door opened and closed again.

The Hawk didn't waste another moment, as he had no desire to deal with any more unscheduled sinners. He scurried out of the con-fessional box and almost ran through the outer sacristy on his way back to the vestry, but he had to slow down when he saw the Cardi-nal Archbishop of Westminster heading toward him. He fell to one knee and kissed his ring. The cardinal made the sign of the cross and said, "Tell me, commander, have you been about God's work?"

"I believe I've saved one sinner today, Your Grace," he replied.

"Then let us hope your reward will be on earth, my child, as well as in heaven."

—◄○►—

"In view of MM's latest revelations," said the Hawk when he chaired the next team meeting, "the commissioner has given us the green light. We can call on any resources within the Met's remit, and we've even got a realistic budget. However, there's one proviso."

"There always is," said Lamont.

"The commissioner insists that our priority is to catch Rashidi and his inner circle, while at the same time securing enough evidence to put them away until they're old men. Simply closing down his drug factory and catching a few runners, even dealers, won't be enough. Rashidi's well capable of just walking away and opening up in another part of town within weeks, possibly days. He's probably got a second factory already set up for just that purpose. Bring me up to date, DS Warwick, on where we are with the investigation."

"DC Adaja and I have been working on the ground in Brixton for the past few weeks," said William.

"That would explain why you're both unshaven and look as if you've been dragged through a hedge backward."

"Got to blend in with the locals," said Paul.

"Not only have we confirmed the block where the slaughter is situated," said William, "but thanks to MM's detailed intel—and by the way, I apologize forever doubting him, sir, because if Jackie and I had arrested him and Tulip in Felixstowe, we'd still be picking up the pieces and—"

The commander waved a hand. "Let's get on with the here and now, DS Warwick, and forget the past." He winked at Jackie, before William continued. "I've visited a couple of local estate agents to find out if I can rent a flat in Block A, so I could come and go without raising suspicion. But it's not possible, because it turns out that the building is registered in the name of a shell company, probably owned by Rashidi."

"However, there are two unoccupied flats in Block B," said Paul, "that are rented by Lambeth council. One of which would be ideal for what we have in mind."

William got up from the table and walked over to a large white-board covered in diagrams, arrows, and photographs, one of which showed two tower blocks with a walkway running between them.

"The flat I have in mind is on the twenty-third floor, not far from the walkway."

"Good work," said the commander. "However, it should be DC Adaja, not you, DS Warwick, who rents the flat, because if he can sneak some of our men in unobserved, when Rashidi attempts to escape across the walkway, he'll find a welcoming party waiting for him."

"Unobserved could be a problem, sir," said William. "We'd need at least half a dozen men to arrest Rashidi and take out his bodyguards, and it won't be easy to get a full firearms division up to the twenty-third floor of Block B before Rashidi has time to escape. But I'll come to that later."

"What about the roof?" asked Jackie. "Is that another way he could escape?"

"Unlikely," said Paul. "The only way he could get out would be via the fire escape and he'd meet us on the way up while he was coming down."

"No," said William, "the walkway will be his preferred escape route, because once he's in his flat in Block B, there'll be no way of linking him with anything that's going on in the next-door building."

"What about the thug who mans the lift in Block A?" said

Hawksby, taking a closer look at the detailed diagram pinned to the wall. "Can we disarm him and take over the lift?"

"Pete Donoghue," said William, pointing to a photograph of a man who could have played an extra in *The Sweeney* without bothering to use makeup.

"He's served time for GBH and armed robbery," said Lamont. "Last time he was arrested it took three officers to hold him down while I handcuffed him."

"You can't get anywhere near the lift without him checking you out," said Paul. "Several of Rashidi's workers would prefer to take the stairs rather than share a lift with that thug."

"Even if you could make it to the lift, there are always lookouts posted here, here, here, and here," said William, pointing to four crosses on the street plan. "If one of them has any doubts about you, the lift disappears to the twenty-third floor, and doesn't return to the ground floor until the all-clear's been given."

"Like an air-raid siren during the last war," said the Hawk, showing his age.

"I'll take your word for that, sir," said Paul.

"How did you manage to pick up so much information without being spotted by one of the lookouts?" asked the Hawk, ignoring the comment.

"Regular journeys on the top decks of buses, sir," said William. "Numbers 3, 59, and 118 pass by the two blocks several times an hour."

"In fact," said Paul, "the number 118 stops right outside Block A, which is how we've been able to pinpoint where the lookouts are posted. I've also identified several dealers, because they are the only ones allowed to head for the lift without being questioned. But I still can't risk getting off the bus in the close vicinity of what is virtually a fortress."

"How long would it take for a unit of armed officers to reach the twenty-third floor if they couldn't make it to the lift in time?" asked Lamont.

"MM did it in seven and a half minutes," said Jackie, "but remember, the lift can get there in forty-two seconds, giving Rashidi more than enough time to escape across the walkway and be back in his flat long before the first officer would reach the front door."

"So how do we get to the twenty-third floor in under forty-two seconds?" demanded Lamont.

"I think William may have come up with the answer to that question," said the Hawk.

25

"My sincere condolences, Miles, on the loss of your unique collection. I know how much those pictures meant to you, and for them to be destroyed in such a cruel way must be devastating."

"Thank you, BW. I appreciate your concern," said Faulkner, trying to sound devastated.

"I know of course that you had planned to buy back Limpton Hall, and in time—"

"The paintings were far more important to me than the house, but I still expect you to get my five-hundred-thousand-pound deposit back as quickly as possible."

"The paperwork's already underway. At least the Vermeer is safe in its new home at the Fitzmolean."

"Not for much longer."

"I don't understand," said Booth Watson.

"No reason you should, BW. Let's just say I have plans for it to be reunited with the rest of my collection."

◄○►

"It was kind of you to agree to see me, colonel," said William when the two men met in the reception area. "I know the commander is looking forward to catching up with you."

"Hawksby was one of my better junior subalterns. He would have made a damn fine soldier," said the colonel, as he followed William into the lift. "It will be good to see the young man again after all these years."

William stifled a smile as he stepped out of the lift and led the colonel down the corridor to the commander's office. He knocked on the door, and as they entered, the Hawk sprang to attention. "It's an honor to see you again, sir," he said.

"At my age, I'm always surprised anyone still remembers me," said the colonel, as they shook hands.

"How could anyone forget," said Hawksby. "My generation was raised on Colditz, Dunkirk, and Navarone."

"So, it wasn't David Niven who led that raid?" said William, playing along.

"No," said the colonel, "but I can't complain. When Niven landed the part it did my reputation with the ladies no harm. So how can I help?"

"May I ask, colonel, if you think DS Warwick's idea has any merit?"

"It most certainly does, and what's more I know the ideal man for the job. He's actually already one of your chaps. When Captain Scott Cairns left the regiment, the Met recruited him to set up its counter-terrorist division, which is more or less the SAS in different-colored uniforms. I think you'll find it's fully operational by now, although it's being kept under wraps."

"Then we'll have to unwrap it," said William. "How do I get in touch with Captain Cairns?"

"I don't know," said the colonel. "But I wouldn't be surprised if he was holed up somewhere in this building."

"Scotland Yard employs over two thousand people in over three hundred offices on nineteen floors, but if he's here I'll have tracked him down before the end of the day," said the Hawk. "Now all we have to hope is our boys are as good as your lot were."

"They're a damn sight better," said the colonel. "We were a bunch of amateurs by comparison. This new lot are highly trained professionals, who'll do whatever it takes to get the job done."

"But are they just as mad?" asked the Hawk.

"Certifiable! It's still the only essential qualification for the job. But now that I've solved your problem, can I ask a favor?"

"Anything," said the Hawk.

"Since I've finally made it to Scotland Yard without being arrested, would it be possible to have a guided tour of the Black Museum?"

◄o►

"When's the baby due?" asked Christina, as William turned off the motorway and followed the signs to Limpton, which brought back so many memories.

"Not long now," replied Beth.

"You must both be so excited."

"William's got one or two other things on his mind at the moment."

"What could possibly be more important than your firstborn?"

"Arson and art theft," said William. "But I hope to have solved both cases before Alexander or Vivien make their presence known."

"Boudicca or Leonardo," said Beth. "As you can see, we haven't yet settled on the name. But let's concentrate on arson for the time being."

"Proving someone has committed arson is never easy," said William. "Unless there are obvious, telltale signs, like traces of accelerant on a floorboard, or a petrol-soaked rag that's been dropped through a letterbox—the sort of crass mistake only amateurs think they could get away with."

"And the professionals?" asked Christina.

"A pile of tissues placed just below a wooden roof next to an immersion heater, and then one match is all it takes. There aren't many people serving prison sentences for arson, as it's one of the easiest crimes to get away with. So, we'll have to concentrate on proving that Miles stole the pictures before the house went up in flames."

"Of course he did."

"However much you believe that's the case, Christina, and I'm not saying I don't agree with you, you'll still need concrete evidence for a case to stand up in a court of law. Without it, vexatious claims from an angry ex-wife tend to be laughed out of court."

"William," said Beth sharply, "that's very harsh after all Christina's been through."

"I'm on her side," said William. "But unless I find what I'm looking for, we'll all be wasting our time," he added, as he turned into the lane that led up to Limpton Hall. This time he drove slowly.

"So where do we start?" asked Christina.

"We go over the site with the proverbial fine-tooth comb."

"What are we looking for?" asked Beth.

"Anything that's survived the fire."

William drove past the abandoned gatehouse and on up the long drive, not quite sure what to expect. He only just avoided crashing into a tree when he first caught sight of what was left of the beautiful Lutyens manor house that had once stood so proudly on the hill dominating the surrounding countryside. All that remained was half an acre of ash and rubble.

William parked the car on the drive, opened the boot and took out three sets of overalls, Wellington boots, and rubber gloves.

Once they had put them on, the three of them walked across to where the front door had once stood.

"Right," said William. "We have to be as methodical as possible. We'll begin on this side and work our way across the site in a straight line, then move three paces to the right and repeat the same exercise on the way back. If you come across anything that has survived the blaze, let me know."

"Does this count?" asked Beth, bending down and extracting the front door knocker from the ashes.

"A promising start," said William, after he'd taken a closer look. He dropped their first find into a large black bin liner.

A few minutes later, it was Beth again. This time a bath tap, followed by Christina who added a marble egg. "I bought it when we were on holiday in Athens," she said, as William took a closer look before dropping the egg into his bag.

Some time passed before William asked, "What's this?"

The three of them studied the latest find for some time before Christina said, "It's the winding mechanism from our old grandfather clock. A wedding present," she added sadly.

"Excellent," said William, dropping it into his bag.

"Why?" asked Beth.

"Later—we still don't have enough. But do you need to rest?" he asked, looking anxiously at his wife, who looked tired. "My son won't thank you if he's born among the ashes."

"While my daughter," said Beth, "for all you know might well be enjoying the search far too much to stop now."

"What have you forgotten to mention, Mrs. Warwick? Dare I ask?" said William, who stood still in the middle of a pile of ash, staring at his wife.

"Oh, did I forget to tell you, Mr. Warwick, that you are going to be a father of twins?"

William and Beth started jumping up and down and hugging each other, while Christina dropped her bag and began to applaud. It was some time before they returned to the task in hand, when William found it hard to concentrate.

"Is this any use?" asked Christina a few minutes later, handing William a picture hook.

"Our best find yet," said William, still not having recovered from the news. "However, we need as many of them as possible," he said, before adding the little hook to his collection.

"Why?" demanded Beth.

"Later," said William.

It was another hour before they'd filled all three large bin liners with countless different objects, when William insisted they should take a break.

"I think we've all earned a celebratory lunch at the Limpton Arms," said Christina, as the bags were deposited in the boot.

"Only if William's found what he was looking for," said Beth.

"Sixty-one of them," said William. "And I think I can now prove the pictures were removed from the house before it was set on fire. Though to be absolutely sure, I'll still need to visit the Fitzmolean."

◄○►

"The colonel has solved one of our problems," said Lamont during the Monday morning meeting. "I attended a rehearsal at a block of derelict flats in Croydon last Friday, and can report that Chief Inspector Scott Cairns and his team have got the whole exercise down to well under five minutes."

"That's impressive," said the Hawk. "But it doesn't solve our problem on the ground, where the lookouts will be able to spot us a mile away, giving them more than enough time to shut up shop and disappear into their boltholes before we can even reach the front door."

"Is it possible we're approaching the problem from the wrong direction?" asked William. "Perhaps we should be considering a simpler solution."

"Enlighten me."

"Our current plan is to have a dozen armed men hidden in the flat we've rented in Block B, and the moment the order's given, they'll take control of the walkway and arrest anyone who attempts to escape through that door."

"And what's wrong with that?" said Lamont sharply.

"Why not do the exact opposite? We know there's little or no chance of breaking down, or even getting anywhere near, the slaughter's reinforced steel door before Rashidi's safely back in his flat in Block B."

"That's exactly why we'll have armed officers waiting for him on the walkway," said Lamont.

"But that puts us at an immediate disadvantage," said William. "First, we have to get at least a dozen men and their equipment up to the twenty-third floor of Block B without anyone spotting them, which in itself would be a minor miracle. Second, even if we did arrest Rashidi and his henchmen as they tried to escape across the walkway, what would we charge them with? Because if they're represented by some scumbag like Booth Watson, you can be sure he'll put forward a convincing argument that his law-abiding clients were legitimately making their way to their flats in the other building. They'd be out on bail the same day. No, we have to arrest Rashidi while he's actually on the premises, or we'll all be wasting our time."

"Anyone can raise a problem, DS Warwick," said Lamont. "It's finding a solution that's a little more difficult."

"Getting a dozen men up to our flat in Block B, along with an armory of guns and other equipment, has always carried the risk of someone working out what we're up to. Why not cut the chances from twelve to one?"

"And like Horatio," mused the Hawk, "will he be expected to defend the bridge alone?"

"No, sir, we don't need Horatio for this job, just a damned good carpenter who, when you give the order, can fix three thick wooden planks across the door on our side of the walkway in a matter of minutes, so the villains will be trapped inside the slaughter, leaving them with only one escape route—the front door. And by the time they realize that, we'll be standing outside waiting for them."

"Ingenious," said Lamont. "But it still leaves us with the problem of what to do about the four lookouts on the ground, and the thug who controls the lift. By the time our boys are halfway up the stairs, Rashidi will be on his way down in the lift, and when he steps out on the ground floor, a picture of innocence, there will be no offense we can charge him with, and the whole operation will have failed. Because one thing's for certain, the chairman of Marcel and Neffe won't have any drugs on him."

"Not if we can make sure the lift is stuck on the ground floor," said Paul.

"How do you plan to do that, DC Adaja," asked the Hawk, "when the moment I give the order to mount the operation, a dozen armed vehicles and squad cars will come roaring into the square, giving the lookouts more than enough time to warn Donoghue, who in turn will warn Rashidi? How do we get out of that one, Houdini?"

"We all have to be hidden in plain sight," said William. "Although I must admit it took me several sleepless nights to figure out something that had been staring me in the face for the past month." No one interrupted. "There's no need for us to go charging in like John Wayne, all guns blazing, when we can drive up and park outside the front door without anyone giving us a second look."

"You're planning to turn into the invisible man no doubt?" said Lamont. "Even John Wayne didn't manage that."

"No, sir. But if Paul were to become a conductor on our own number 118 bus, he would be invisible along with everyone else on board!"

The Hawk and Lamont looked at each other.

"The sleepless nights were worth it, DS Warwick," said the commander. "I think the commissioner's going to be impressed by my latest idea."

They all started banging on the table.

"Right," said the Hawk, bringing them back to order. "We've got our bus conductor, now we need a driver."

"It has to be Danny Ives," said William without hesitation.

"Along with sixteen handpicked specialist arms officers from PT17," said Lamont, "who'll occupy the lower deck, ready to move at a moment's notice."

"However," said Paul, "the first of them shouldn't be in uniform or armed to the teeth but in tracksuits and trainers, as they'll need to take out the four lookouts in under ten seconds, while three other officers tackle Donoghue and commandeer the lift."

"By which time a dozen heavily armed passengers will be on their way up the stairs, which is when I'll call upon the counter-terrorist specialists to play their part."

"We'll also need a dozen WPCs," said William, "dressed in civilian clothes."

"Enlighten me," said the Hawk.

"Rashidi's lookouts might become suspicious if they see a passing bus entirely packed with fit young men with crew cuts, not on their way home from work but on their way to work. So, I want there to be a scattering of women dressed like housewives, commuters, shoppers—looking like anything but police officers."

"Nice touch, William," said the commander. "But we'll also have to remove all the seats from the upper deck and set up a command center from where I can oversee the entire operation. Which leaves me with the problem of how to get my hands on a double-decker bus."

"I'm so glad we've found something for you to do, sir," said Paul, immediately regretting his words.

"As we have for you, DC Adaja. Because once this operation is over, you'll be well qualified to apply for a job as a bus conductor. But before then, try not to forget who'll be conducting the orchestra."

◄○►

Once the meeting had broken up and his team had returned to their offices, Hawksby sat back and thought carefully about how he could increase the operation's chances of success. After a few moments, he pulled open the bottom drawer of his desk, took out an unopened Marlboro packet and a felt-tipped pen. He tore off the cellophane wrapping, flicked the pack open, and emptied the cigarettes onto his desk.

He removed the foil and thought carefully about the simple message he needed to convey. After a few moments he wrote, *11 p.m., 12th,* then put the foil back into place. He closed the top and slipped the pack into an inside pocket, then made his way out of his office and took the lift to the basement. He left by the back entrance of the building, turned right, and headed for Westminster Cathedral. This time he went in by the front door, not as a priest but a parishioner.

He walked slowly down the left-hand aisle, admiring Eric Gill's *Jesus Is Nailed to the Cross*. When he reached his target, he looked around before unlocking the offertory box and placing the cigarette packet in one corner. He then closed the lid and locked it, finally dropping fifty pence through the little slot to assuage his guilt.

He decided to walk home. Quite some distance, but he needed the exercise, and time to think about his speech.

◄○►

"Superintendent Lamont has been in touch," said Booth Watson, taking a seat opposite his client in the prison's private consultation room. He opened his briefcase, extracted some papers and placed them on the glass table between them. "He's applied for a production order under the Police and Criminal Evidence Act, and he wants to interview you as soon as possible."

"So, am I to be transferred to an open prison?" asked Faulkner. "Or is my sentence going to be halved for good behavior?"

"Neither. Lamont wants to question you about two other crimes they think you might have been involved in."

"Like what?" said Faulkner.

"Arson, for starters. They have reason to believe you were responsible for burning down your own home."

"While I was locked up in here?"

"Along with the theft of seventy-two paintings from the house before it was burned down, valued at approximately thirty million pounds," said Lamont, ignoring the outburst.

"But they went up in smoke with the house."

"Lamont doesn't think so, and claims he can prove it."

"Sherlock Holmes couldn't prove it."

"But William Warwick has."

"Not that damn man again."

"He spent a day raking through the ashes of Limpton Hall, and has found sixty-one picture hooks."

"That only proves the paintings were there at the time of the fire."

"On the contrary, he says it proves they weren't. It's not what he's found that's important, but what he didn't find. And before you say anything, Miles, I suggest you remain silent until you've answered a couple of questions I feel sure the superintendent is likely to ask you."

Faulkner reluctantly held his tongue.

"If the pictures were hanging on the hooks Warwick found in the rubble, what was holding them up?"

"Picture wire of course. Except for the larger paintings, which would have needed ch—" He paused for a few moments before saying, "Ah, yes, now I remember. I had them all changed to rope a couple of years ago."

"Enough to hang yourself with," said Booth Watson, "because your ex-wife claims—"

"It will be her word against mine."

"I only wish it was. But unfortunately, Warwick has recently paid a visit to the Fitzmolean, where he found the Vermeer Christina donated to the museum hanging by a steel and brass interwoven picture wire, and both the Rembrandt and the Rubens that you so generously presented to the gallery last year were still hanging on their original brass chains. So, before I fix a date for Superintendent Lamont to question you under caution, Miles, you'd better come up with something more convincing than rope. Otherwise the only way you'll be getting out of Pentonville will be to face a new trial for arson and the theft of seventy-two paintings worth over thirty million pounds. In which case, your present accommodation could end up being permanent well into the next century."

26

"In an hour's time the battle will be over, one way or another," were the commander's opening words to his troops on the ground.

The Hawk had assembled a crack team of specialists from every field of law enforcement in the Met's armory. They had all played their individual roles on smaller stages across the capital many times, but this was the first time they'd come together to form the biggest gang in town.

The previous night they'd taken part in a dress rehearsal with only the commander sitting in the audience.

At ten o'clock, that wretched hour when more drugs and money change hands than at any other time of the day or night, and well hidden from the public gaze, they had all assembled at Battersea power station. Four fully equipped armored vehicles, six Black Marias, a dozen squad cars, four ambulances, and a double-decker bus. Inside the power station were eighty-three men and women who had been given strict orders to remain silent about where and when this covert army would be assembling the following night, including their colleagues.

The commander surveyed his troops. As with everything else connected with Operation Trojan Horse, he'd gone over his speech again and again.

"Fellow officers, we are about to take part in one of the biggest operations in the Met's history. Every one of you was handpicked because you are recognized as the acknowledged leaders in your particular field. Drugs are the scourge of our society, and have caused the biggest rise in crime for decades. They indiscriminately kill the young and the vulnerable, while a small group of ruthless individuals line their pockets, untroubled by the human suffering they're causing, and arrogantly convinced they're above the law.

"Tonight, we have a chance to strike a blow against these vile individuals, by capturing one of the most prominent of their leaders, Khalil Rashidi, and closing down his empire, which stretches from one end of London to the other. Let's put this monster behind bars for the rest of his life."

Everyone rose to their feet and cheered, and William was reminded why he'd always wanted to be a copper. It was some time before the commander was able to continue.

"If our operation goes to plan, we will also arrest his four closest acolytes, preventing the hydra from simply replacing its lost head. And finally, we will permanently shut down the drugs factory where Rashidi's deadly wares are prepared before they're released onto the streets."

Once again, the commander was held up by the eager response of his troops.

"If we succeed, you will be able to tell tales of heroic deeds performed tonight that will become part of police folklore. Many of your colleagues will claim they were members of the Capital Gang, when drug barons became drug serfs, when our young were freed from being victims of these cynical predators. But you yourselves will never talk of the role you played, other than to those who stand by your side tonight.

"As the one chosen to lead you into battle—for a battle it will surely be—this is unquestionably the high point of my career. So now let's go about our task, and in the great tradition of the force, let's make a difference."

The Hawk stepped down from the stage to a storm of cheers that only died down after he had climbed aboard the battle bus to join his inner team, who had spent so many months preparing for this moment.

"This wouldn't be St. Crispin's Day by any chance?" said William, suppressing a grin when the commander joined them on the top deck.

"If it is, let's hope we achieve the same result as Henry the Fifth," replied Hawksby as he took his place in front of a command center that looked capable of delivering a man on the moon rather than just a couple of dozen armed officers to the top floor of a tower block in Brixton.

"Time to discover just how efficient this piece of kit is," said the commander, tuning in to a frequency that would keep him in touch with everyone on the ground, although they'd all been warned to maintain radio silence once the convoy was on the move.

Danny sat astride the Trojan horse, stirrups ready, impatient to spur the beast into action, while Lamont, William, and Jackie remained by the commander's side. Paul was in position on the lower deck, determined that he would be the first off the bus the moment they drew up outside the entrance to the tower blocks.

The commander checked his watch, pressed a button on his two-way radio, and said, "Let battle commence."

The number 118 bus led the troops out onto Brixton Road, with its well-ordered convoy following closely behind. No flashing lights, no sirens, no screeching tires. At various prearranged points along the way, other vehicles peeled off to disappear down unlit streets and await further orders.

A mile from the target the Hawk said, "Time for you to leave us, DS Warwick, and begin directing operations on the ground. Don't report back until the job is done."

"On my way, sir," said William, who ran down the spiral staircase to join Paul on the lower deck, where the assembled troops were waiting impatiently for the order to move. One young officer, chosen because he could run a hundred yards in under ten seconds, was standing next to the conductor waiting for the starter's pistol to sound. Paul hadn't told him that he was determined to reach the lift ahead of him, and personally take out Donoghue before he could press the alarm button.

One step behind the sprinter stood two squat square-shouldered men, who played in the front row of the scrum every Saturday afternoon. They would only be a few yards behind, and their orders were clear: play the man and not the ball, because there wouldn't be any referee giving penalties for foul play.

The two rows of seats near the back of the bus were occupied by eight young officers in tracksuits and trainers, whose sole purpose was to disarm the four lookouts before they had a chance to warn the gatekeeper. In the next three rows were a dozen officers from the Specialist Firearms Command, hydraulic kits strapped to their backs, who once they'd leaped off the bus would head straight for the stairs, determined to reach the twenty-third floor in under seven minutes. Bets had already been placed as to who would make it to the front door first.

In the front rows sat a larger group of men and women who were in no particular hurry. Trained specialists from the drugs unit, their job was to meticulously gather the evidence and bag it up before sending it to the lab for analysis. It would be their evidence that would decide the length of the sentences, not the courage of the foot soldiers.

Scattered at random among the other officers were a number of WPCs, of whom the Hawk had said, *they also serve who only sit and wait.* William had smiled when he heard his boss misquote Milton.

The carpenter was already in position near the walkway on the twenty-third floor of Block B, ready to put up his own personal no-entry sign the instant the order was given, so that one line of escape from the factory would be completely cut off.

The tactical firearms team was out of sight, but Hawksby was confident that, like unwelcome guests, they would appear the moment they were least expected.

So far, everything had gone like clockwork, but the Hawk knew only too well that you can't plan for the unexpected. On that, at least, he would be proven right. The bus continued its steady progress along Coldharbour Lane carrying a silent group of nonpaying passengers on their way to work. Danny had carried out two dry runs the previous evening, so he knew how long every red light took to change, where the pedestrian crossings were located, and where the road narrowed, making it impossible to overtake or be overtaken. He drove past puzzled and irate clusters of would-be passengers at each stop, ignoring their insistent waves. Would they work out why he hadn't stopped when they read their morning papers?

"Five minutes from the target," said Hawksby, breaking radio silence for the second time. William could see that the passengers who would be getting off at the next stop were now poised tensely on the edge of their seats, waiting for the command, *go, go, go!*

The sprinter was already set, desperate to burst out of the blocks and be on his way with his two heavier colleagues following close behind. Paul, still determined to reach Donoghue first, had ditched his ticket machine and peaked cap, and was unbuttoning his jacket. Leaping off the bus had been endlessly practiced to make sure no one would trip or bump into each other.

"Three minutes," said the commander, as they rounded the next bend and the two tower blocks came into sight for the first time.

William could feel a rush of adrenaline flood through his body, accompanied by a moment of fear and apprehension, as they inched closer and closer to their target.

Hawksby checked his stopwatch, a thumb poised on its button, aware that a few seconds either way could spell the difference between success and failure.

Two minutes, Red. "Board them up," said the commander.

The carpenter stepped out of his overnight accommodation, having completed all his preliminary work during the day. He rested three thick wooden planks up against the wall, then took a battery-powered drill and a handful of screws out of his large kit bag. He placed the first plank across the door. A perfect fit. He inserted the first screw into its prepared hole and set about his task, confident that no one on the other side of the heavy reinforced metal door would be able to hear him going about his work.

One minute, Blue. "Prepare for landing."

The carpenter was screwing the second plank into place when a Gazelle helicopter appeared out of the clouds, banked steeply, and hovered above the roof of Block A.

Thirty seconds.

The carpenter finished screwing the final plank into place, and stood back to admire his handiwork. Anyone who was thinking of leaving the slaughter by that route could think again. He picked up his bag, and whistled as he began making his way down the stairs. He'd told his wife he might be a little late for supper, but hadn't told her why.

Fifteen seconds.

Danny began to slow down as he approached the bus stop; CI Scott Cairns leaped out of the helicopter and fast-roped down onto the roof. Another officer was only seconds behind him, while two more waited impatiently to join them.

Danny put his foot on the brakes when he reached the entrance to Block A.

"Go, go, go!" said the commander, finally releasing his troops from the Trojan horse. He was painfully aware that the game was no longer in the coach's hands, and he would have to remain on the touchline while the players determined the final outcome.

Paul and the sprinter flew out of the blocks together and began running flat out toward the lift, with the two front row forwards doing their best to keep up, while at the same time, eight track-suited young constables moved swiftly in four different directions toward the lookouts.

One of them was so high he wouldn't have noticed if a space-ship had landed. The second was deep in conversation with a girl who was offering him sex in return for a joint. The third had been overpowered before he realized what was happening, but the fourth saw them coming, and had time to contact Pete Donoghue, who was sitting by the lift listening to Pink Floyd on his radio.

"Raid, raid, raid!" came crackling over his intercom, and Donoghue was suddenly back in the real world. He was reaching for the FOP button when the sprinter dived head first as if reaching for the try line. He hit him squarely in the stomach, knocking the radio out of his hand. Donoghue fell backward, but quickly recovered and caught the sprinter with a well-aimed knee under the chin that sent him into touch.

The two front row forwards were only yards away when the sprinter came tumbling back out of the lift, clutching on to the radio. Donoghue staggered to his feet and quickly jabbed at the top button. The doors slowly closed, clamping shut with the two props only a yard away. Their sole task that night had ended in failure. One of them punched the closed doors in frustration, but could only watch helplessly as the lift indicator passed the second and third floors. The other knelt down beside the sprinter, who was writhing in pain. "Officer down!" he shouted into his radio. "I need an ambulance immediately! Repeat, officer down!"

The last of the eight counter-terrorism officers landed on the roof moments later, as the twelve armed officers on the stairway reached the sixth floor.

By the time the lift passed the seventh, Donoghue could hear the sound of heavy footsteps thundering up the stairs. He looked around for his radio, but it was nowhere to be seen. He cursed, but he was still convinced he could reach the slaughter and raise the alarm long before the Old Bill got there.

As the lift was passing the twenty-first floor, the counter-terrorism unit began abseiling down the side of the building, confident that no one in the slaughter would have thought it possible an intruder could appear from above, not least because every window on the top three floors was covered with tightly fitted black mesh blinds to make sure even a passing pigeon couldn't see what they were up to.

When the lift reached the twenty-third floor and the doors began to slowly open, Donoghue ripped them apart, leaped out, and banged frantically on the small metal grille in the front door with a clenched fist. The gatekeeper peered through the grille, and when he saw the sweat pouring off Donoghue's face, he quickly undid the three locks and wrenched open the heavy door.

"We're being raided!" Donoghue screamed at the top of his voice as he barged past the gatekeeper and began looking for the one person he was responsible for, just as the Specialist Firearms Command reached the fourteenth floor.

Rashidi was stacking piles of cash into wads of a thousand pounds, before placing them into a sports bag, when the door of his private office was flung open. The moment he saw Donoghue's face, he didn't need to be told a raid was in progress. He'd rehearsed for this moment several times, knowing that one day they must surely come.

Rashidi followed Donoghue into the boiler room, where he was confronted by something he hadn't been able to prepare for: pandemonium. While his workers streamed in panic toward the front door, he moved swiftly in the opposite direction, accompanied by Donoghue and two armed guards, as the SFC passed the nineteenth floor.

Rashidi quickly reached the door that led to the walkway and the safety of his flat in Block B, but it soon became clear that, despite the three heavies' best efforts, their escape route had been blocked. There was now only one way out. While those around him continued to panic, Rashidi remained calm and headed quickly back toward the front door in the hope that he could reach the lift and be on his way down to the ground floor before his nemesis appeared. His lawyer had told him that although it was the less desirable alternative, once he was in the lift it could be argued in court that he was simply an innocent resident caught up in the cross fire, and that he'd never taken a drug in his life. The last part of the prepared statement had the virtue of being true.

Back in the boiler room, Rashidi found his progress blocked by workers all struggling like lemmings to desperately cram through the same narrow doorway as they attempted to reach the stairwell or the lift. His bodyguards and Donoghue began hurling them aside to make a gangway for their master, and he was within a few feet of the door when the first of the counter-terrorism officers came crashing through the window, knocking Donoghue off his feet. Moments later a second intruder crashed the party and threw a stun grenade into the middle of the room, shouting, "On your knees!"

Rashidi had just reached the front door when a third paratrooper took out one of his armed guards. He could only watch helplessly as the lift doors began to close. His last remaining protector thrust an arm into the gap in a vain attempt to hold up a lift, which was built to accommodate no more than eight passengers but already had at least a dozen desperate escapees crammed inside, jabbering away in several different tongues. Rashidi spotted the first of the armed officers emerging from the stairwell below, and immediately fell back on the "plan of last resort." He made his way back into the boiler room, where he threw off his jacket, put on a discarded face mask and a pair of rubber gloves that he found on the floor, and joined the workers who were meekly kneeling, hands behind their heads, passively accepting their fate. He, too, was prepared to accept their fate.

The first of the armed officers reached the top of the stairs, and with one movement he disarmed the last of Rashidi's remaining bodyguards by thrusting the butt of his Heckler & Koch into his jaw. Only Donoghue was still putting up a fight, but the police light heavyweight boxing champion put him out for the count, then handcuffed him and read him his rights—not that he could hear a word.

Armed officers continued to pour into the slaughter, and began to round up what was left of Rashidi's workforce, while half a dozen policemen dragged Donoghue and the two bodyguards unceremoniously down the stairs to the ground floor, where the first of a row of Black Marias was waiting to accommodate them. William was disappointed to find that the last of the resistance had already been dealt with by the time he reached the twenty-third floor.

He strode into the slaughter as one of Rashidi's lieutenants was being led away, shouting and cursing, but not before he was able to throw a punch at William that landed a passing blow and stunned him for a moment. He quickly recovered as another officer slapped a pair of handcuffs on his assailant. As the smoke from the stun grenade attack began to clear, he turned to survey the carnage of what was left of Rashidi's empire. A dozen or so menial workers wearing face masks and rubber gloves were kneeling on the floor. No doubt most of them were illegal immigrants who hadn't been working there by choice, and who might even be relieved to have been rescued. The lower ranks of the drugs world always ended up carrying the can for their masters, and they knew they could never open their mouths. There was always another Tulip, always another gouged eye.

William was sure he hadn't passed Rashidi as he came up the stairs, and Jackie had informed him on the radio that he wasn't among the frightened passengers in the lift who had been rounded up as soon as they reached the ground floor. As there was no other way out, he began to look more closely at the pathetic rabble who remained in the slaughter. And then he noticed a couple of them were stealing fearful glances at one particular worker. William took a closer look, but could see no difference between him and the others kneeling in front of him. But he tapped him on the shoulder and told him to stand up. He didn't move.

"Probably doesn't speak English, sarge," said a young constable, yanking the man to his feet.

"I think he speaks several languages," said William. He removed the man's mask, but even then he couldn't be certain.

"What are you looking for, sarge?"

"The Viper," said William, but not a flicker of recognition crossed the man's face. "Take the glove off your left hand," he said slowly and clearly. Again, no response.

The constable ripped the man's glove off, to reveal that part of the third finger was missing. "How did you know that, sarge?" he said.

"His mother told me."

The man continued to stare blankly at William, as if he didn't understand a word he was saying.

"If you hadn't hugged her, Mr. Rashidi, I might never have known you were her son."

Still not a flicker of comprehension.

"I wonder how she'll react when I visit her in The Boltons tomorrow morning to tell her what her son really imports from Colombia, and then exports onto the streets of London, not from an oak-paneled office in the City as the respected chairman of Marcel and Neffe, but from a depraved drugs den in Brixton, where he's known as the Viper."

The man continued to stand there impassively, not even blinking.

"The attentive son, who never misses an appointment with his mother on a Friday afternoon but doesn't care how many young lives he destroys, as long as he makes a profit week in and week out."

Still nothing.

"One thing's for certain, Rashidi. After I've told your mother where she'll be able to find you for the next ten years, hopefully longer, don't expect her to visit you in prison, because she'll be too ashamed to admit to her friends at the Brompton Oratory that the real reason they haven't seen Khalil recently is because he's brought a new meaning to the word evil."

Rashidi leaned forward and spat in William's face.

"I've never been more flattered in my life, Mr. Rashidi," he said. The constable stepped forward, thrust Rashidi's arms behind his back, and handcuffed him as William read him his rights. He still didn't speak.

"Don't let him out of your sight," said William. "There's an armored van waiting outside for Mr. Rashidi, and a cell awaits him at Brixton police station. It may not need fumigating now, but it certainly will after he's spent the night there."

Rashidi leaned forward and said, "Your days are numbered, sergeant. And I'll be the one to tell your mother."

"No, Mr. Rashidi, it's you whose days are numbered, and I'll be telling your mother why in the morning." Rashidi was unceremoniously led out of the room by two armed officers and escorted to the lift he hadn't quite reached in time.

When he heard the noise of a helicopter somewhere above him, William walked across to the smashed window and looked out to see a chopper disappearing into the clouds. The colonel would be pleased to have it confirmed that the new lot were indeed every bit as good as the old.

He turned his attention back to the room, now a crime scene that had already been taken over by a different breed of policeman: an exhibits officer, who wouldn't be joining his wife for supper, and probably not for breakfast; photographers who were snapping anything that didn't move; and the scene of crime officers in their white boiler suits and latex gloves, who were carefully collecting evidence and depositing it into plastic bags. Even a Polo Mint would be taken back to the labs for closer examination. A cocaine press, scales, sieves, rubber gloves, and face masks awaited inspection by the backroom boys and girls, who would be among the last to take the lift back down to the ground floor.

After writing down Rashidi's words in his notebook—not something he'd be telling Beth—William went through to the next room, which could only have been Rashidi's office. Three bulky sports bags were lined up against the far wall. He picked one up, and was surprised at how heavy it was. He put it back on the floor and unzipped it.

He wouldn't have thought that anything could surprise him after what he'd just witnessed, but the sight of so much money, probably just a single day's takings, reminded him why modern criminals no longer bother to rob banks, when their victims will hand the cash over to them willingly.

He unzipped the second bag to see still more fifties, twenties, and tens neatly stacked in large bundles. He was about to unzip the third when a voice behind him said, "I'll take care of that, DS Warwick."

He turned to see Superintendent Lamont standing in the doorway.

"Meanwhile, the commander wants you to report to him immediately."

"Of course, sir," said William, trying to hide his surprise.

"And well done, DS Warwick. I know you'll be pleased to hear that Rashidi's already on his way to the nearest nick, where a welcoming party awaits him."

"Thank you, sir," said William, as Jackie entered the room.

"Congratulations, sarge," she said. "A triumphant night for everyone." She paused. "Well, everyone except DC Adaja."

"Why, what happened to him?"

"I think it might be better if he told you himself."

William took one last look at the havoc and squalor of what had once been the heart of Rashidi's empire. He reluctantly left the boiler room and began to jog down the stone steps, past graffiti-covered walls where one word was repeated again and again. He ignored the stench of urine as he continued on down to the ground floor, passing several handcuffed prisoners who would not be profiting from the drugs trade for a long time, if ever again.

When he emerged onto the street, he took a deep breath of fresh air and watched as another Black Maria that couldn't accommodate any more occupants was driven away. He walked over to the bus and made his way upstairs to the command center.

"What are you doing here, DS Warwick?" snapped the Hawk. "I made it clear that you were not to leave the crime scene until the job was done."

"The super has taken over, sir, and he said you wanted to see me."

"Did he indeed?"

27

"*The Observer* has done you proud, William," said Sir Julian, "and it's not always complimentary about the police. And as you've never once mentioned Operation Trojan Horse during the past year, it must have been a tightly guarded secret."

"Not even Beth knew until she heard about it on the news this morning."

"The raid has even made the first leader," said Sir Julian. "I quote: 'The arrest of Khalil Rashidi is a genuine breakthrough in the war against drugs, and the Metropolitan Police are to be congratulated on their relentless pursuit of these ruthless criminals who do so much harm to our society.'" He looked up from behind the paper. "There's a photograph of Commander Hawksby sitting on a bus. Not his normal mode of transport, I suspect." He put down the paper and looked across at his son. "You don't appear to be overwhelmed by your triumph."

"The press only has one side of the story."

"And the other side?"

"Isn't quite as commendable. In fact, it's something I need to seek your guidance on."

"Take me through your concerns slowly, and don't leave anything

265

out," said his father, as he sat back in his chair and closed his eyes, as he always did during a consultation.

"While I was in the slaughter—"

"Slaughter?"

"Boiler room, drugs factory . . . I came across three sports bags filled with cash—hundreds, possibly thousands, of pounds. By the time I got back to the Yard, there were only two."

"And you think you know who removed the third bag?"

"I'm in no doubt who did. But I can't prove it."

"Can't have been anyone particularly bright, that's for sure," said Sir Julian.

"What makes you say that?"

"It would have been more sensible to have taken the same amount of cash from each of the three bags, then no one would have been any the wiser."

"You even think like a criminal."

"I'm a QC," said Sir Julian, "a Qualified Criminal. But tell me, did you leave the bags where they were?"

"Yes, I did," said William.

"Then why did you leave the boiler room?" asked Sir Julian, his eyes remaining closed.

"Superintendent Lamont ordered me to report to the commander, who was overseeing the operation from the top of the bus. Told me it was urgent."

"And it wasn't?"

"No. In fact, the Hawk wasn't pleased that I'd left the crime scene without his permission."

"Circumstantial at best. If that's all you've got to go on, you should give Lamont the benefit of the doubt. However, I can see your dilemma. Do you tell Commander Hawksby that you suspect a senior officer of stealing a large sum of money from a crime scene?" He still didn't open his eyes. "If I recall correctly, Super-intendent Lamont is due to retire in a few months' time."

"Yes, but what difference does that make? If there's one thing worse than a professional criminal, to quote the Hawk, it's a bent copper."

"I agree with him. But I do like to know all the facts before I pass judgment."

William pursed his lips.

"Has Lamont ever come under investigation before?"

"Once, many years ago. But since then he's received three com-mendations."

"Ah, yes, I remember he turned a blind eye when he was a young sergeant. And now you're wondering if you should do the same."

William was about to protest when Sir Julian added, "How do you get on with Lamont?"

"Not that well," admitted William.

"Which only adds to the problem, because if you were to report a senior officer for such a serious offense, it would have to be in-vestigated at the highest level, although I suspect Lamont would resign before a disciplinary hearing was held—if he was found guilty, he would undoubtedly be dismissed from the force, lose his pension, and might even end up serving a prison sentence."

"I've already considered that, and I realize turning a blind eye would be the easy way out."

"Not for you it wouldn't," said his father. "However, if you do report him, whether he's found guilty or not, you might well have to consider your own position."

"But why? I've done nothing wrong."

"I accept that without question. But it's the one thing your fellow officers will remember about you. They might never say anything to your face, but behind your back you'd be called snitch, traitor, or worse. And friends of Lamont will go out of their way to derail your chances of promotion. Never forget, the police are a tribe, and some of them will never forgive you for turning against one of their own."

"Only the dishonest ones, in which case I'm in the wrong profession."

"Possibly, but I hope you won't do something in haste that you'll later regret."

"What would you do, Father?"

"I would . . ." began Julian when there was a knock on the door, and Beth walked in. "Lunch is ready," she said. "And Marjorie is looking for a carver."

"We'll have to talk about this again, my boy. And soon," said Julian, rising from his chair.

"Don't you think William's black eye is rather fetching?" said Beth, as she linked arms with her father-in-law and accompanied him through to the dining room.

◄◦►

Faulkner smiled up at Rashidi, and waved a hand to indicate he could join him for breakfast. The first inmate he'd treated as an equal, even if he didn't trust him an inch.

"Why are you dressed in civilian clothes?" asked Rashidi, taking the seat opposite Faulkner. "Are you about to be released?"

"No. I'm going to a funeral."

"Whose?"

"My mother's."

"I adore my mother."

"I hadn't spoken to mine for over twenty years," said Faulkner, as a warder placed a cup of tea on the table in front of him.

"Then why bother to attend her funeral?" asked Rashidi.

"It's an excuse to get out of this place for the day," said Faulkner, dropping a couple of sugar lumps into his tea.

"I won't be seeing the outside world again until my case comes up in about six months' time."

"And what are your chances?"

"Zero, while one of my so-called mates has turned Queen's evidence in exchange for a lesser sentence."

"There are people in here who can take care of that little problem," said Faulkner.

"Not while the filth have two other witnesses in reserve who'd be only too willing to take his place should he fail to turn up."

"So who's running your empire while you're away?"

Rashidi pointed to a young man seated at the next table smoking a cigarette. "One of the few who stood by me when the shit hit the fan."

"But he's also stuck in here, Khalil, in case you haven't noticed."

"Not for much longer. He pleaded guilty to possession of a half-smoked reefer, the only thing they found on him other than a packet of Marlboro. And as he has no previous convictions, he won't get more than six months, possibly less, so he could be out of here in a few weeks' time."

"But surely someone has to run the business while you're away?" said Faulkner.

"My deputy wasn't even on the premises when the raid took place. Doesn't usually take over from me much before midnight. So he'll keep the business ticking over in my absence."

"Can you trust him?"

"Can you trust anyone?" said Rashidi. "However, it's not all bad news. Since I arrived here, I've discovered a new bunch of even more desperate customers. Did you know there are a hundred and thirty-seven prisons in Britain?" he continued. "And they're all about to become branches of my new company."

Faulkner looked interested.

"Give me a year, and I'll control the supply of drugs to every last one of them. I've already identified the officer I'll use as my go-between, while Tulip will be my main prison dealer, so all I need now is a phone."

"Not a problem," said Faulkner. "I'll point you in the right direction when you go to chapel on Sunday."

"I'm Roman Catholic."

"Not any longer, you aren't. You're the Church of England's latest convert. That is, if you want to control the drugs scene in this place. The Sunday morning service is the only time we're all gathered together in one place, when the business for the following week is sorted out during the sermon."

"How does the chaplain feel about that?"

"He fills in another Home Office form reporting how well his services are attended."

"Speaking of the Home Office, what's the latest on your appeal?"

"Couldn't be much worse. They're now accusing me of burning down my own home, but not before I'd removed my art collection."

"What motive could you possibly have for doing that?" asked Rashidi, as another officer poured him a cup of coffee.

"Revenge. I did it to make my ex-wife penniless."

"And did you succeed?"

"Not yet, but I'm still working on it. In fact, I've arranged a little surprise for her this morning."

"So what are your chances of getting off the latest charges?"

"Not good. My lawyer tells me they've got enough evidence to bury me, and it doesn't help that the detective in charge of the case, a certain DS Warwick, is a friend of my wife's."

"Detective Sergeant William Warwick?" spluttered Rashidi, spilling his coffee.

"The same."

"He was the officer who arrested me. But I'm not expecting him to give evidence at my trial."

Faulkner smiled. "That's a funeral I would like to attend. By the way, if you need a lawyer, I can recommend one," he said, as another warder appeared by his side.

"Your carriage awaits, Mr. Faulkner."

"No doubt accompanied by three police cars, six outriders, and an armed escort."

"Not to mention a helicopter," said the warder.

Rashidi laughed. "Only you and the Royal Family get that sort of treatment. I'm going to have to come up with a funeral they'll let me go to."

"The Home Office regulations only allow you to attend the funerals of your parents or children, not even other close relatives."

"Then I won't be going to any funerals," said Rashidi, "because they certainly aren't going to allow me to attend Detective Sergeant Warwick's."

◄○►

"What's the problem, grumpy?" asked William.

"Today's the day," said Beth.

"You're going to give birth today?" said William, sounding excited.

"No, Caveman. It's the day we have to give the Vermeer back to Christina."

"I'm so sorry," said William, as he wrapped his arms around her. "No wonder you had such a restless night."

"However much Christina says she needs the money, I can't pretend I'm looking forward to parting with one of the gallery's finest works."

"Is she picking it up herself?"

"No. Christie's are sending a representative around to collect the picture this morning, as she's putting it up for sale. Tim will be responsible for handing it over, but I intend to be there as it's probably the last time I'll ever see the lady."

William couldn't think of any words to comfort her, so he just continued to hold her in his arms.

◄○►

It wasn't until the last painting had been stored safely in the hold that the captain gave the order to cast off.

He set out on the voyage to England at least a couple of times a year, always docking in Christchurch, but not tonight. The *Christina* slipped out of the bay that morning in broad daylight without attracting any unwanted attention. But then several far grander yachts were making their way into the harbor to watch the Monte Carlo Grand Prix the following week, so why would anyone give them a second look?

The captain had locked the villa and handed over the keys to the estate agent, along with clear instructions as to which Swiss bank the funds should be deposited in once the sale had been completed.

All the valuables, including the fabled art collection, were already on board, and when they eventually came under the hammer the boss would have more than enough money to begin a new life in any country he chose, while the police would be convinced he was dead and buried.

The *Christina* would only drop anchor once, to pick up a passenger who would instruct the captain where his next port of call should be.

The voyage across the Bay of Biscay was calmer than usual. As he sailed into the English Channel a ball of fiery red disappeared in the west, and by the time it reappeared in the east, his boss would have escaped, or be back in jail.

—◦—

William had described the problem as urgent after they'd left Nettleford on Sunday afternoon.

His father had suggested they meet in his chambers at eight o'clock the following morning, as he would be appearing in front of Mr. Justice Baverstock at ten.

William arrived at Lincoln's Inn Fields long before the appointed hour. He walked slowly across to the Victorian building that could have passed for a fashionable private residence—and probably was a hundred years ago—on the far side of the square.

As he entered Essex Court Chambers he stopped to study the long list of names printed neatly in black on the white brick wall. SIR JULIAN WARWICK QC headed the list. His gaze continued on down, only stopping when he reached the name MS. GRACE WARWICK. How long before QC would be added to her name, he wondered. His father would be so proud, though he'd never admit it. He spent a moment thinking about where his name might have appeared if he'd taken his father's advice and joined him as a pupil in chambers, and not signed up to be a constable in the Met.

William climbed the well-worn stone steps to the first floor and knocked on a door that he'd first stood outside as a child. He was no less apprehensive now about how his father would react when he told him his news.

"Come," said the voice of a man who didn't waste words.

William entered a room that hadn't changed for as long as he could remember. The picture of his mother as a beautiful young woman stood on the corner of his father's desk. Prints of Sherborne, Brasenose, and Lincoln's Inn hung on the walls, alongside a photograph of Sir Julian dining with the Queen Mother at High Table, when he'd been treasurer of Lincoln's Inn. There was even a photograph of William running the one hundred meters at White City when he was an undergraduate. He'd never told his father he'd come last in that race.

Julian stood up and shook hands with his son as if he were a client, while Grace gave her brother a huge hug.

"You clearly require the advice of two of the leading advocates in the land, my boy, so be warned, the clock is already ticking and, on your salary, I suspect we can spare you about ten minutes."

"I've got all morning," said Grace, giving her brother a reassuring smile.

"Unfortunately, I haven't," said William. "I have to be back at the Yard by nine for the Trojan Horse debriefing. But I wanted you both to know, before I tell the commander, that I'm going to resign."

Julian didn't look surprised and simply said, "I'm sorry to hear that."

"I thought you'd be delighted," said William. "After all, you never wanted me to join the police force in the first place."

"True, but a lot of water has passed under the bridge since then."

"Not least your triumph as a leading member of the Trojan

Horse team," suggested Grace. "And there are rumors you're about to become the youngest inspector in the force."

"It's that so-called triumph that's the cause of my current dilemma."

"What do you mean?" said Grace.

"One of the senior officers involved in that operation turns out to be just as crooked as the criminals I'm trying to put behind bars."

"I've given the problem a great deal of thought since we discussed it over the weekend," said Julian, "and have reluctantly come to the conclusion that you'll have to expose him."

"I agree with you," said William, "but I wouldn't be surprised if he decided to brazen it out until he's due to retire in eighteen months' time."

"Given the circumstances," suggested Sir Julian, "the Hawk might consider it politic to move him to a less high-profile department before he retires."

"Like burglary perhaps?" said William, which at least brought a smile to his father's face.

"So, what do you plan to do instead?" asked Grace. "Because you're still young enough to consider a new career."

"I'll do what Father always wanted me to do. Apply for a place at King's College London to read law. Though the timing isn't ideal . . ."

"Don't worry about the money," his father assured him.

"And once you've graduated," said Grace, "you can join us in chambers."

"Only if, like your sister, you're awarded a first-class honors degree," said Julian. "I don't believe in nepotism, so there will be no 'Bob's your uncle' in these chambers."

"Remind me, Father," said William, playing a game that had begun in the nursery.

"The saying derives from the days when Sir Robert Peel, later Lord Salisbury, was prime minister and put two of his nephews in the cabinet. Hence, Bob's your uncle. But can you tell me which one of them went on to also become PM?"

"Sir Anthony Balfour," said Grace.

"Correct," said Julian. "But as you're in a hurry to get back to the Yard, may I suggest that we discuss your future in greater detail when you and Beth join us for lunch on Sunday?"

"By which time I will have resigned," said William, as he rose from his place.

"Then you'll need to get your application into King's College fairly quickly if you're hoping to join the law faculty in September."

"I've already filled in the application form," said William. "All I need to do now is hand it in."

"Would you like me to have a word with Ron Maudsley, who's the law professor at King's? We were contemporaries at Brasenose and—"

"If you do that, Father, I'll go to Battersea Polytechnic and take up basket-weaving." He'd closed the door behind him before Julian had the chance to reply.

"How disappointing," said Grace. "I agree with you, Father. He made the right choice in the first place."

"But it's not without a silver lining. He'll make a fine barrister, and all that knowledge gained as a policeman will serve him in good stead whenever he comes up against a hardened criminal in the witness box."

"Or a police officer for that matter. But I still think he should have remained in the force and gone on locking up criminals rather than joining us and trying to get them released."

"Don't ever tell him, but I agree with you, and will try and talk him out of it on Sunday."

"It may be too late by then."

◄○►

Tim Knox picked up the phone.

"There's a Mr. Drummond from Christie's downstairs," said his secretary. "Says you're expecting him."

Knox glanced at his watch. "He's early, but then so would I be if I was collecting a masterpiece worth several million. Tell him I'm on my way, and please ask Beth to join us."

The director reluctantly left his office and made his way slowly down the wide marble staircase to the ground floor, where he saw a smartly dressed man carrying a large blue Christie's bag.

"Good morning, Dr. Knox," the man said as they shook hands. "Alex Drummond. Mr. Davage asked me to stand in for him as he's in New York for the autumn sales, but said he'll phone as soon as he wakes up," he added, handing the director his business card. "You probably won't remember, but we met at the Christie's summer party last year. You asked me what price I thought Teniers's *Night and Day* might fetch."

"And remind me," said Tim, "what was the hammer price?"

"Just over a million."

"Well beyond our resources, as I feared. Where did it end up?"

"The Getty Museum in California."

"Petty cash for them," said Tim ruefully, as Beth joined them, wearing a pair of white cotton gloves. "This is Beth, the gallery's assistant keeper of paintings."

"An unfortunate title, given the circumstances," said Beth.

"Nice to meet you, Mrs. Warwick," said Drummond.

"Well, let's get on with it, shall we?" said Tim. "I'd like to get this over with before we open the gallery to the public."

Beth carefully lifted the painting off its hook before handing it to the director. At the same time, Drummond removed a small wooden box from his canvas bag, and opened it so Beth could place the picture inside.

"A perfect fit," she said.

Drummond closed the lid, snapped the clasps shut, and slipped the box back into his bag.

"How much do you expect it to fetch?" asked Tim, after he'd signed the release form.

"The low estimate is one million, but Mr. Davage thinks it could make as much as two."

"More than enough to solve Christina's problems," muttered Beth.

"Divorce, death, and debt," said Drummond. "The auctioneer's three best friends. With the added irony on this occasion that it will probably be our client's ex-husband who ends up buying it. Mr. Faulkner has made it clear that he wants it back at any price."

"Then I hope he has to pay way over the top for it," said Beth with feeling. "Although I can't see the prison authorities allowing him to hang it in his cell."

Drummond smiled after he signed the release form. "If either of you would like me to reserve a seat for you at the auction, just let me know."

"I couldn't face it," said Beth.

"Nor me," said Tim. "Not least because I know only too well that we can't afford to join in the bidding."

"And on that note, I'll leave you," said Drummond, shaking hands with them both before taking his leave.

"A sad day for the gallery," said Tim, as he and Beth walked back up the stairs together.

"It was inevitable, I suppose," said Beth, "after Faulkner stole all Christina's other paintings. But at least she got the better of him this time."

◄◦►

After William had left his father's chambers in Lincoln's Inn Fields, he walked up the Strand and hesitated for a moment before dropping into King's College.

He handed in his application form to join the law faculty in September to the senior porter in the lodge. The porter's expression suggested that he thought William looked a bit old to be an undergraduate.

William checked his watch. He didn't need to be late for the commander's meeting, when he intended to expose Lamont.

◄◦►

Back in his office, Tim Knox began to go through the morning's post. Too many bills and not enough donations. *A museum director's perennial problem,* he thought, as the phone on his desk began to ring.

"There's a Mr. Davage waiting for you in reception."

"What? I thought he was meant to be in New York," said Tim. He immediately called Beth and asked her to join him, and this time they both ran down the stairs.

"Good morning," said Davage after they'd caught their breath. "Though not a particularly good one for you, I fear, which is why I decided to come over and collect the painting myself."

"But one of your colleagues has already picked it up," said Tim, pointing to an empty space on the wall.

"One of my colleagues? What are you talking about?"

"Alex Drummond," said Tim nervously. "He said you were in New York."

"I was, but I caught the red-eye, and came straight to the gallery from the airport. And I can assure you, there's no one at Christie's called Alex Drummond."

An embarrassed silence followed before Beth said calmly, "Faulkner's done it again. And this time he didn't even have to put in a bid for the painting." After a moment's pause, she added, "I should have asked him how he knew . . ."

"Knew what?" demanded the director.

"That I was Mrs. Warwick, when you introduced me as Beth."

"And that box he had with him," said Knox, thumping his leg in anger. "The painting fitted in so neatly."

"Far too neatly," said Beth. "But then it was supplied by the previous owner."

"But Faulkner's in jail," said Davage.

"That wouldn't stop him issuing orders to his flunkies on the outside," said Beth. "Like the so-called Alex Drummond."

"This isn't the time to stand around chatting about what fools we've made of ourselves," said Tim. "Beth, you'd better call your husband immediately, and tell him what's happened."

Beth walked slowly back to her office, clinging onto the banister. She feared the lady in *The White Lace Collar* would already be in the arms of another.

28

THROW AWAY THE KEY, screamed the *Sun's* banner headline.

The team sat around the table in the commander's office, perusing the morning papers. William had chosen the *Sun* because Beth wouldn't allow him to have it in the house. Half a million pounds in cash, thirty arrests, and five kilos of cocaine discovered in a Brixton drugs den. Beth would have pointed out that Brixton was about the only word in the article that was accurate.

Jackie was reading the *Daily Mail*. MET ARREST LEADING DRUG BARON IN MIDNIGHT RAID. A flattering photo of the commander adorned the front page. Profile, page sixteen.

Lamont had settled for the *Express*. A VIPER TRAPPED IN HIS NEST! ran the headline, above a photo of Rashidi being dragged out of the building by two armed police officers.

The Hawk was reading *The Guardian's* leader, WAR ON DRUGS, while Paul was the only one who didn't appear to be enjoying the morning's press coverage.

"That's enough self-indulgence for one day," said the Hawk finally. "Time to move on."

"Great coverage, though," said Lamont, tossing the *Express* back on the pile in the center of the table. "Even if, search as I did, I couldn't find a single mention of DC Adaja and the pivotal role he played in the whole operation."

"It's bound to be in the small print somewhere," said the commander masking a smile, "if one had the time to look for it."

Paul bowed his head and made no attempt to respond.

"Did you witness the sad event, DS Warwick?"

"No, sir," said William. "The last time I saw DC Adaja he was still on the bus."

"Which is where he should have stayed," said Lamont.

"How about you, Jackie?"

"The whole tragic incident unfolded right in front of me, sir. DC Adaja jumped off the bus before it had even come to a halt. He hit the ground running, but unfortunately he tripped and fell. Luckily, I was able to drag him to one side so he wasn't trampled on in the stampede that followed. I shouted 'Officer down!' and an ambulance appeared within minutes and immediately whisked him off to A and E at St. Thomas's."

"And once they'd examined the patient, what was the diagnosis?" asked the commander, barely able to keep a straight face.

They all turned to face Paul.

"A sprained ankle," he eventually managed. "Truth is, I played absolutely no part in the success of the operation."

"You most certainly did," said the Hawk. "Don't forget the hours you spent tracking Rashidi. And, frankly, without your input the whole operation might never have got off the ground."

The rest of the team began to bang the table with the palms of their hands in recognition of the role Paul had played, and within moments the familiar grin reappeared on his face.

The Hawk turned to William. "DS Warwick, I'm puzzled as to how you got that black eye."

"One of Rashidi's thugs punched me in the heat of battle," said

William proudly. "But it was worth it, because I arrested and charged the little bastard."

"It certainly was," said the Hawk. "In fact, that particular little bastard was Marlboro Man."

William was momentarily stunned, but quickly recovered. "Are you telling me your UCO was in the slaughter the entire time?"

"The entire time. In fact, when you arrested him, he was trying to let you know which one was Rashidi."

"Then I'm blind, as well as stupid," said William. "So where is he now?"

"Pentonville, where he'll stay put for the next few weeks while he awaits trial."

"That's a bit rough, isn't it?"

"Not when he's still got work to do, which is why he's on the same block as Rashidi."

"But if Rashidi were to suss him out . . ."

"Why should he? He only knows MM as a loyal lieutenant who tried to help him escape. We're rather hoping that while he's on the inside he'll be able to gather enough evidence for us to nail the rest of the bastards."

"But won't it look suspicious when he's found not guilty?"

"He won't be. He'll be found guilty of the possession of a couple of reefers, sentenced to six months, and sent back to Pentonville."

"What about actual bodily harm?" said William, pointing to his black eye.

"He'll probably get a couple of months knocked off for that," said the Hawk. DC Adaja laughed. "No. MM will be transferred to an open prison after a few weeks, and released soon afterward so he can get back to work. But not before he's taken a holiday somewhere warm."

Jackie smiled. She even knew where.

"Quite right too," said Lamont. "No more than he deserves."

"Agreed," said the Hawk. "Now, let me bring you up to date following my meeting with the commissioner."

◄○►

"Ashes to ashes," intoned the priest.

Miles Faulkner showed little interest as the body of his mother was lowered into the grave. After all, he hadn't spoken to the damn woman in years, and he had more important things on his mind. Christina had made no attempt to contact him once she'd signed the postnuptial, as Booth Watson described the contract. She would receive a thousand pounds a week as long as she made no attempt to contact him, and was well aware that the payments would cease if she so much as crossed his path.

Miles never told his friends or business associates that he was the son of a railway porter, who fortunately had died before he'd won his scholarship to Harrow, and that his mother was a hairdresser from Chelmsford in Essex, a county he'd never entered since leaving school. Although in truth the only reason he'd been awarded a scholarship to Winston Churchill's alma mater was because of his background, Harrow trying to appease a recently elected Labour government.

He looked around at the small gathering that circled the grave. Miles recognized none of them, although every one of them knew him.

During the funeral service, three prison guards had sat in the row behind him while another had been posted by the church door. They had removed his handcuffs just before they accompanied him into the church, which hadn't come cheap. They did their best to melt into the background when he joined the other mourners to witness the burial. The guards were dressed in dark suits, black ties, and similarly ill-fitting raincoats, so all the mourners knew who they were. At least they'd had the decency to stand a few paces back while the burial service took place. A police helicopter hovered above them, almost drowning out the vicar's words.

"Dust to dust . . ."

The priest was declaring the final blessing when a white Transit van drove slowly through the main gates at the far end of the cemetery. One of the prison guards took a closer look at the van as it trundled slowly past them before coming to a halt some fifty yards away. A sign in large black letters on the side of the van read:

DESMOND LEACH & SONS

STONE MASONS AND ENGRAVERS

FOUNDED 1963

The senior guard took an even closer interest when the driver jumped down from behind the wheel, walked to the back of the van, and unlocked the doors. Moments later a younger man joined him and clambered into the back. All four guards were now watching carefully until they saw the younger man heaving a gravestone out of the van, which the older man took hold of before the two of them lugged it off to the far side of the graveyard.

They turned their attention back to Miles Faulkner, whose head remained bowed as the coffin was lowered into the ground. The priest made the sign of the cross, and as the first spade of earth was thrown onto the coffin three black Norton 750cc motorbikes shot out from the back of the van. Seconds later they skidded to a halt by the graveside, engines turning over.

The senior guard didn't move, but then he knew what was going to happen in the next thirty seconds. The prisoner turned and began to run toward the center bike, the only one without a passenger. All three riders wore identical black leather outfits and black helmets, visors down. The two pillion passengers, who were seated on the back of the first and third bike, wore dark-gray suits, white shirts, and black ties, identical to the clothing Faulkner was wearing.

Faulkner leaped onto the back of the middle bike, grabbed the proffered helmet with one hand and the waist of the driver with the other. He shouted, "Go!" One of the younger guards leaped at them as the bike took off, but was a moment too late. He rolled over and over, nearly ending up in the grave.

The senior guard stifled a laugh as the motorbikes zigzagged in and out of the gravestones toward a partly concealed pedestrian entrance, which led out onto a busy street. He then walked quickly, but not too quickly, back to his car, climbed in, and barked out an order. His driver headed for the main entrance but he knew it would be a hopeless task, because by the time they reached the main road, the bikes would have already covered the first mile. However, the two officers in the helicopter had witnessed exactly what had taken place below them. The compliant guard had already warned Faulkner he had no control over them.

The pilot banked and swept down toward the three bikes, closely following their progress, while his colleague radioed back to the command center in New Scotland Yard to let them know what had happened. Moments later, every patrol car within a five-mile radius had been alerted and began listening to the instructions from the helicopter—something else the three motorcyclists had anticipated.

Once they reached the main intersection, the bikes began a maneuver known as the "three-card trick." Every few seconds they swapped places, until the pilot in the helicopter no longer could be certain which of the motorbikes Faulkner was on.

When the three bikes reached the next junction, the lead rider turned left, the second turned right, while the third carried straight on.

The pilot decided to follow the one that was heading for the motorway, while giving Scotland Yard the exact locations of the other two, and their direction of travel. The police got lucky. The first of the patrol cars spotted the bike that had gone straight on coming toward them. The driver switched on his siren, swung around, and pursued the suspect, who to their surprise slowed down and came to a halt by the side of the road. The two police officers got out of their car and cautiously approached the suspect.

The rider had removed his helmet long before the two officers reached him, but they were only interested in the passenger. She slowly removed her helmet and smiled warmly at the policemen. "How can I help you, officers?" she asked innocently.

When the second bike reached the motorway, it moved into the outside lane and quickly accelerated away, reaching speeds of well over a hundred miles per hour, while the helicopter stuck with him. When the rider heard the siren, he glanced in his wing mirror to see a police car speeding toward them. He slowed down, moved across to the inside lane, and took the next slip road off the motorway, only to be met by three police cars blocking the exit.

This time the bike was surrounded by a dozen officers, two of them armed. The driver removed his helmet and said, "I don't think I broke the speed limit, officer."

"We're not interested in you," barked one of the officers, pushing up the passenger's visor to be greeted by a teenager, who gave him a huge grin.

"Yes, you did, Dad, but it was worth it."

The third motorcyclist slowed down as he approached an underpass. Once the bike was out of sight it skidded to a halt, while a fourth took off like a seamless relay runner, emerging from the tunnel just seconds later. The driver swung left at the next junction and sped away in the opposite direction to the helicopter. His instructions couldn't have been clearer: lead them a merry dance for as long as you can.

Miles climbed off the back of his motorbike and handed his helmet to the driver.

"Hang around for fifteen minutes, and then drive slowly back the same way you came," he said, as a Ford Escort entered the underpass and pulled up next to them.

The driver got out and said, "Good morning, sir," as if he was picking up his boss from the office.

"Morning, Eddie," Faulkner replied, as his chauffeur opened the front door and he climbed inside.

The Ford Escort emerged from the underpass a few moments later, and when it reached the junction, Eddie turned right. Miles looked out of the back window to see the helicopter flying in the opposite direction.

◄○►

The commander opened the thick file in front of him. "First, and most important, Khalil Rashidi is, as you know, safely locked up in Pentonville. You'll also be glad to hear he was refused bail, so he'll spend the next six months or so in jail, waiting for his case to be heard. Until then, his lawyer is the only person who'll be allowed to visit him."

"Do we have reliable witnesses this time?" asked Lamont.

"The Crown will produce a doctor who's already under the witness protection scheme and will give detailed evidence as to what Rashidi's been up to in exchange for a lighter sentence."

"That's good news," said Lamont. "We don't need another Adrian Heath."

"I can assure you," said the Hawk, "this one will be better protected than the Royal Family. And even if he should change his mind at the last moment, we've got two other potential witnesses in reserve, whose lawyers are also trying to make deals with the CPS."

"What about Rashidi's mother?" asked William.

"She's locked herself in her home in The Boltons," said Jackie, "and won't open the door to anyone."

"And who can blame her?" said William. "It must have come as a dreadful shock to discover your only son is a notorious drug dealer, and not the respectable chairman of a successful tea company."

"Ironic really," said the commander. "If he hadn't hugged his mother on her doorstep that Friday evening, we might never have been able to identify him."

"She betrayed her only begotten son," said William. "But, unlike Judas, she didn't mean to."

The commander turned a page. "A total of twenty-seven other suspects have been arrested and charged, including Marlboro Man and four of Rashidi's closest associates. One who, as I said, is singing like a canary. An added bonus, Jackie arrested another runner who turned up after the raid was over with enough wraps of cocaine on him to make sure he joined the rest of the villains in Pentonville."

"Did anyone get away?" asked William.

"Thanks to the carpenter and the counter-terrorism officers, it seems unlikely. But three of those who were arrested have been released on bail and are now threatening to sue the police."

"Let me guess," said William. "Three of the lookouts?"

"So, what's their story?" asked Lamont.

"They claim they were walking home peacefully after enjoying a drink at their local when they were attacked without provocation by the police. Their lawyer is threatening us with unlawful arrest and police brutality."

"Spare me," said Lamont.

"But if we were to drop the charges, they won't take the matter any further."

"Which means they must have previous as long as your arm," said Jackie.

"You're right," said the Hawk. "But, frankly, they're pretty low down the food chain. This time we've caught the shark, so I think we can allow a few minnows to escape."

"What about the fourth lookout?" asked Lamont.

"He was stoned out of his mind," said the commander. "He should be in a hospital bed, not a prison cell."

"And Donoghue?" said William.

"He's been charged with assaulting a police officer. He was refused bail, and with his record he's looking at four to six years at least."

The banging of palms on the table lasted for some time.

"I do have one piece of sad news to report, however," continued the Hawk. "The lad who so nearly stopped Donoghue, but managed to get hold of his radio—allowing us those vital forty-two seconds—was badly injured, and may have to spend the rest of his life in a wheelchair."

"On a constable's pension," said William. "Ending up as just another statistic on an internal report and forgotten by the public in a few days. He should get one of those three holdalls full of cash. That's the least he deserves."

"Two holdalls," said Lamont. "The third one was empty, probably waiting to be filled with the rest of the night's takings."

"I didn't open all three of them," said William, looking directly at Lamont, "but I picked up the third one, and could have sworn it was just as heavy as the other two."

An uncomfortable silence descended around the table.

"You're mistaken, DS Warwick," said Lamont firmly. "It was empty, as DC Roycroft will confirm."

Jackie gave a perfunctory nod, but didn't speak.

"Perhaps Marlboro Man is not the only person hoping to spend a long holiday somewhere warm," said William, unable to restrain himself any longer.

"Watch your tongue, laddie!" barked Lamont. "I've already told you, there was nothing in the third bag, so just leave it at that."

"Gentlemen, gentlemen," said the commander. "This is not the way colleagues should behave after such a triumph."

"Unless one of us has behaved as badly as the criminals," said William, looking directly at Lamont.

The superintendent rose from his place, clenched his fist, and leaned threateningly across the table just as there was a knock at the door, and the Hawk's secretary came rushing in.

"Now's not a good time, Angela," said the commander.

"It's just that a Mr. Knox has called from the Fitzmolean to say DS Warwick's wife has been rushed into hospital."

William leaped to his feet. "Which hospital?"

"The Chelsea and Westminster."

"And there was another call I thought you would all want to know about . . ." But William had already left the office before Angela could pass on the news.

He ran along the corridor, down the stairs, and out onto the street, where he hailed the first taxi he saw.

◄○►

A car's headlights beamed across the water, but only for a brief moment before they were turned off.

The captain gave the command to lower the RIB. Moments later he and a young deckhand climbed into a bobbing motorboat. They began to motor toward the shore, the navigator guiding them toward a narrow inlet—not for the first time—as the captain scanned the water to spot anything that shouldn't be there. A couple of seagulls squawked above them, clearly enjoying their company, while a flock of sheep on a nearby hill showed no interest.

And then he saw him standing on the beach.

The captain changed direction and headed for the shore.

◄○►

"Where to, guv?"

"The Chelsea and Westminster hospital," said William. "And I'm already late."

Even Danny would have been impressed by the side streets and back-doubles the cab driver took to get his passenger to the hospital in the shortest possible time.

"Going to have a baby, are we?" said the cabbie, as William handed him a five-pound note.

"Two in fact. How did you guess?"

"'I'm already late' was the first clue, and then the expression on your face clinched it."

William was about to say "keep the change" when the cabbie handed the note back to him and said, "Have this one on me, guv. And if you know anyone who was involved in catching those bastards last night, pass on my congratulations."

"Will do," said William, before rushing into the hospital and heading straight for the front desk.

"Warwick, Beth Warwick," he said to the woman seated behind the counter. "I'm her husband."

She checked the screen in front of her and said, "Cavell ward, fourth floor, room three. Good luck!"

William avoided the group of people waiting for a lift, aware that hospital elevators were built to move slowly. Instead he took the stairs two at a time. By the time he reached the fourth floor, he was out of breath. A nurse was waiting for him in the corridor, clipboard in hand.

"I can only hope it was something important that kept you, Mr. Warwick," she said. "Because your wife has just given birth to twins."

William began jumping up and down. "Boys? Girls? One of each?" he asked once he'd landed back on earth.

"A little girl, six pounds three ounces—she was first out—and a boy, six pounds one ounce, followed, as I expect he'll do for the rest of his life," said the nurse with a grin.

"And Beth, how's she doing?"

"Follow me and you can see for yourself. But you're not to stay for too long, Mr. Warwick. Your wife is exhausted, and needs to rest."

She led William into a ward where Beth was sitting up in bed, a baby cradled in each arm.

"You're late," she said.

"And you're early," said William.

"Sorry about that. But in the end they were in rather a hurry to get out. They must take after you. This is Daddy," she said, looking adoringly at the twins, "who's already missed the main event. He believes he was put on earth to save the world, a modern superman, which is the reason he also missed the second major decision in your lives."

"And what was that, superwoman?" asked William, wrapping his arms around all three of them.

"We've already had a serious discussion about names," said Beth, handing one of the babies to William.

"And what names did the three of you decide in my absence?"

"For your son, we settled on Peter Paul."

"Rubens," said William. "I approve. But will he be an artist or a diplomat?"

"As long as he's not a policeman, I don't care."

"And his sister?"

"Artemisia."

"Gentileschi? A genius, way ahead of her time."

"And more important, she had a father who acknowledged her talents, and encouraged her to use them. So beware."

"Hello, Artemisia," William whispered, stroking her nose.

"Good try, but that's Peter Paul, who's keen to know if you've given any more thought to applying for the job at the Fitzmolean? Applications close at the end of the week, the director reminded me."

"You can tell Tim I've been giving the idea some serious thought recently," said William quietly.

A puzzled look appeared on Beth's face. "Why recently?"

"We've got a bent copper on our team, and one of us will have to go."

"But why should it be you? You haven't done anything wrong."

"Because I'm not willing to turn a blind eye, and that's what I'd have to do if I decided to remain on the force."

"How sad," said Beth, almost to herself.

"I thought you'd be delighted to learn that I'm thinking about packing it in."

"I am. But I wouldn't want to wake up every morning with a disgruntled caveman beside me, especially now the press are saying you're in line to become the youngest detective inspector in the Met's history!"

"But at what price?"

"Perhaps you should talk it over with your father before you come to a decision you'll later regret."

"Almost his exact words. But I can't think of anything that would make me change my mind."

Artemisia began to cry, quickly followed by Peter Paul.

"They're clearly going to work in tandem to attract our attention," said Beth.

She and William handed the twins to the midwife, who quickly calmed them down before placing them gently in their cots. "Perhaps it's time for your wife to rest," she suggested before leaving the room.

"But not before we've checked to see if you're already yesterday's news," said Beth, flicking on the television to see a red double-decker bus disappearing off one side of the screen.

"Well, I guess that's the last we're going to see of you," she sighed. She was about to switch off the television when the newsreader said, "Some breaking news has just come in. A prisoner has escaped from Pentonville jail."

Miles Faulkner's face filled the screen.